C000163689

Ian Cook was born in the county of Devon, England, grew up in Hertfordshire and took a degree in crop science at the University of Reading. During his subsequent worldwide travels, he became intrigued by the universal mythology associated with red hair and acquired more knowledge about the subject than is strictly necessary for everyday social purposes. His first novel, *Redhead*, was published in 2012 and a revised second edition in 2018. He lives in London with his wife, Maggie.

The Future
Is
Red

[signature: Ian Cook]

IAN COOK

Matador
9 Priory Business Park,
Wistow Road, Kibworth Beauchamp,
Leicestershire. LE8 0RX
Tel: 0116 279 2299
Email: books@troubador.co.uk
Web: www.troubador.co.uk/matador
Twitter: @matadorbooks

ISBN 9781800464858

British Library Cataloguing in Publication Data.
A catalogue record for this book is available from the British Library.

Printed and bound in Great Britain by 4edge Limited
Typeset in 10.5pt Adobe Garamond Pro by Troubador Publishing Ltd, Leicester, UK

Matador is an imprint of Troubador Publishing Ltd

To Maggie,
with love
and thanks

"The Sun is God."
J. M. W. Turner

"Start with the sun, and the rest will slowly, slowly
happen."
D. H. Lawrence, *Apocalypse*

"… and this stone which I have set up as a sacred pillar
shall be a house of God."
Genesis 28: 22–24, *New English Bible*

1

Great Serpent Mound, Ohio, c. 350 BCE

Shrouded by a blanket of mist, the Serpent slept under a brilliantly clear, starlit sky. High above, a crescent moon was hanging as if suspended by an invisible thread and it seemed to be watching the scene below in anticipation of the events ahead. Far below the head of the Serpent, at the base of a rugged cliff, a river flowed languidly, indifferent to the affairs of mortals.

As the sky lightened along the eastern horizon and the mist began to lift, they started to arrive for the ceremony they believed could save their lives. A single sparrow chirped and broke the silence, but no dawn chorus followed. Hovering above, an owl in desperate search of prey eyed the vast, undulating earthen body of the Serpent stretched out on the landscape, then sensed a powerful energy awakening in it and veered away.

Groups of dark-haired men and women were approaching the three coils of the Serpent's tail. After reaching the tip, they continued along its length on both sides, positioned themselves and waited quietly.

As the procession came into sight, all heads turned. It was led by the medicine man of the tribe. Dressed in full ceremonial regalia, he wore a bark-cloth coat decorated with designs inspired by the wild animals that had once inhabited the surrounding woodland. His headdress was bizarre: a helmet fashioned from copper, surmounted by a pair of copper antlers. He stopped at the tip of the Serpent's tail and waited for the others to catch up.

Grim-faced, the six elders of the tribe then arrived, richly attired in long, decorated skirts and wearing necklaces of animal bones and coloured beads over their chests.

But it was the next figure who commanded the most attention. A giant of a man, nearly seven feet tall, strode up behind the elders. His head held high, he gazed impassively with pale green eyes over the heads of the others at the colossal earthwork snaking into the distance. His hair made him seem even taller. A fiery red in colour, it was arranged in a coil on top of his head to reveal long, stretched earlobes, studded with the jade stones passed down by his ancestors. He was dressed simply in a plain buckskin coat and trousers, his only ornaments six copper bangles on each wrist. The more perceptive of the onlookers would have noticed that he was holding something hidden in his clenched right hand.

Six warriors came next, wearing loincloths and adorned with bone necklaces. Each one armed with a stone axe, they stood back at a respectful distance.

The medicine man waited to ensure that everybody was ready. He then nodded and stepped up onto the very end of the Serpent's tail. The others followed him and proceeded slowly in a twisting line for nearly 400 long strides. As they passed by, the onlookers lowered their heads in deference.

By the time they reached the Serpent's gaping mouth, the sky was glowing red behind them. Now an expectant silence fell and all eyes turned towards the east. The tip of the golden orb broke over the tree-covered hills, bathing the scene in a soft light. Instantly the onlookers knelt down and raised their arms, reaching upwards towards their god. The chant of "Ra… Ra… Ra…" echoed around the landscape.

The medicine man held up his hand and the crowd instantly fell silent. Beyond the Serpent's wide-open jaws, as if it were poised to swallow it, lay an egg-shaped embankment, fully forty strides in length and with a mound of stones at its centre. It was a sacrosanct place, which only a chosen few could enter.

With a further nod from the medicine man, the procession climbed over the embankment into the sacred area and stood there looking at the sun as it cleared the horizon.

The medicine man now reached up, placed his hand in the small of the red-haired man's back and guided him to the mound of stones. Feeling a little more pressure from the medicine man's hand, the red-haired man unprotestingly knelt down and lowered his head.

With an increasing sense of foreboding, everybody waited, facing the sun and shielding their eyes as they watched it rise slowly in the clear sky.

3

The red-haired man knew what was about to happen next. He had foretold that on this very morning there would be a full eclipse of the sun.

Closing his eyes, he thought about the fate of his own tribe and yearned for its lost glorious past. The tribe of tall white men had been here long before the newcomers arrived from the land of the Pole Star. He thought about the legends of his tribe and how they had arrived long, long ago in boats from an island across the Great Sea to the east. Renowned for their tall stature and red hair, the island civilisation had thrived in peace. They had learned how to grow crops and domesticate wild animals, so that they had time to study. They had built a great city, studied the movements of the sun, moon and stars, and constructed magnificent temples to their glory, believing their souls would return to the heavens when their bodies died. Using their knowledge of the skies, they had taught themselves advanced navigational skills, which enabled them to trade across the known world.

The catastrophe had occurred without warning. They had felt the tremors days earlier, but only a few had managed to prepare and board their ocean-going boats before the massive earthquake finally struck and the resulting deluge engulfed the island.

His distant ancestor, a priest-king, had sailed to the west with his wife and children and discovered a vast uninhabited land where they had decided to settle, cultivating crops of the useful plants they found. Here they had led peaceful lives. They had no need for the arts of war; the only weapons they kept were those to defend themselves from wild animals and predators. His priest-king ancestors had preserved their sacred understanding of the heavens, passing it on over the generations.

Then the others had arrived: men who hunted wild animals for food while their womenfolk gathered berries, fruits and roots.

There was no problem at first; there was plenty of land and the newcomers were in awe of the white men's learning. Worshippers of the sun, the new tribe had feared the eclipses, believing that the sun could disappear forever. Not only did the white men seem to know in advance when an eclipse would occur, but the incantations of their priest-kings always made the sun reappear.

Over the generations the power of the white men had grown. Their tribe had built the great Serpent at this sacred place where the earth was alive with energy. For them, the Serpent was the embodiment of that energy: an energy his people could sense and use to communicate with their ancestors. But the newcomers saw the egg-shaped enclosure as representing the sun and the Serpent as threatening to swallow it. For them, it was a symbol of the power of the priest-kings over the eclipse.

The terrible disaster had spared nobody: the drought had lasted for ten long years now. Slowly the rivers had dried, the wild animals had almost disappeared and the land had become so parched that when the wind blew, everything was covered in a fine dust. Everybody was hungry and had looked to the priest-king for help. But he could do nothing. The newcomers became angry and turned against the white men. One day, when the white tribe was holding a ritual at the Serpent to beg for guidance from their ancestors, they had been attacked and slaughtered. He alone had been spared, but they kept him captive, knowing that he held secrets of the newcomers' god, the sun; secrets that they did not understand.

The priest-king was now the only survivor of his tribe, the last of the giant white men. And he knew his only chance of survival was that his incantation would convince them that he alone held the power to stop the sun disappearing forever.

He was deep in thought, his eyes closed, when he heard a great gasp from the crowd. He opened his eyes and looked up. The tiniest black bite had been taken out of the sun. He had already calculated that the eclipse would be long and that the people could become impatient and restless.

Very slowly, like an eternity, the moon edged over the dazzling orb. As the sky grew darker, nobody moved and a deathly quiet fell over the land. Now only a sliver of the sun remained. The air chilled and there was a gust of wind. People's faces turned a ghoulish yellowish-green, with purple lips and circles around their eyes.

From the depths of the woodland, the long piercing howl of a coyote drifted over the site, but there was no reply. The medicine man turned his head in the direction of the sound and shuddered.

It was at this point that the sun disappeared completely and the stars and the moon shone again, as if the night had returned.

This was his moment. The priest-king stood up and raised his left hand towards the black disc. With his other hand, he held what appeared to be a small, rough stone against his right temple. Staring intently at the disc, he chanted slowly and softly in a language that nobody could understand. But the black disc did not move; it seemed to be frozen in place. The crowd was now becoming agitated. The priest-king chanted more stridently, but when the wailing began, his voice was drowned.

It happened quite suddenly. An orb of white light rose from the tip of the Serpent's tail, hovered for a while, then shot up high into the sky and disappeared. Instantly, another orb appeared from the tail and drifted slowly over the terrified crowd, before shooting horizontally over the heads of the medicine man's entourage to explode with a loud bang at the edge of the cliff. Now the Serpent seemed to come alive, about to slither across the landscape, an invisible current flowing through its earthen body.

Panic-stricken, the medicine man rushed over to a warrior and grabbed his axe. The priest-king was still calmly chanting, staring up towards the black disc. The medicine man raised the axe high in the air and brought it down with a dull thud on to the back of the priest-king's head. The priest-king stood there for a few seconds, before raising his arms high in the air towards the black disc, still holding the stone between his finger and thumb, as if directing it to the heavens. Very slowly, his knees buckled and he fell forwards to collapse face-down on the ground, the axe deeply embedded in his skull.

A split second later, a star, conspicuous by its red colour, momentarily twinkled more brightly than the others. Then a brilliant shining halo appeared around the black disc and rays of blinding white light shot out into the heavens.

2

Antarctica, present day

The captain couldn't help feeling tense as he lined up the plane with the distant ice-covered runway and the landing gear clunked down. The enormous C-130 Hercules was fully laden with just about everything needed for the Antarctic research stations dotted over the Norwegian territory of Dronning Maud Land.

In the jargon, visual flight rules applied with Troll Airfield and there was no instrument landing system. In other words, he was in full manual control of the aircraft. His co-pilot picked up on his colleague's tension and they both stared straight ahead, grateful that the sky was clear and the landing conditions were perfect.

The co-pilot saw it first in the distance: a glowing white ball hurtling down towards the plane from the heavens. Before he could say anything, the fireball rocketed past in front of them, so close that the plane shuddered. There was a roar as it flashed into the distance, leaving a trail of white smoke.

"Jeez, what the…" was all the captain could mutter as they saw a flash of light in the distance.

They barely had time to talk about it as he landed the plane perfectly and it taxied to a standstill. The pair of them slumped and stared at each other with a look of disbelief. The co-pilot found himself shaking uncontrollably.

"Did I imagine it or did we just have a near miss?" said the captain. "Definitely not something I would like to experience again."

"I doubt if either of us would," his co-pilot replied, trying to maintain a professional cool despite continuing to shake. "I wonder what the odds are of seeing that."

"It looks as if it went down in the British sector," said the captain, looking into the distance. "That should really give their meteorite search team something interesting to look for."

"Perhaps we should be heading back now," shouted Amanda Holness, wiping the snow from her goggles with a gloved hand. The katabatic wind had seemingly blown up from nowhere and the sun had faded to a dull glow appearing intermittently through the driven particles of ice and snow.

"One more pass, then that's it," shouted back Pete Hughes. He shielded his eyes as the wind momentarily dropped and he caught a glimpse of the mountain range in the distance. From there the intensely cold, dense air was rushing down to the ice plain below, picking up the surface snow as it descended.

The news of the meteor sighting had excited Amanda's team. Though nobody in the British sector had actually seen the meteor, they had now been diverted to the area where the Norwegians estimated any fall would have occurred. So far, the search had been unsuccessful and now the weather was closing in.

Amanda had been thrilled to be chosen as one of the two women to be based at the Halley Research Station, sited on an ice shelf right on the edge of the desolate Antarctic ice-covered land mass. The highly original design of the research centre was already famous, but her first sight of it from a plane banking over it had made her smile with delight. The line of eight colourful modules raised high on hydraulic legs really did look like an army of AT-AT walkers straight out of *Star Wars*.

The small team drawn from Manchester University in the UK had a special mission. In recent years it had been increasingly recognised that the Antarctic was an ideal place to hunt for meteorites. Not only were they easy to spot on the surface of the ice, but as the ice flowed slowly from the interior of the land mass to the sea carrying its treasures from outer space, it occasionally came up against barriers such as mountain ranges. At places like these the meteorites were forced to the surface to be concentrated in so-called "stranding zones".

But the UK team had a slightly different purpose to that of other meteorite teams on the continent. Out of 35,000 documented meteorites around the world, more than two thirds had been found in Antarctica. However, the ratio of iron meteorites, as opposed to stone, found in Antarctica was far lower than that found in the rest of the world. It was believed that this was because the sun heated the iron and so the meteorites melted the snow immediately beneath them. They then sank down and became hidden from view. Now the team had successfully adapted mine-detecting technology in order to find the iron meteorites. They had already found four specimens that very morning in a known stranding zone where the four snowmobiles had been methodically conducting a search before they had been diverted.

As they sped back to their base camp through flurries of snow, it was Amanda who spotted the hole in the ice just ahead of her. She swerved her snowmobile round and stopped sharply, waving eagerly to Pete, the team leader. He spun his snowmobile into a tight turn and drew up alongside her, signalling to the two other team members. She looked around, and though visibility was limited, she could see no other holes in the ice. It was almost as if something were waiting to be discovered.

Very tentatively, she looked down into the hole. And there it was: a freshly fallen meteorite that had been hot enough on impact to have melted the ice and sunk down a full foot. "I nearly ran over it. It's definitely a meteorite," she called out as her colleagues walked over.

Pete bent down to inspect it. "Well I never," he said. "Let's bag it." He trudged back to his snowmobile and fetched the collection kit. After taking a GPS reading, he took out a pair of tongs, to avoid contaminating the meteorite, painstakingly extracted it from the hole and placed it into a bag as carefully as he could.

He passed the bag to Amanda. Barely able to control her excitement, she held it up and inspected the contents. It was no bigger than a clenched fist, but it was the pitted surface that intrigued her – evidence of material being burnt away as the meteorite hurtled through the Earth's atmosphere. "I think it's stone," she said. "It's not heavy enough for iron."

"God, we would have to find it in a snowstorm," grumbled Pete, fumbling for a pen to write the label. He scrawled a few key details and attached the label to the bag. "Okay, all done. Let's go," he called out, walking back to his snowmobile. "I'm hungry."

By the time they made it back to the base camp, the storm was abating. Andy Dunning emerged from the biggest of the six tents to greet them. "Any luck?" the burly Yorkshireman called out.

"Four iron and one stone one," yelled back Amanda. "And guess what? We think the stone one is the one that came down yesterday."

Andy was officially responsible for the maintenance of the team's equipment, but he could best be described as a general factotum. Although he was originally trained as an electrical engineer, it seemed he could turn his hand to anything, whether fixing broken snowmobiles, general plumbing, sorting out computer problems or, what he liked most, a spot of cooking. A huge, jovial presence who liked a drink, his practicality and bonhomie made him very popular. Though he was now just about bald, his luxuriant ginger beard supported his claim to be of Viking stock, a claim

13

he found useful if he sensed any trouble brewing between teammates. "Okay, let's get the machines under cover," he called out genially. "Have you got the meteorites, Pete?"

Pete passed him the bags. Andy checked the label on the bag containing the stone meteorite. "Well, that's a stroke of luck finding this." He moved the bag up and down. "Definitely not iron. Perhaps we should send it to Ben Harrington at the Natural History Museum. Grub's up in half an hour," he yelled over his shoulder as he took the bags to the equipment tent.

Fortunately for him, no one on the team was vegetarian and he had been able to indulge himself in preparing a chicken curry, his favourite dish and a meal he considered ideal for an evening in the Antarctic.

After the meal in the communal tent when everybody was feeling mellow and relaxed, Andy, with a theatrical flourish, produced a bottle of malt whisky.

It was not long before Pete, well-pleased with the success of the past couple of days and slightly inebriated, was regaling his colleagues with stories of ancient meteorites and how they had been worshipped. "Well, just think about it," he said, "if you didn't know better and saw a bright light streaking over the heavens towards you with a roaring sound and landing with an enormous bang. And then you found it and it was still hot and smoking. Wouldn't you think that whatever sky gods you believed in had sent it down and perhaps it was an omen – maybe good, maybe bad? Wouldn't you have worshipped it?" He paused and looked at everybody in turn. "And did you know it could be that the memory of meteor worship still lives on?"

"Where?" asked Amanda.

"Mecca, of course," replied Pete, dramatically. "Legend has it that the Black Stone in the Kaaba is a meteorite, and that originally Mecca was a pagan site where the stone was worshipped. Naked priestesses were supposed to have danced around it seven times in an anticlockwise direction – what pagans call widdershins. Mohammed is said to have destroyed all the other idols, but he left the stone alone. Even now, pilgrims doing the Hajj try to touch it, but they usually have to content themselves with walking around it seven times."

Pete was still in full flow as he walked, a little unsteadily, with Andy back to the tent they shared. "Did you know the goddess Aphrodite was worshipped as a stone in ancient Cyprus? The stone is still there, in a museum near Paphos."

Andy yawned and was ready to sleep, despite the fact that it was still very light and would be staying light throughout the night. The snowstorm had abated and just odd flurries swirled around them. The sun, still well above the horizon, was trying unsuccessfully to break through dirty yellow clouds, creating an eerie, ghostly atmosphere.

Sitting on his camp bed, Andy held out the now near-empty bottle of whisky. "One more dram each to finish it?" he ventured.

Pete held out a plastic cup and nodded. "The world's largest meteorite is estimated to weigh sixty-six tonnes. It was found in Namibia and is called Hoba…" He noted that Andy had drained his cup, lain down on his bed and closed his eyes. "Tell you tomorrow," Pete whispered, and stretched out on his own camp bed.

Andy normally slept well, and especially after a drink. He liked to relax his mind thinking about some technical problem and how he would tackle it the next day.

Perhaps it was the snoring of his colleague that disturbed him, together with the images of Mars fed back from the exploration rovers that he had been looking at on his computer. The technical aspects of the programmes had always fascinated him and he had avidly followed their investigations over the years. Maybe the desolation of the Antarctic had played on his mind, knowing the workers based at the research station were the only people around for hundreds, possibly thousands, of miles. Or perhaps it was something else.

His dream, or was it a vision, was as vivid as if he were there. He was aware that the sky was a dull orange and that a dust storm was blowing. Occasionally a small sun appeared and then disappeared, occluded by the dust. A sense of desolation overwhelmed him.

Slowly the storm abated, the dust settled and the Martian scene he had studied so often suddenly appeared. It was a dull, desolate, bleak landscape, devoid of any signs of life: just rocks, more rocks and a mountain range in the distance.

It was then that he heard it. It was a *clang*, like somebody hitting a bell. It faded slowly, until it disappeared. But he sensed in his dream state that something profound was happening to his mind. Now he heard a low murmuring mixed with odd squeaks, followed by a rumble, almost a groan. Something intangible, something at the limits of his senses, was speaking to him, trying to communicate with him. He felt a sudden flash of fear, then a feeling of dread, yet he did not know why. Instinctively, his mind battled against it, until at last the sensation faded and he opened his eyes.

He lay there wide awake, listening to Pete snoring, until Pete eventually woke up in the early morning and stretched out his arms.

Pete looked over at Andy, bleary-eyed. "Have you made coffee yet?" he asked.

Andy ignored his question. "You didn't feel it, then?"

"Feel what?"

"Something trying to make contact."

"What the hell are you talking about?"

Andy didn't say anything; he got up and sat on the edge of his camp bed. He looked bewildered.

"Something just happened. Something happened just now."

"What do you mean, 'something happened'?" said Pete. "Look, do you want a coffee? I'll make it."

Andy ignored him. "It was like I was on Mars, Pete. It was like a dream, but more real."

Pete was now looking worried. "Are you all right?"

"I don't know," said Andy. "Then I heard the sound of something like a bell being struck. It was as if something was trying to hypnotise me – trying to take control of my mind."

Pete stared at him, not knowing what to say.

"I fought against it until it stopped," Andy went on. "But I know something's here – something that wasn't here before. And it's not far away." He paused. "I don't know what it is, but nothing like this has ever happened to me before. Whatever it is, it was trying to force itself into my mind – like it was trying to take over my mind. I'm scared, Pete. I think it's evil."

3

NASA Johnson Space Center, Houston

The chair creaked ominously as he leant back in it and put his feet up on the desk in front of the giant screen.

His assistant stopped typing into her computer and glanced over at him. "Strictly speaking, Dr Gallagher, that's a misuse of government equipment."

Dan Gallagher stood up, switched off the screen and swung around to face her. "Yeah, yeah, I know. It was a crap game anyway." He reached out, took a sheet of paper from the printer, read it, groaned, screwed it into a ball and threw it into the bin in the corner of his office. He grunted with satisfaction as he scored a direct hit. Then his face broke into a broad, appealing smile. "Any chance of a coffee, Ginge?"

Taking off her tortoiseshell glasses, his assistant glared at him, her green eyes glinting. "Don't call me 'Ginge' – it's gingist. And if you keep saying it, I'm going to report you to a ginger-support group. We are special, you know."

"So Ben Harrington over in the UK keeps telling me. His redhead girlfriend sounds real scary." He smirked, whirled around a couple of times in his chair, got up and leapt over to her. Sinking down on one knee, he gazed into her eyes. "Okay, you win. I am your most obedient servant, special ginger person," he said, and reached out to kiss her hand. With that, he jumped up, ran over to the office window overlooking a lawned quadrangle, waved his arms around in the air and shouted, "Gingers rule, okay," to nobody in particular. An attractive blond girl walking below his office looked up and waved back.

Putting on a hurt expression, his assistant passed her hand over her short, neatly cut hair to smooth it down. "Actually, my hair is not ginger – it's pepper and salt, in case you haven't noticed."

"Once a ginger, always a ginger," he said.

She raised her hand up as if to hit him, but picked up a sheaf of papers instead and handed them to him. "There you are – one draft paper. You can type it up yourself next time – I stayed late last night doing it. And don't forget you've only got two days before it has to be submitted."

"Thanks, honeybunch," he said, taking the papers.

She drew in breath sharply. "And don't call me 'honeybunch'. That's sexist."

"All right, then, 'Dr MacDougall' it is," he said, hanging his head down in mock apology, so that his long dark hair fell around his face, revealing the odd grey strand.

"Mary will do just fine," she said quietly. "And you should get your hair cut, *Dr* Gallagher," she went on. "I don't know how you can represent the department looking like that. You could at least get a new pair of jeans – there are holes in those."

"It's the fashion," he countered. He raised his eyebrows. "Mind if I smoke a joint?"

"Don't be stupid. And stop trying to wind me up. Anyway, you look like something left over from Woodstock."

"You sound just like my mother," he said.

"She has my sympathy," Mary MacDougall retorted. Then she giggled. "I expect you'd like a doughnut with your coffee?"

"Yum, yum," he said, smiling, and started reading the first page of the paper. "'Recent Advances in the Curation of Antarctic Meteorites,'" he read out. "More routine stuff. Boring, really."

"Well, you are supposed to be a cosmic mineralogist. It's all part of the job," said Mary.

"I know, I know," he replied. "But it's the fieldwork I love, not curating meteorites."

"Hankering after the Antarctic again?"

"Now that's what I call real adventure. Out there in the wilderness, never knowing what the weather will do. Never knowing what you will find."

"It'll be your turn again soon," said Mary sympathetically.

"There's a whole bunch of people wanting to work in the Antarctic."

"But you're special. After all, you actually worked on the Allan Hills meteorite they found in the Antarctic."

"Yeah, that was good fun. Trouble is, most people now

agree that the so-called nanobacteria they found on it were inorganic structures formed here on Earth. Not evidence of microbial life on Mars."

"Not everybody agrees, though – you're not alone," said Mary. She was about to continue when Dan's phone rang.

He picked it up and looked at the display. "Ben Harrington," he mouthed to Mary. "Hello Ben," he said. "We were just talking about you—"

"Then you haven't heard yet," Ben cut in. "Talk about a coincidence…"

"What do you mean?" said Dan.

"In the Antarctic – we've just heard. A Norwegian supply plane actually witnessed a meteor strike. It landed in the British sector – we've already found it. Thought you might like to know."

"God," said Dan. "That must be a first. Has it been classified yet?"

"Not yet," said Ben. Just then there was the sound of a dog barking loudly over the phone. "Quiet, Daisy!" Dan heard Ben say. "Sorry about that," Ben continued. "Holly's dog wants to go walkies. Listen, I'd better go. I'll keep you posted about the meteorite. It'll probably be sent to me for identification and curation."

"Typical Ben wind-up," said Dan, putting his phone down. "A Norwegian plane actually witnessed a meteorite fall and the British found it in their sector. He just wanted to let me know that our search teams are not the only success story."

Mary smiled. "Perhaps he's wanting to get you involved, Dan. He knows you're at a loose end." Intending to walk

21

over to the coffee machine, she stood up and smoothed down her skirt. As she reached out to pick up Dan's empty coffee mug, somehow her hand got caught on a computer cable and pulled it so sharply that it sent the mug skittling along the desk. She tried to grab it but missed, and it fell off the desk to crash loudly on the floor, sending pieces bouncing away in all directions.

Dan sat bolt upright in his chair. Then his body started to shake. Turning away from Mary, he closed his eyes, as if retreating into a world of his own. He sat there quietly for a full minute, breathing deeply, before opening his eyes, standing up slowly and walking to a window. Gazing out, he watched people walking past below, some chatting in groups, some laughing or just rushing along, late for a meeting.

Mary studied him anxiously as he slowly relaxed, consciously resisting the temptation to go over and put an arm around him. "Sorry," she whispered.

He turned around. "It's okay," he said with a thin smile. "It's me who should apologise."

4

There is something that seems strangely out of place in the south porch of the parish church of St Peter and St Paul in Long Compton near Oxford. The light, airy church sits at the edge of the Cotswold village and, in common with the local cottages, is built from warm, welcoming, honey-coloured limestone. But there are many visitors who say that the effigy in the porch is decidedly chilling and scary.

A leaflet in the church describes it as a "fourteenth-century tomb of a recumbent lady with an exotic headdress and her feet resting on a small dog". Some people, though, are not so sure and there is much speculation about who really might have been in the tomb. The effigy is so badly worn that it is difficult to discern the facial features and only the eyes can be clearly made out. More than one observer has commented that they seem to follow you around wherever you stand.

It could be argued that as the monument is so dilapidated, it could be far older than the existing church. Inside, there is a plaque listing the vicars from the thirteenth century onwards, but the present building is said to be have been constructed on the site of a fifth-century Anglo-Saxon church, where it is reputed that St Augustine once preached.

Now, inside the church on Easter Sunday, a class of children was learning about the resurrection of Jesus from his stone tomb.

If the scene in the church concerned matters of the soul, that in The Black Dog at the other end of the village was centred on more earthly pleasures. In fact, its primary function as a meeting place centred on the consumption of alcohol and food had remained the same for the nearly 300 years since the inn was built.

In the middle of the afternoon the diners who had packed the place for the traditional Sunday roast lunch had now drifted away, leaving a group of regulars who had gathered to enjoy the locally brewed beer and the week's gossip.

On this occasion, however, there were two additional customers. Reflecting the easy-going ambience of a place that, over the centuries, had seen it all, they barely attracted attention.

The two women were chatting animatedly at a corner table where they were sharing a bottle of wine. One, in late middle-age, her hair hanging long and loose and obviously dyed, was wrapped in a deep green cloak over a full-length crimson velvet dress. A multitude of brightly coloured bangles rattled as she spoke and her long silver pendant earrings shook whenever she laughed.

Her companion could not have been more different. She was in her early twenties, and her clothes proudly marked her out as a British Goth. She was wearing a glistening, ankle-length, black dress with button-up Victorian boots. On her coal-black hair, she wore a black fascinator with a fine veil that covered half her white face. The dramatic image was heightened by the heavy use of black mascara and eye-liner, plus purple lipstick and matching fingernails.

Both women stopped talking and stared at a man who had just walked into the pub and was looking around. His new green tweed jacket, brick-red trousers and brown brogues marked him out as a man who worked in the City and was enjoying a weekend jaunt in the countryside. The Goth giggled and put her hand over her mouth.

The older woman tried not to smirk. "Stop it, Greta," she said.

The newcomer stopped in front of a large, black Labrador that was sprawled out between him and the bar. It had appeared to be asleep, but opening one eye, it turned over onto its back with the clear expectation of being tickled.

"Just ignore Satan," said the landlord, Dave Taylor, from behind the bar. "He's being soppy again."

The man stepped over the dog, which lazily turned back over onto its stomach and closed its eye again.

Dave cleared a couple of empty glasses from the bar and looked up at the man.

"Yes, sir?"

Reaching out, the man touched the label on a pump handle. "Half of that, please." He watched the landlord as he filled the glass. "Interesting name – Satan?"

Dave looked up. "Pub tradition. There's always been a

black dog called Satan here. Probably to do with the local folklore."

"Folklore?"

"You know, since time immemorial people have said there's a phantom black dog around here, and if you see it, someone close will die. Maybe even the person who sees it."

"Satan doesn't look much like a phantom to me."

"No, don't worry, old Satan's real enough – especially if you tread on his tail."

Dave had already recognised the man as someone who had just bought a dilapidated cottage in the village and was doing it up; his job ensured that he was familiar with all the latest village news, though for him the newcomer was simply a fresh customer. Approaching thirty, the newcomer had a pallid, tired face, sharply at odds with the weather-beaten faces of the three farmers at the other end of the bar, who were busy complaining about the rising cost of the soya that they were feeding to their animals.

"Here for the weekend, are you?" asked the landlord, as he put the beer on the bar.

"Yes, up from London," replied the man, handing over a twenty-pound note. "I'm doing up a cottage here. I expect it'll take some time."

"That's the one down at Witch End, then," said the landlord, giving him the change.

The newcomer smiled sardonically. "Yes, I was told all about Witch End after I bought the cottage. It's a lovely village, though," he went on. "I'm just reading up on the history."

"Yes, there's clubs and societies for just about everything here, including the Historical Society if you really want to get stuck in."

"I've been reading about the history of witchcraft here," said the newcomer, taking a sip of his beer.

Dave laughed. "An awful lot of people come here asking about that. You should have a chat with William over there," he said, indicating an old man sitting at a table by himself and nursing a near-empty beer glass. "He's a mine of information.

"William – have you got a moment?" the landlord called over. "Gentleman here is interested in our reputation for witchcraft."

William just nodded and touched the empty chair next to him.

"I hope you don't mind my disturbing you," said the newcomer, standing by the chair. "I've just bought a cottage here – I'm doing it up. I'm Henry – Henry Bentley-Overton," he added, sitting down.

William briefly shook hands with Henry Bentley-Overton. "Pleased to meet you, Henry," he said, with a twinkle in his eye. He nudged his glass forwards, almost as if by accident.

"Another pint?" asked Henry, getting up.

While Henry was at the bar, William winked at another old regular sitting on a bar stool, who rolled his eyes towards the ceiling.

"Wasn't there once a murder here connected to witchcraft?" Henry asked, as he passed over the beer and sat down.

"Jake, over there," the old man said, raising his arm to catch his friend's attention, "he knows all about the history of witchcraft round these parts. He's better than me." He beckoned to his friend, who quickly drained his glass and joined them. His gnarled hands indicated that he was a manual worker.

"What'll it be?" asked Henry, slowly getting up again.

"Very kind of you. My usual, please. Dave behind the bar knows."

Henry returned with another pint.

"Interested in witchcraft, are you then?" asked Jake.

"Only in that I've just bought a cottage in Witch End," replied Henry.

"Not one of those politician types who've been moving in here, are you?" asked Jake.

Henry looked taken aback. "No, no, I'm a banker," he said. "I need some fresh air for a couple of days after a week in the City. And it's nice and peaceful here."

Jake grunted. "Wasn't always so peaceful here."

Henry looked at him expectantly.

"Witchcraft. Put us on the map, it did," said Jake, leaning towards Henry.

"I did read something about it—" said Henry.

"It was 1875," cut in Jake. "Local farm boy. A bit weak in the head. There was this old lady – Anne Tennant was her name. Her house was at Witch End as well. James Hayward shoved his pitchfork right through her throat and pinned her to the ground. Then he carved bloody crucifixes on her face and chest with a billhook. Well, it petrified people, didn't it? They knew, you see – that's how you kill a witch. When the police got him, he said there were sixteen other witches in the village. The inquest was held in The Red Lion down the road. Wilful murder, the jury found. Anyway, he didn't swing. They said he was mad, so they locked him up in the loony bin. Died there, I believe."

"What about now? Are there still witches here?"

Jake took a deep swig of his beer and raised his eyebrows quizzically. "Well, you never know."

"You see, around here witchcraft ran very deep," said William. "All to do with the Rollright Stones up the road. They were always having pagan ceremonies up there. All around here – it was a sacred place for the pagans, even before Christianity arrived. Still is. The whole area was covered in burial sites, they say. Ploughed over now, I guess."

"You been up there?" asked Jake.

"Yes, a couple of times," said Henry.

"So you'll know all about the legend, then?"

"Tell me again."

"Well, there's the King's Men – that's the stone circle. Then there's the Whispering Knights – that's the ruined burial chamber about four hundred yards away. On the other side of the lane that runs through Rollright, there's the King Stone, all by itself.

"So the legend says a Danish king came to the Stones with his army and was accosted by a witch. So she says to him, 'If you take seven long strides and can see Long Compton, then you'll be king of England.' Well, he can't resist it, can he? He takes seven strides, but this mound rises up and blocks his view. So he couldn't see the village, could he? Well, she's got him, hasn't she? So she turns him into stone – that's the King Stone – and his army as well – they're the King's Men. The Whispering Knights are five knights who were plotting against the king, who she also turned to stone. After that, she turns herself into an elder tree. And do you know what? A few years ago they found the grave of a woman nearby. They also found this bronze ladle in the grave. They reckoned it was used for pagan ceremonies and that she was a witch." With that he glanced up at the clock above the bar. "Got to go and pick up my granddaughter from Sunday school – better be going."

"Yes, I suppose I'd better be off myself," said Henry, looking at his watch and standing up. "Got to drive back to London." As he made his way out, the Goth girl and her friend smirked at each other and then ostentatiously cackled.

Dave looked up from pulling a pint and winked at them. William just smiled and briefly raised his glass.

At the Church of St Peter and St Paul, a group of parishioners was standing in the porch chatting as they waited for their children. What happened next happened so briefly that nobody noticed and, if they had, they would probably have put it down to a gleam of sunlight reflected from a passing car. Because, just for a second, the stone animal at the feet of the effigy of the woman seemed to light up and glow.

5

On the Thursday night after Easter, just a few hundred yards from the parish church of Long Compton, Dr Ben Harrington was sitting, half-dressed, at the small desk in the bedroom of his rented terraced cottage. He was completely absorbed in checking his emails.

Holly Fraser was perched on the end of his bed, wearing his dressing gown, clearly wondering how she could attract his attention. "You must be pleased," she said. "The village hall was packed last night. Not bad for a Wednesday evening."

Ben pressed a key on his computer and looked up. "Yes, it was a good turnout," he agreed. "Especially seeing that it was the local history society. I think people like the mystery associated with meteorites – that they've travelled for millions of miles from outer space." He picked up a lump of rock on his desk. "And this is what they really loved – the chance to actually hold a meteorite that's come from Mars."

"And you were able to tell them a great story about it," said Holly.

"Well, it was quite something," said Ben. "I mean, for it to flash past a plane and then for a British team to find it."

"Doesn't Manchester Uni want it back?"

"They're in no rush – they're now more interested in the iron meteorites they're finding. They only wanted me to confirm what type it is." He gently turned the meteorite around in his hand, inspecting it. "This one's stone. It's an achondrite. Not the usual SNC categorisation though – it's an orthopyroxenite."

"And what on earth does that mean?" said Holly, opening a cupboard and eyeing a neat stack of sweaters.

"You know," said Ben. "The same as Allan Hills 84001, the meteorite from Mars they thought contained fossilised signs of life – primitive bacteria. President Clinton actually made an announcement about it being the first evidence of extraterrestrial life."

"I thought in the end they decided it just looked like bacteria?"

"But not everybody accepts that," said Ben. "There's still research going on trying to prove they were life forms. Dan Gallagher knows more about it than I do." He noticed an email from his boss and muttered, "Oh no, not another bloody departmental meeting."

"I liked the bit about the mythology," said Holly. "I didn't know about all that." She selected a pale blue sweater and arranged it next to a navy skirt lying on the bed.

"Yes, that did seem to go down well," replied Ben. "The science bit was okayish, but it was the mythology that really caught their imagination. You could tell from the questions."

"What?" Holly laughed. "You mean 'stellar structure and evolution' wasn't a turn-on?"

Ben gave her a wry smile. "You try and make the development of your photovoltaic solar power cells of interest for a talk in the village hall."

"You had Charles to help," said Holly.

"True," Ben replied. "I'm so lucky he lives in the village. What he doesn't know about ancient civilisations and their beliefs about the heavens isn't worth knowing."

Holly went back to the cupboard, selected a pink sweater and placed it next to the blue one. She studied them both and shook her head. "Where is Charles, by the way?" she said, perching on the end of the bed.

"He's in Ireland, doing a spot of tour guiding around the Neolithic sites. It keeps him busy."

"I just hope he's okay. He must get lonely since Alice died, being by himself at his age." She turned back to Ben. "Do you really like my hair?"

He sat down beside her on the bed. "Of course I do. I love everything about you – you know that."

"Would you like a new dressing gown for your birthday?"

Ben looked surprised. "Why? What's wrong with this one?"

"I suppose it does match the bedroom curtains."

"I know it's getting on a bit," he said, shrugging his shoulders. "I haven't really thought about my birthday."

"You're going to be thirty," said Holly, shifting closer to him.

"So?"

"Perhaps we should have a party – we've still got time to organise it."

Ben checked the date on his watch. "But my birthday's not for a month – there's loads of time."

Holly got off the bed, sat down in front of the small table-top mirror on the chest of drawers and started to brush her hair again. She gazed at her reflection. "Do you prefer my hair up or down?"

"Either way," replied Ben, going over to her and kissing the top of her head. "But I love the way you have it at the moment."

She pulled a handful of hair across her face. "Do you still think redheads are special?"

"Oh, absolutely no doubt about it," he said, smiling and pretending to wipe sweat from his brow.

She got up and put her arms around his neck. "As long as it stays that way." She pulled him closer. "Ben – I've got something to tell you," she whispered in his ear.

"What's that, then?" he said.

"Well…" She kissed him on the cheek.

"Well, what?"

Holly was about to reply when a loud howl came from downstairs.

"Is that Daisy?" asked Ben. "Did you forget to feed her?"

"Of course I didn't. I wonder what's up with her," said Holly, looking concerned. She took her arms from around him and went down into the front room.

A brown and white cocker spaniel was lying on the carpet, whining. It stood up, barked at Holly and lay down again, its head on the carpet so that its long floppy ears spread out on either side. Holly knelt down and put the dog's head in her lap. "What's the matter, Daisy, darling?" she said.

The dog looked up appealingly at her owner and moaned quietly.

As Holly stroked her head, Daisy seemed to relax. "There, is that better now?" said Holly, and she got up. She studied Daisy for a while, but the dog seemed to have recovered.

"What was wrong with her?" asked Ben, as Holly came back into the bedroom.

"I don't know," said Holly. "A bad dream, maybe. She seems all right now."

"What were you going to tell me?"

Holly was about to reply when her expression changed to mild annoyance. "Does your neighbour have to have his radio on so loud?"

Ben listened for a few seconds. "What radio? I can't hear anything. Anyway, Al is away – he's been in Switzerland for the past week doing a geological survey."

"Perhaps someone else is in there," said Holly.

"I don't think so. It seems dead quiet there."

"Oh, now it's stopped."

"I heard nothing," said Ben. "Anyway, what is it you were going to tell me?"

Holly shook her head. "I've forgotten now." She sat down again on the end of the bed. "We're going out tomorrow night, aren't we? Perhaps I'll remember by then."

"Yes, we're going out for a meal at The Plough. Are you all right? Is that still okay with you?"

"Yes, yes, of course it is," she said, and stood up. "I'm going to get ready for bed." Before Ben could reply, she frowned. "That bloody radio is on again. It's Stravinsky's *Rite of Spring*, isn't it? Probably BBC Radio 3."

"I can't hear a thing. Really…"

"But it's getting louder. Perhaps there's a burglar there…"

Ben shrugged his shoulders, did up his shirt and put on his trousers. "I don't think a burglar would bother to put the radio on. But okay, I'll check next door – if you really want." He raised his eyebrows at Holly, headed downstairs to the front door and went outside.

He stood and listened in front of his neighbour's house. Hearing nothing, he rang the bell and called out, "Al? Are you there?" Nobody answered, so he tried the door handle. The door was firmly locked. Ben stood there for a while, listening, before returning to his own house. "Nothing," he said. "Al's still away. I couldn't hear a thing and there's nobody there."

Holly sat down on the bed and clasped her hands to her ears. "Ben – it's back again. It's getting louder and louder. Now it's blasting in my head. Do something! Please!"

6

Professor Charles Gresham was miserable. There was no wind or breeze and the drizzle was still falling steadily and vertically. In fact, it had hardly stopped during the entire three days he had been in Ireland.

An archaeologist, he had specialised in the Middle East and he was more attuned to coping with the rigours of the heat and dust in Syria and Iraq. Wars had put paid to any fieldwork in these countries and he had progressively switched to interests that were closer to home. Theories concerning migrations during the time of the Neolithic, over 5,000 years ago, westwards from the Near and Middle East, eventually to the Atlantic seaboards of Western Europe, had increasingly intrigued him. Now he had gravitated to almost an obsession with the stone circles and standing stones still dotted all over the British Isles.

Charles shivered, aware that the raindrops dripping from his waterproof jacket were starting to soak his shoes. He yearned for the sunshine that had once lit up his life. Alice, his wife and a fellow archaeologist, had often accompanied him on field trips. It was nearly a year ago that she had died and he was still waking up in the middle of the night feeling desperately lonely. Recently retired at sixty-five, he was grateful that his emeritus status allowed him to give the occasional lecture and to participate in the activities of the School of Archaeology at Oxford University.

It was the research on the rock art scattered over the wilds of Britain that was now starting to intrigue him in more positive moments. He had found that similar motifs and symbols were present all over Western Europe and he had previously seen others as far east as Azerbaijan around the Caspian Sea. This, naturally, gave him the opportunity to explore remote landscapes, to commune with nature and recollect the good times he had had with Alice. If he occasionally burst into tears, perhaps it was only a solitary hawk that would be a witness.

He was starting to feel the need for human company, possibly people who were unaware of his loss. Their only son, a banker living in Hong Kong, was preoccupied with his own family and career. Though Hugo was always ready to talk, Charles was conscious of burdening his son with his own sadness.

When a sympathetic and concerned friend had introduced him to a tour company specialising in Britain's rich heritage of Neolithic monuments, knowing that they were looking for a knowledgeable guide, Charles had needed little persuasion to accept an offer. Making travel plans, giving talks and sometimes looking after elderly tourists kept him busy during the daytime.

The Neolithic temple of Newgrange was in the

Boyne Valley, not too far from Dublin. It was rightly acknowledged as a masterpiece of the Neolithic world. Older than the Pyramids, the temple had been left to decay over the millennia. Only in the past sixty years or so had its importance been fully recognised, and it had since been methodically studied. Now that it had been rebuilt and given protected status, tourists were required to register at a visitor centre and taken to the monument in buses.

The six tourists in Charles's group were pleasant enough. The white-haired American was clearly fascinated by the achievements of his ancient Irish ancestors and his wife seemed content that he was happy. The three British men, two of whom had long, straggly, grey ponytails, were decidedly eccentric and were clearly drawn to a place that resonated with the spirituality of a lost civilisation they yearned would return. The tall Swede just kept himself to himself.

Even in the rain, the sight of Newgrange inspired awe. Dome-shaped and topped with grass, it was almost the size of a football pitch. The façade on the entrance side was covered in quartz pebbles that would have glittered in sunshine. Guarding the entrance to the temple itself was a huge recumbent boulder, covered with abstract carvings that commanded attention. Perhaps these were the predecessors of Celtic art, with swirling spirals intertwined in a possible reference to another world, the world of the dead. In truth, no one really knew their true meaning and what archaic beliefs they represented. The debate had continued and, in more positive moments,

Charles sometimes dreamt that he would be the one to crack the mystery.

Perhaps it was the grey skies of Ireland and the constant rain that were affecting him. More likely it was the subconscious awareness that Newgrange had been built to honour and actively commemorate the dead. All Charles knew was that a deep melancholia had settled over him and that he desperately needed to break out of it.

"Our turn now," he said, with a slightly forced smile as the official guide raised her arm in the air to the next group of tourists.

The guide was young, in her early twenties, and full of life. She held out her hand to test the rainfall, looked up at the heavens and shook her head, smiling. "Let's just get inside, shall we?" she called out in an attractive Irish lilt to the twenty or so visitors assembled at the entrance.

Charles couldn't help but instantly warm to her youthful enthusiasm. She was wearing jeans and a bright red cagoule and, together with her cropped dark brown hair, her appearance was almost boyish. No one, though, could doubt her femininity as she warmly welcomed and chatted to the tourists entering the temple.

It was then that Charles noticed her eyes. Emerald green, they sparkled and seemed to draw him to her, almost as if he were being hypnotised. He wondered later whether Alice had had such an instant effect on him when they first met and felt a pang of conscience.

He let his party go ahead in front of him and followed them down an artificially lit passageway, until they were in the central chamber deep inside the temple. The guide waited until the group settled down and then pointed out the three smaller side-chambers, each containing a large, shallow stone basin.

"Nobody really knows what they were used for," she said. "It is possible that they put the bones of their ancestors in them to make contact, maybe to ask their advice. Or it could have been just to remember them."

It was then that she pointed out the rock carvings. Echoing the designs on the boulder outside the entrance, the carved spirals seem to draw the eye into the living rock.

It was the three spirals linked together, like a three-lobed clover leaf, that attracted most attention. She explained that it was known as a triskelion and that the design is still found repeated in various forms the world over, from the three-legged emblem of the Isle of Man to the seal of the US Department of Transportation.

The excitement was almost palpable as the guide approached the climax of the tour. She pointed out that the passageway was orientated towards the sunrise on the winter solstice and that a remarkable discovery had been made in 1969. With that, she doused the lights, plunging everything into darkness. The group fell silent. A thin light appeared through a slot in the stones above the entrance. Slowly, the light grew and crept along the passage, until the central chamber was filled with artificial sunlight. As it fell on the triskelion, the group watched entranced.

At that point something strange happened. In a side-chamber, Charles imagined – or did he actually see? – a figure with long white hair, wearing a full-length cloak woven from undyed wool. The figure had its back to the group and was leaning over the stone basin. It slowly turned around to reveal the ghostly image of a priest, his beard almost touching a glittering gold torc at his neck. His blue eyes radiated a sense of benign authority. With a hint of a smile, he nodded once towards Charles, then faded away. The apparition was there for merely a few seconds. Charles blinked and looked around for a reaction from the others. None of the tourists appeared to have seen it, but he noticed that the guide was looking at him with interest. As the group shuffled back down the passage to the grey skies and rain, he thought in vain for an explanation. Shaking his head in bewilderment, he took off his glasses and cleaned them with his handkerchief. Putting them back on, he decided he needed a cup of tea.

The guide was standing just inside the entrance answering questions. "Excuse me," she called to Charles as he approached her.

Charles wondered what she could want, but he had intended to thank her, anyway. "That was excellent," he said.

"I'm so pleased," she answered. "Do you mind if I ask you a question?"

Charles was slightly taken aback. "Of course not."

"When we lit up the inner chamber, you seemed distracted by something?"

Charles looked embarrassed.

"It's just that there's an interesting legend associated with Newgrange. It's said the place is haunted."

"Haunted by what?" said Charles.

"The ghost of a priest. An ancient priest who is conducting a ceremony in the central chamber…"

Charles went pale.

"You saw something, didn't you?" said the guide.

"I thought I was going mad," said Charles. "Has anybody else seen it?"

"Only one person I know of, personally," she replied, smiling. "But Newgrange is a very sacred place," she continued, "and visions in sacred places aren't exactly rare, are they?"

"I don't think my vision is quite in the same category as St Bernadette's visions of Mary at Lourdes."

The guide laughed and held out her hand. "My name's Gráinne O'Connor. Is that your tour group over there?" She pointed to his group, who were standing together in the rain, talking and occasionally throwing him a glance.

"They are indeed," he said, and introduced himself, explaining his background and interests in the Neolithic. "But it's the rock art that really fascinates me," he couldn't help telling her.

"I'm the same," she said. "In fact, I'm doing a doctorate on it at Trinity College. I work here part time." The group was now looking over to him more and more frequently.

Gráinne waved to them in acknowledgement. "Look," she said. "Have you got a notebook?"

Charles fumbled in his pockets and handed his notebook and pen to her.

Gráinne jotted something down and handed them back. "Here's my mobile number and email address. Let's stay in contact. And if you're over here again, let's meet up."

For Charles, it was as if the sun had come out again.

He shook hands with her. "I'd like that," he said, and turned towards the tour group. "Coming," he called out.

When his group got into the bus to return to the visitor centre, he noted with pleasure that they were all talking enthusiastically to each other.

The group sat together in the visitor centre café, nursing hot drinks, as Charles explained the astronomical significance of many of the Neolithic monuments and their links to heavenly bodies. His phone vibrated. He looked at the number, but there was no name associated with it. "I'm so sorry, but I'd better answer it," he said before getting up and walking quickly to a quiet corner.

"Charles Gresham," he said and looked bewildered for a moment, before his eyes lit up. "Well, well, well – Warren Treadwell. What a pleasant surprise. My God, it's been a long time. How are you? Where are you phoning from? How did you get my number?"

"Fine, Charles, fine. One of your colleagues at Oxford University gave me your number. And I'm still here at Boston University – still teaching archaeology." They chatted amiably for a few minutes, updating each other on their lives since they had worked together at the British Museum at the start of their careers, though Charles carefully skirted around the death of Alice.

"So when are you coming to the UK?" he asked.

"I was rather hoping you could come to the States." There was a brief silence. "That's really why I'm phoning. It's not actually something I wanted to put on the record – rather a delicate matter."

"Sounds intriguing," said Charles.

"Possibly the most intriguing thing in my career," replied Warren. "Down in Ohio – near the Serpent Mound – I've found something I think is very important. Look, Charles, I know this is unorthodox, but can you get yourself over here?"

"Could you tell me just a little more?"

"Charles." He paused. "Charles, it's so important that it can change our thinking on American history. It's dynamite. And it's going to attract a lot of attention. Some welcome, some unwelcome."

Charles didn't say anything, but glanced over at his group. They were still deeply involved in discussion.

"Charles, I need somebody with your knowledge and expertise. And I need someone I can trust. I can't say more now. Can you get yourself over here? We will cover all your expenses – make you a consultant or whatever."

"I have to admit I'm intrigued," said Charles. "What's the weather like with you?"

"Beautiful," replied Warren. "Sun's shining and not a cloud in the sky."

There was a long pause at Charles's end.

"Good," said Warren. "Then I'll see you in three days' time at Northern Kentucky International Airport at Cincinnati. You won't be disappointed, I promise."

Charles shook his head, smiling, slipped his phone back into his pocket and walked back slowly to his group. They were all still engrossed in conversation and nobody even looked up at him. "Shall we take the bus to see the other temples at Knowth and Dowth?" he said cheerfully.

7

Holly retched into the washbasin again. She groaned, brushed her hair away from her face and ran cold water into the basin. "Morning sickness – just my luck."

Ben put his arms around her shoulders. "You poor thing. Come and sit down," he said, steering her towards an armchair. He puffed up a cushion and helped her sit. "Is there anything I can get you?" he asked.

Holly shook her head. "I just hope I don't have months and months of this."

"At least it's Sunday," said Ben. "You don't have to worry about work and I've got a couple of magazines for you to read. Let's just take it easy today."

Holly nodded and slumped back into the chair.

"I read morning sickness when you're pregnant can cause confusion," said Ben. "That could be why you thought you heard the radio on next door."

Holly looked up blearily. "No, I know I heard music from a radio," she said emphatically.

"But you haven't heard it again, have you?"

"No, thank God. But just believe me, please, Ben. I know I heard it – okay?" She looked around. "Where's Daisy?"

"I'll go and have a look," said Ben, heading towards the kitchen. He came back shortly, looking guilty.

"You left the back door open again, didn't you?" said Holly.

"I'm sorry," he replied. "She's probably next door in Al's garden. He's always giving her bones. He said he once found one in his rhubarb patch."

"Can you check, please?" asked Holly, wearily.

Ben returned after a couple of minutes. "No, she's not there. I'll go and have a look out the front. She may have got into the street to try and cadge a treat. Everybody seems to love her round here."

He opened the front door and looked up and down the street. Again, no sign of the dog, not even a neighbour or a delivery van. He came back into the house, looking mystified. "I couldn't see her," he said. "I'll go and have a proper look." As he was putting his jacket on, his phone rang.

"Ben, it's Joanne Clayton here. I'm up at the Rollrights, taking Snowy for a walk. Did you know Daisy's here by herself?"

"Oh, thanks, Joanne," he said, breathing a sigh of relief. "I was just going out to look for her. I'll come right up." He mouthed "Daisy," to Holly. "Is she okay?" he asked.

"Yes, she's fine. Actually, I'm not sure – she's over at the Whispering Knights, going round and round the railings and whining. Shall I try to get her into my car?"

"No, no," said Ben. "I'll come and get her. Thanks so much for letting us know. So lucky you were there." He put his phone down and looked at Holly. "She's up at the Rollrights. I'll go and get her."

"I can get her," said Holly. "I need some fresh air." She heaved herself up out of the armchair. "Have you got her lead?"

Ben fetched it from a hook near the front door. "Are you sure?" he asked.

"I'm fine," she said, reaching for a coat. "I won't be long."

"Any problem, just call," Ben said.

Holly drove the short distance up the hill to the Rollright Stones. Even early in the morning, the lay-bys were practically full, and she parked the car in the only available space.

Noting a large group of German tourists gathered inside the stone circle and being addressed by their tour guide, she walked quickly to the track that led to the Whispering Knights. Even from a distance she could see Daisy walking round and round the monument, trying occasionally to get through the railings. "Daisy!" she called out as she approached the collapsed burial chamber, relieved there were no visitors there. Yet Daisy seemed unaware of Holly's presence. She had now sat down and seemed to be whining at the stones.

"What's the matter, Daisy?" she said, stroking the dog's head. Daisy still didn't react and kept on whining.

Holly quickly clicked the lead on to Daisy's collar and pulled gently. "Come on, Daisy. Time to go home. Your dinner's waiting," she added, smiling encouragingly. "It's a nice bone, a very special bone."

In the end, it was only by getting hold of Daisy's collar

that Holly managed to forcibly drag her away. Yet the dog still tried to turn back and whined as she reluctantly followed Holly back down the track. If Holly had looked back, she would have noticed the tiniest wisp of mist rising from the centre of the Whispering Knights.

The group of Germans had now left and only a few cars remained in the lay-bys. Daisy seemed to relax as they neared Holly's car and jumped into the back without any persuasion.

However, just as Holly was about to start the car, Daisy started to bark. "Shush, now, Daisy," said Holly, slightly irritated. Daisy continued to whine softly and lay down flat on the back seat.

It was at this moment that Holly heard the gentle *clip-clop* of a horse's hooves and a trundling sound, getting louder as something drew closer. She looked in the rear-view mirror and saw a horse and cart approaching them.

As the horse and cart passed by, she was confused. The horse she recognised as a Shire, a traditional workhorse of the English countryside, widely used before the advent of tractors. Huge and grey, its lower legs were white, with feathered hair covering the hooves. But it was the driver who completely threw her. He resembled something out of *The Hay Wain*, the famous painting by John Constable, painted 200 years ago. Dressed in a smock, with leather gaiters around his legs, he was wearing a battered straw hat. The cart was heavily laden with a cargo of hay, which bounced up and down as if it were on a rutted country track.

Holly watched incredulously as it passed, the driver

staring straight ahead, seemingly completely unaware of her existence. When Daisy started barking again, Holly turned around. "Stop it, Daisy. That's enough." Daisy lay down again on the seat, quiet. Holly turned back again and stared at the road ahead in amazement. The horse and cart had completely disappeared.

8

At two o'clock the following Monday morning, an elderly VW Westfalia camper van eased into the deserted lay-by close to the entrance to the Rollright Stones. John Bowman switched off the ignition and sat there, letting his eyes adjust to the darkness. He opened the door, got out, took a deep breath of the cool air and stretched out his arms to the sky to release the tension after a two-hour drive. The sky was clear and, although moonless, peppered with stars. He gazed upwards, soaking in the atmosphere, for a full five minutes.

He reached in for a Thermos flask on the passenger seat and poured himself a cup of hot tea. He had taken a late evening ferry from the Isle of Wight to Southampton, driven through Newbury and Chipping Norton, and was now well over halfway to the cathedral city of Coventry. A native of the Isle of Wight and a proud "caulkhead", John chose to commute weekly to Coventry and his job as a telecommunications engineer. A break at the Rollright Stones had become a habit and reflected his interest in anything concerned with the so-called "Old Religion" of Britain.

As was also his custom, he liked to stroll around the stone circle at night when it was deserted and at its most magical. Cup in hand, he casually walked a short distance along the road, the stone circle shielded by trees and shrubs, until he reached the entrance to the site. However, as he reached the entrance, something made him stop in his tracks. He could see a distinct glow coming from the direction of the stones.

At first, he thought that maybe a witchcraft ceremony was in progress and that it would be unwise to be spotted. But he couldn't control his curiosity and cautiously crept forwards to where he could see the stones more clearly. What he saw made his senses spin: the tops of all the seventy-odd stones were glowing with a phosphorescent blue light, making them seem taller than they already were.

He tried to think of a rational explanation. Had someone put blue lights on top of each stone? Not likely, as the blue lights flickered like flames. They were clearly not man-made, and besides, no one else was there. He would tell just a few friends later that the lights reminded him of the "will-o'-the-wisp" phenomenon that sometimes occurs on marshland and that country folk used to believe were fairies or elemental spirits.

Entranced, he gazed for a few seconds in wonderment at the stones. Then the cold reality of what he was witnessing kicked in. He muttered an expletive to himself, turned and started walking quickly away. Halfway from the entrance, without looking back, he started to run in pure fear towards the camper.

If he had not been so overwhelmed by the whole experience and had by chance looked towards the Whispering Knights in the distance, he might have noticed the stars disappearing from view just above the collapsed capstone, as a dark cloud formed.

Then, just as he reached the camper something swept past him like a swarm of demented bees, yet completely silent, as if not of this world. He grabbed the door handle and stood there, petrified, as the swarm moved quickly over the road. There, it abruptly stopped. Amoeba-like and about the size of his van, its ever-changing form pulsated, strands of the nebulous body occasionally stretching out across the road in his direction, as if sensing his presence.

He instinctively clicked the door open and whatever it was seemed to make a decision. Without a sound, it moved unimpeded through the gate that led to the King Stone.

If John had been able to see the King Stone through the thick hedgerow, he would have seen that the whole pillar of stone was emitting a pulsing light. Like a lighthouse, it seemed to be broadcasting a warning over the landscape.

He fell back into his van, yanked the door shut and locked it. Shaking, he fumbled in his jacket pocket to find his car key and went to start the van. Nothing happened. Swearing to himself, he nervously dared to glance in the direction of Long Compton, praying that whatever it was had gone. Seeing nothing, he turned the key again and shuddered with relief; the van started instantly. As he slammed it into gear and let the clutch out too quickly, it jerked forwards before accelerating away into the darkness.

Shortly afterwards, unseen by him, the porch of the Church of St Peter and St Paul momentarily lit up as the stone at the foot of the ancient effigy glowed a phosphorescent blue.

To this day John Bowman has been guarded about recounting his experience, aware that the incident was too bizarre to be readily believed. But he knew that what he had witnessed had been very real.

9

John Bowman was not the only person who had a profoundly disturbing experience that night.

In the early hours, Holly was lying on her back, unable to sleep. Alongside her, Ben was snoring gently. Holly envied him. She had always been a light sleeper and, as she lay there, a mixture of feelings tumbled through her mind. She was deeply conscious of the new being growing inside her and of her deep responsibility for it.

Then she couldn't help worrying about her strange mental state. Had those recent weird experiences really happened or had she just imagined them as a result of her new physical condition? Eventually, the comforting influence of the tiny baby inside her calmed her mind and her body and she relaxed enough to drift off into a light sleep.

It didn't happen straight away. She was aware something was happening when she sensed something alien, something primaeval, attempting to break through into her mind. It was as if it were outside a door, tapping insistently, asking to be let in.

She never knew how it happened, whether she herself

opened the door or whether it was forced open, but she found herself present in a scene so realistic that she was not just an observer, but part of it.

Initially, she sensed the air around her becoming cooler and she shivered involuntarily. It was the dazzling vista of a crystal-clear night sky that she noticed first. There was no moon, but high above her the Milky Way seemed to flow like a celestial river.

Now she became aware of myriad other stars. Two points of light, though, were brighter than the others. She recognised one immediately: the planet Venus, the Evening Star, seemed friendly and welcoming.

It was the other, though, almost directly above her, that quickly drew her attention. It could not have been more different, and the sight of it baffled her. A glowing red dot of flame, it blazed angrily. A memory flashed into her mind: she had seen it once before. When she was a young girl, her father had taken her into the garden and shown her the star, explaining that Mars hadn't been so close to the Earth for 60,000 years.

As her eyes adjusted, she realised that she was standing on the top of a cliff, overlooking a secluded sandy beach. A calm sea stretched out to a barely discernible distant horizon and glistened with reflected starlight.

She turned around to see behind her a flat landscape of coarse grasses, gradually merging into sparse woodland consisting mostly of birch trees.

It was at this point that she noticed a movement. Emerging from the woodland was a group of shadowy figures, which were coming in her direction. Intrigued, she watched the figures come closer until they assumed the shapes of four human beings walking in single file.

She now knew instinctively, as if in a dream, that she would be able to integrate herself into the group and, instantly, she found herself among it. There was no response to her presence and, like an invisible spirit, she moved alongside the figures.

At the sight of a man in front, however, her mood of wonderment changed to one of apprehension and fear. She quickly realised that she was witnessing a scene that must have happened 60,000 years ago.

The leader emanated a brutish power and strength. He was wearing animal furs, crudely stitched together, that barely contained his massive barrel-shaped chest. Reaching just below his knees, the furs revealed huge calf muscles that seemed to harden with each step and, like his arms, were covered in dark hair. On his feet he was wearing moccasins made from tough animal skin. In his right hand he gripped a long wooden spear, tipped with a shard of flint bound in place by a length of twisted fibre.

But it was the sight of his headdress that made her shudder. The head of a wolf covered most of his face, and though clearly desiccated, it still induced the ancient dread of the totemic animal. Jutting out over his bearded face, the wolf's mouth hung open so that the teeth were bared in a permanent snarl. The eyes were sunken pits in the fur, but the ears still stood upright and its fur pelt hung down over his hunched shoulders, adding further to the sense of menace. With obvious authority the man was purposefully leading the three others towards the beach.

Of the three, two were clearly men, dressed similarly in furs, but wearing no headgear, so that Holly could discern their massive heads covered with straggly dark hair that hung down over their shoulders. Pronounced ridges of bone shielded dark, alert eyes that missed nothing. Their noses were broad and fleshy, with flared nostrils that twitched like those of the seasoned hunter.

But it was the other figure walking between the two bare-headed men that startled her when she realised it was a girl, clearly no more than fifteen years of age. Unlike the men, she was fair-skinned, slightly built and carried herself upright with a natural elegance. But, most distinctively, even at such an early age, she was already much taller than the men.

Holly felt an immediate empathy with her. Even though she could not determine the colour in the starlight, she knew instinctively that the girl had red hair, perhaps because of the freckles scattered around her fine features. Worn long and plaited, her hair hung down to her waist.

Her garment indicated that someone had taken great pride in its design and preparation. Judging by its soft and supple appearance, it was almost certainly made from the fur of a deer. Around her waist she wore a belt of carved stone spheres through which was threaded a long strip of fur tied in front of her so that it reached down to her knees.

To Holly it seemed that the girl was certainly from a different tribe to the three men and could even be a member of an entirely different species. She knew enough to guess that the men could be Neanderthals, or possibly a race she knew nothing about. But the girl? She didn't know. Whatever her tribe or species, though, Holly could only think of one word that characterised her, and that was "regal". Intrigued, she watched the girl as she delicately picked her way through the rocks and odd shrub.

Something then struck Holly. The girl's pale eyes rarely looked around and she seemed unaware of her surroundings. It immediately entered her mind that the girl must be drugged, though with what she had no idea.

Occasionally the leader stopped, raised his spear, and pointed it towards the red star. His two followers halted at the same time. One joined his leader in pointing a spear in the same direction, but Holly noticed the other man was carrying a thick stick with what appeared to be a ball of fur tied to the tip. She wondered what it was.

The group now descended along a pathway to the beach and walked along the sand until they came to the end of the bay, where boulders had fallen at the base of the cliff.

The cave entrance was concealed by a large boulder, and certainly would not have been found except by someone with an intimate knowledge of its location.

The wolfman stopped and paused to get his breath back, before gesturing to the man carrying a spear. He immediately put it to one side and grasped the top of the boulder. With one heave, it rolled back to reveal a hole large enough for someone to crawl through.

Passing his spear back to the man carrying the stick, the wolfman reached inside his fur hide and produced what looked like a miniature archery bow, a stick and a piece of dried, crumbling wood. Within two minutes the primitive fire-making device had produced a glowing ember. Now it was evident to Holly that his follower had been carrying a torch and that the ball of fur was probably soaked in animal fat.

When the wolfman put the ember onto the fur ball, it flared instantly, producing a plume of black smoke. He raised the torch in a further salutation to the red star, before lowering his head and disappearing through the entrance to the cave.

One of his followers gently edged the girl forwards, as if he had great respect for her. Nervously, he reached up and put his hand on her shoulder. Bending double, she entered the cave. Within seconds the two men had followed her.

Again, in the same mysterious way, Holly found herself as an unseen presence inside the cave and alongside the group.

The girl apprehensively stood upright, her head just short of the cave roof. The light from the torch flickered on the cave walls, which Holly could see were quite smooth. The wolfman swept the torch around, pointed into the blackness ahead and nodded. Almost reverentially, the man with the spear lightly touched the girl on the shoulder. Expressionless, she still betrayed no emotion as she walked forwards, instinctively negotiating the few rocks on the floor.

Holly found herself moving along with the group, sometimes within it, sometimes behind it. It was after only twenty or so paces that she felt a current of air and noticed a ghostly light beaming through a hole in the roof of the cave, lighting up the walls and floor. She stood in the shaft of light and, gazing upwards, caught a glimpse of the Milky Way. To Holly, the stars seemed friendly and benign, in contrast to the growing feeling of impending danger surrounding the girl.

It was when the light from the torch caught the girl's face that the girl too seemed to become aware that something was wrong. She glanced around anxiously.

The wolfman continued walking and, grim-faced, the other two men quickly fell in behind the girl to edge her on into the gloom.

A feeling of dread and doom now overwhelmed Holly, as she realised she was witnessing an ancient ceremony concerned with something that lay ahead in the depths of the cave: something possibly connected with the planet Mars that she had seen glowing furiously in the sky and that the men had saluted.

As they moved on, the patch of starlight fell behind them and the tunnel grew wider and higher. Only the soft padding of moccasins on the cave floor and the occasional cough broke the silence. Holly felt the air chill and the light from the torch now picked out recesses and protuberances on the wall, casting eerie moving shadows.

The girl continued to stare straight ahead.

Shortly, the tunnel came to a dead end and the flare lit up a wall of fractured rock. The light moved down to illuminate a large and almost spherical boulder, wedged at floor level into the rock face.

The air of tension heightened when the wolfman

nodded to a follower and stood back while a rock underneath the boulder was removed. The boulder shifted slightly with a nerve-jangling grating sound, before it fell away from the wall of rock and rolled of its own volition to settle in front of the girl.

The stench was overwhelming. Invisible fumes poured out from the black hole and the effect on the men was instant. They put their hands to their faces as tears streamed down into their beards.

The girl reacted as if smelling salts had been waved under her nose. She stared around trying to work out where she was and what was happening. Then, as if all her senses had suddenly been switched back on, her face contorted with pure fear. She jumped round and made to run back into the darkness, but the two men behind her grabbed her. They held her tight as she struggled to free herself.

Holly knew exactly what was going to happen next. The hole that had appeared was just large enough for a person to crawl through. The wolfman passed the torch to one of the men, knelt down and disappeared into the hole. Then his hand reached back and took the torch, leaving the others lit only by a faint light from the other side.

Still struggling, the girl was forced to her knees and, with the wolfman pulling and the other two pushing, she was literally manhandled through the hole. The two men, still grimacing at the stench, followed the girl.

As the girl got up from her knees and stood upright, she seemed to freeze, overwhelmed by the sight that awaited her. The wolfman was standing there holding the torch high above his head, the light straining to reach just a fraction of a huge cavern.

Perhaps it was the sound of a rock dislodged by one of the men, echoing into the distance, but the girl instantly reacted and spun round.

Holly saw it at the same moment as the girl.

The wolfman had turned so that the light picked out a skeleton lying against the cavern wall, close to the entrance they had crawled through. Scraps of rotting flesh were still adhering to the bones and strands of long hair were hanging from the skull. Even though it was in the foetal position, as if trying to protect itself, it was clearly the skeleton of a tall person.

For just an instant, the girl froze, before she tried to run back to the cave entrance, only to see more tall skeletons pressed against the edges of the cavern. She struggled briefly when she was caught.

Holly could see the look of pure terror on the girl's face as the cruel truth now forced itself on her. It was obvious that people like her had died trying to escape from something nightmarish and that their terrible fate would soon be hers. The men sensed that the girl had realised what was about to happen and tightened their hold on her.

The wolfman now strode ahead into the cavern and stood in front of a rock ledge. The girl was pushed forwards to stand behind him for a moment, before he moved aside so that she was alone. Involuntarily, she started shaking.

In a naturally formed alcove behind the rock ledge was a black object. It was shaped like a huge teardrop, about three feet tall, tapering towards the top and pitted over its entire surface. Holly instantly recognised what it was: a magnificent meteorite.

With the assurance of familiarity with the ritual, the wolfman held the torch high in the air, so that the smoke rose straight upwards. The other two men moved in and stood on either side of him. The wolfman now took the proffered spear in his other hand and held it in front of himself, pointing it upwards, halfway between horizontal and vertical, the symbol of Mars, God of War.

Raising his head, so that the snout of his headdress was almost vertical, the wolfman began to howl; the sound bounced around the cavern. Slowly, it faded away. Now the three men raised their heads together and howled in unison. Again the echoes resounded around the cavern.

Terrified, the girl tried to run once again, but the wolfman stepped up and blocked her. Finally, the three men howled once more.

To start with, it was just a wisp of mist that crept from the base of the meteorite.

Seeing it, the three men responded quickly. As the girl was pushed forwards, the wolfman stepped a pace back, stopped, and nodded to the meteorite. Then he turned and walked purposefully back towards the hole through which they had entered. The other two men immediately followed him, clearly resisting the temptation to run. Shortly afterwards, there was a dull thud as the boulder was rolled back into place.

As the blackness enveloped the girl, Holly found herself beside her, desperately trying to comfort her. The girl cried out in some strange tongue, but in response there were only the other-worldly echoes of her own voice. She broke down, wailing, with tears pouring down her cheeks.

The girl was unaware that the mist was now flooding from the base of the meteorite, flowing over the rock ledge and spreading over the cavern floor towards her.

It was the foul smell getting stronger that first alerted her to its presence. Sobbing, she edged backwards, but within seconds it caught up with her, burning her nostrils. Choking and on the verge of vomiting, she tried to run, but she tripped on a boulder and fell to the ground. Staggering upright and touching her forehead, she felt the stickiness of blood seeping from a gash. She moved cautiously now, her hands in front of her, trying in vain to retrace the way to the cave entrance. But wherever she went, the stench stayed with her.

Only when she stumbled up against a wall of rock did she stop. Reaching out sideways, she edged around the wall of the cavern, but was moving in the wrong direction.

Holly tried and tried to guide her back. She put her arm around the girl, but it went right through her body. She shouted, she implored, but the girl didn't respond.

It was then that the girl stepped on the femur of a skeleton. There was a *crack* as it snapped. Tripping over the rib cage, she lost her balance and fell to the ground again. The mist flooded into her nostrils and, gasping for air, she struggled to get to her knees.

But it was too late. The last thing she saw was two red eyes appearing in the blackness, growing ever larger as they approached her.

Holly's eyes flicked open and she sat up in bed, trembling. She turned to Ben, but he was deeply asleep. When she shook his shoulder, he groaned, turned towards her and blearily opened his eyes.

She was almost crying. "Ben, I've just had a horrible nightmare…"

He slowly sat up, looking totally bewildered.

"I don't know what's going on, Ben. It wasn't just any old nightmare. It was as if something had taken control of my mind. It was so realistic, like I was there…"

Ben put his arm around her. "Tell me," he said, calmly.

He listened carefully as she described everything in detail. He was obviously lost for any explanation. "It does sound very terrifying, but it's all over now."

"No, you don't understand, Ben. The cavemen were like Neanderthals. The girl was completely different. I felt she was something to do with me…"

Ben lay back down, gently pulling Holly down beside him. "You must try and get some sleep," he said, softly. "There are two of you now." He reached out and took her hand. "It's all right," he said. "Just early pregnancy symptoms."

Even as he tried to sound reassuring, he was now clearly deeply worried and wondering what on earth could be happening to her.

10

Charles Gresham emerged from baggage reclaim in Northern Kentucky International Airport and stood there, looking for his friend Warren. He burst out laughing when he saw a board with his name on it being raised up and down by a grinning white-haired man. They chuckled as they warmly shook hands. "At least we've still got some hair, even if it has faded a bit," said Warren. "Wasn't yours black?"

"Light brown, actually," replied Charles. "At least I've still got a memory."

Well over six feet tall and wearing a beautifully cut suit, smart tie and polished brogues, Warren exuded an Old World charm and elegance.

Charles self-consciously did up a button on his old tweed jacket, one pocket laden with his glasses case, phone, odd coins and a tube of mints. He surreptitiously pushed the crime novel he had been reading down into the other pocket. They slapped each other on the back and chatted amiably as they made their way to the airport car park.

"Emeritus professor now, I suppose?" asked Warren.

Charles nodded. "It allows me to keep up-to-date and I still give the occasional lecture. Better than complete retirement."

"Same with me," said Warren. He decided to switch the conversation to their time together in London at the British Museum. "Do you remember the lady who brought in that little vase for identification? The one who said her father had been using it for his toothbrush? It turned out to be from Nineveh. Totally unique."

"I do, I do," replied Charles. "But wasn't it from Babylon?"

"Perhaps we should just agree on Mesopotamia," said Warren, laughing, as they reached his hire car.

Charles tried to get into the car on the driver's side, shook his head and went round to the passenger side.

"Well, what's it all about?" he asked, as they emerged from the slip road on to the freeway. "Why all the mystery?"

Warren looked pensive. "I've been involved in a dig near the Serpent Mound. It's an untouched burial mound – quite a small one. That's probably why it had been ignored. But as far as I know, what I've just found there is totally unique."

"What is it?" asked Charles, bemused.

"You'll see soon enough. I want to see your reaction."

Charles smiled. "Still the same old sense of drama. But why me? I still don't understand."

"You will," replied Warren. "And very soon – it's not that far. We've got an arrangement with a local college. Students from the college help out on digs – they get an introduction to all the fun of archaeology and we get cheap labour. Unfortunately, the students didn't find anything interesting. But I did…" He stiffened as a car swept past at high speed. "Why are people always in such a hurry?" he said, as he took out a bag of toffees from the glove compartment and held it in front of Charles.

"No thanks," said Charles. "You could at least give me a clue about what you've found."

"Okay," he said. "What do you know about the Serpent Mound?"

"Well, as you know, I'm really a Middle East man," replied Charles. "I looked it up on the net as best I could, but there are so many theories about the Mound. Even about who built it."

"Most people would put their money on the Adena culture," said Warren, "but, personally, after what I've found, I'm not so sure. The most recent carbon analysis on charcoal samples makes it at least 2,500 years old. It was probably just maintained by the Hopewell and Fort Ancient peoples who came later."

"It's the astrobleme connection that fascinates me."

Warren popped a toffee into his mouth and chewed ostentatiously. "You've got it in one," he said, eventually. "The Mound is on the site of an ancient meteorite impact. There's not much evidence in the land features. It happened about a quarter of a million years ago and there's no crater to see. But deep core samples show the evidence. And they have picked up geomagnetic anomalies."

Charles turned to him. "What do you mean by 'geomagnetic anomalies'?"

"Usually we're talking about local variations in the

Earth's magnetic field – they are often associated with geological fault lines and stresses in rock formations. But just recently odd people have been reporting something else – something quite remarkable…" He glanced at Charles. "They've been seeing earth lights – balls of light whizzing around and then disappearing."

"That's very strange," said Charles, sitting up in his seat. "What do you think is going on?"

"We don't really know," replied Warren. "It may be that the stresses in the fault lines are increasing. There's a theory that earth lights are sometimes seen before an earthquake. But it's only a theory…"

"As long as there's no earthquake while we're visiting the place," said Charles, turning to study the passing scenery.

After a few moments' pause Warren asked after Charles's wife and family.

Charles didn't answer immediately, as if trying to find the right words. "Alice died nearly a year ago, Warren. She was ill for a long time, but it still shattered me."

"I'm really very sorry, Charles," Warren said, quietly. They drove on in silence for a while, before Warren spoke again. "I never married, Charles. Guess I got stuck in my bachelor ways. Now I've got used to living by myself. You were very lucky to find the right girl."

Charles nodded and changed the subject, asking about the indigenous cultures of the mound builders and the latest findings.

An hour later they drove into the staff car park of Hillsboro Community College. They were met just inside the entrance by the beaming middle-aged school secretary.

"Good morning, Barbara," Warren greeted her. "May I introduce Professor Gresham – he's over here from the UK. We're just going to have a look at the dig and need a few things from the storeroom."

"It's so sad you haven't found anything interesting," said Barbara. "The students are very disappointed."

"There's time yet," replied Warren. "There might be something there just waiting to be discovered. Don't worry, I've got the key." He led the way down some stairs to the basement, unlocked a door, and reached inside to switch on the fluorescent lights. He held the door open for Charles.

There was a large table in the centre of the room, covered in polythene sheeting under which Charles could discern the outlines of bones.

Like a magician, Warren lifted the polythene with a flourish. "What do you think?" he said. "I've pieced it together as best I could."

"My God, but he was tall," said Charles.

"Practically seven foot," replied Warren.

The skeleton was in excellent condition, with jade ear studs displayed neatly on either side of the huge skull. Warren gently picked up the skull to show Charles the gaping hole in the back.

"He certainly died a violent death," said Charles. "And jade ornaments must have been quite rare in this part of the world." Then he noticed the small tufts on the skull. "Red hair!" he exclaimed. "You're right. As you said on the phone – this really is dynamite!"

Warren nodded. "It could be chemicals in the soil that changed the hair colour to red, but I've managed to take samples for DNA analysis. I'm going to check if the gene for red hair is present." He carefully placed the skull back in position. "He was buried in a dedicated mound," he continued. "He was special, Charles. He's completely different to any of the Native American skeletons that have been found – and an awful lot have been found. We're talking about a different race. There are various reports of giants being found during mound excavations, but when you ask where the remains are, nobody seems to know. So now you've got all sorts of conspiracy theories. But here we are – the actual evidence."

"Who else knows about it?" asked Charles.

"Only us, nobody else. Last week, I went to check the dig by myself in the evening. That's when I noticed the finger bone. It was barely visible. I couldn't resist excavating around it. Then I really got carried away. It took me all night to excavate the whole skeleton."

An enigmatic smile spread over his face. "There's something else," he said, and went over to a cupboard in the corner of the room. He brought out a small cardboard box, opened it and passed what appeared to be a stone to Charles.

Charles held it up and studied it. It was about the size of an orange, but almost black and with a pitted surface. "If it's what I think it is, it's a meteorite, isn't it?" He looked intrigued. "Where does it come from?"

"I'm impressed," said Warren. "Yes, when I excavated the skeleton, he was holding it tight in his hand. It was obviously very special to him and whoever buried him decided to let it stay with him."

"What are you going to do about it?" asked Charles, placing the meteorite very carefully on the table. "Are you going to make an announcement? Where are you going to publish?"

"For the time being, I'm not going to do anything."

Charles looked perplexed. "Why is that?"

Warren looked him straight in the eye. "Think about it, Charles. As we've agreed, this is dynamite. If I went public now, it would be worldwide news."

"What happens if somebody else sees the skeleton here? Somebody else must have another key. You won't be the only one."

"That's why tomorrow I'm taking him away. Then I'm going to quietly put him into storage in Boston." He ignored Charles's look of disbelief. "Look at it this way," he went on. "He was regal, wasn't he? Think about his size, his burial circumstances. And look at the beautiful ear studs. I've checked – the jade is not from the Americas. It's from the Far East."

Charles nodded.

"If we go public now, it will all become politicised," said Warren. "I know I have an academic duty to go public, but first I really want to get to the bottom of this. I want to do it properly and get as many facts as possible to minimise conjecture. I want to know where he came from and what he was doing here. But it's got to be handled sensitively."

"I can understand your predicament," said Charles, "but it's your reputation that's at stake – your lifetime's work. You'd be taking one hell of a chance."

Warren sighed. "I'm an old man, Charles, and I'd rather go out with a bang. That's why I invited you over – and I'm grateful you've come. Mainly because you're a friend and a man of integrity – I can trust you." He paused and smiled. "Just think – a spot of real adventure at our age."

Charles didn't look entirely convinced.

Warren pointed to the tufts of red hair on the giant's skull. "I think the red hair could be one clue. And you could be pivotal in all this. I mean, the mythology of the ancient world is your specialty and even I know there's a lot of mythology associated with red-haired people. You might be able to help work out where he actually came from."

"Yes, it is odd," replied Charles, "but red-hair mythology does crop up all over the world. There's barely a country that doesn't see redheads as different. Not just the hair colour, but something deeper than that. What's your attitude to redheads, for instance?"

"Me? Even at my age, the thought of a redheaded woman brings me out in a sweat."

"There you are – typical. But there's more to it than that, isn't there? Redheads have always punched above their weight. Just look – the scientist and astronomer Galileo – the artist Van Gogh – leaders like George Washington and Churchill. Then there are monarchs like Henry VIII, his daughter Elizabeth I, and even Egyptian pharaohs such as Seti I and his son, Ramesses the Great. And they're just a few of the big hitters. There are so many more…"

"But you're not even a redhead yourself," said Warren.

"Ah, but I'm definitely biased," replied Charles. "That's because my mother was a redhead. I probably carry the gene for the red hair in its recessive form." He smiled and added, "Even if my hair is white now."

Warren shook his head indulgently, then looked serious. "But there's this as well," he said, picking up the meteorite. "No way am I going to hand this over. This stays with me. This could be another key to unlocking the mystery of this person. And I know that you know all about the ancient worship of meteorites."

Charles went quiet for a moment. "Warren – why not make life easier for yourself? You need to know all about this meteorite, right? What type it is? Where it came from? I've got a friend who works at the Natural History Museum in London. He specialises in meteorites – it's his job. After all, if you hand it over for identification here, you'll have to explain where you found it. And that means you'll have to disclose all this." He gestured towards the skeleton. "Perhaps it would make much more sense to let me help with the meteorite."

Warren looked relieved and didn't hesitate in agreeing. "Good idea. I was wondering what to do with it, anyway." He grinned wickedly. "This could be an awful lot of fun, Charles."

Charles burst out laughing.

"So, we're in this together?" said Warren, handing over the meteorite.

Charles weighed it up in his hand, studied it briefly and then wedged it into his jacket pocket alongside his book. "Together," he said, and held out his hand.

Warren gripped Charles's hand, smiling at the sight of Charles's bulging pockets. Then he opened the door and put his hand on the light switch. "Time to go and have a look at the Serpent Mound," he said.

After a short drive, they were pleased to find the site of the Serpent Mound was quiet and the few visitors present were spread out along the pathways running the length of the winding, grass-covered mound.

It was as they were standing together by the egg-shaped embankment at the head of the Serpent that Charles put his hand to his forehead. "Sorry, Warren," he said, "but I'm feeling a bit faint. It must be jet lag."

Warren looked concerned. "I was going to show you the dig. Perhaps we should do it tomorrow. I must have already given you enough to think about."

Charles looked at the body of the Serpent stretching into the distance and blinked. "You know, I think I'm beginning to see things," he said. He looked again. "I could swear I saw the Serpent move. It definitely trembled."

Warren now looked alarmed. "Let's go and find somewhere to sit down. Would you like a coffee?"

Charles shook his head. "I think I'm going mad. Look, Warren, the Serpent is moving. Can't you see it? It's as if it's coming alive."

11

As usual, the Natural History Museum was thronged with tourists from around the world and different troupes of wide-eyed schoolchildren were being shepherded by harassed teachers, keen to remind their charges that the museum was home to exhibitions of plants, animals, fossils and rocks, as well as the scary T. rex that roared in the dinosaur gallery. Less well appreciated by the public was that the museum was also a renowned research centre and home to over 300 scientists engaged at the forefront of life and Earth sciences.

Ben Harrington was busy in the Earth Sciences Department preparing a section of a meteorite for study under a scanning electron microscope, when, out of nowhere, Charles peered over his shoulder.

Ben swung around, startled. "Charles! What a surprise. How the hell did you get in here?"

Charles beamed smugly. "Oh, I've still got some contacts here. Alf in security used to work at the British Museum." He looked with interest at the meteorite Ben was preparing. "Where's it from?"

Ben was still shaking his head in disbelief at the

surprise visit. "It's a lunar meteorite. It was found in the Outer Hebrides. The Isle of Lewis, to be precise."

"Can I tempt you to a coffee?" asked Charles. "I need your help and it's a rather delicate matter. Is there some place where we can talk without being overheard?"

Ben couldn't help being intrigued. "Okay, then," he said. "Just let me tidy up here." He decided on the Coffee House in the museum, where he knew they would be quickly served and would find a quiet corner.

They chose a table well away from other people. Ben watched, amazed, as Charles emptied four sachets of sugar into his cappuccino. "So, how was Ireland?" he asked.

"Wet," replied Charles. "So I decided to go to the States."

"Just like that?" said Ben, suppressing a laugh.

"Almost," said Charles. "An old friend of mine, Warren Treadwell, wanted some help with a project. He actually made me a consultant to Boston University. It paid for my trip." He looked around before reaching into an old carrier bag to fetch out the meteorite that Warren had given him. After removing the bubble wrap from around it, he put it on the table. "I need to know about this," he said. "What type it is and where it came from. Anything you can tell me about it."

Ben picked it up and felt its weight. "It's not an iron meteorite – I can tell you that straight away. Where does it come from?" he asked.

"It was found in Ohio."

"Then why don't you get it categorised in the States?"

"I don't want it to go through the system there," said Charles.

Ben looked surprised, but said nothing.

"I can't tell you why – not yet, anyway."

Ben was puzzled. "This is rather unorthodox."

"How did your talk about meteorites go in the village hall?" asked Charles.

"Really well," replied Ben. "They were quite taken by all the mythology you told me about. There were loads of questions. I wished you were there."

Charles said nothing, but just sat there smiling.

"All right, all right," said Ben, eventually. "I'll fit in some overtime this week."

"Good man," said Charles. "And how's Holly?"

"I've got some news for you, Charles," said Ben, and he took a deep breath. "Holly's pregnant."

"What marvellous news," said Charles with a broad smile. "And when are we talking about?"

"She's seven weeks gone," said Ben. He bit his lower lip.

Charles looked concerned. "You don't seem very happy about it. Is everything okay?"

"She's suffering very badly from morning sickness," said Ben.

"But that's not uncommon," said Charles, relieved. "It usually stops after a few weeks. I remember when Alice had it."

"But there's something else," Ben said. "I don't know whether it's to do with her pregnancy – with the morning sickness."

Charles didn't say anything, but waited.

"It started when she said she'd heard music on the radio. The radio wasn't on, Charles. The house was completely quiet." He went on to tell Charles the details of the incident.

Charles took a sip of coffee.

"But it didn't stop there," continued Ben. "Her dog, Daisy, ran away up to the Rollright Stones for some reason. When Holly went to get her, Daisy was over at the Whispering Knights, behaving oddly. Then, when Holly got her back to the car, Holly swears she witnessed a time slip." He described the details of Holly's experience exactly as she had related them to him. Finally, he told Charles about Holly's horrifying nightmare. "I'm really worried about her, Charles," he said.

Ben waited for Charles to respond, but he just sat there silently as if deciding what to say. Finally, he leant forwards. "I don't know if it's a coincidence, Ben, but I've had a couple of disturbing experiences myself. Have you heard of the Serpent Mound in Ohio?"

"Yes, of course – it's famous. It's the American equivalent of Stonehenge."

"Well, I've just been there with Warren Treadwell. I'm still trying to come to terms with it, but something very strange happened to me there." He looked around the café before continuing. "I swear I saw the Serpent move."

"What?"

"I saw it move. The Mound seemed to come alive and writhe like a snake."

"You have to be joking," said Ben.

"I wish I were joking. At first I thought it must have been jet lag, but nothing like that has happened before when I've been jet lagged. I tell you, the Serpent definitely seemed to be coming alive."

Ben looked incredulous. "What about your friend?" he said. "Did he see anything?"

"No – nothing. Warren didn't see or feel anything. He reacted just like you did. It was all rather embarrassing."

"Did you ask if anyone else had had similar experiences there?"

"We discreetly asked around. Nothing. Just the usual reports of New Agers feeling earth energies there – usually when they're high on something, no doubt. Warren said there'd been the odd reports of earth lights – just recently. But what I experienced – whatever it was – was overwhelming. And that wasn't the first experience I've had." He looked down at his coffee before looking up again. "Something happened to me when I was in Ireland."

Ben looked intrigued as Charles told him about his vision at Newgrange. "The thought of it all still keeps me awake."

"I'm not surprised," said Ben. He sat there, deep in thought, before he spoke. "The only thing I can think of straight away is that when you and Holly had experiences, you were both at, or at least near to, a sacred site. I haven't seen any reports in the media of people having the same type of experience, though. But that doesn't mean much – there've always been odd reports about strange happenings like that at sacred sites, so I doubt they would make the news – unless there was an epidemic."

"Has anybody else in the village seen or heard anything unusual at the Rollrights?" asked Charles.

"No, nothing as far as I know. At least, nobody's talking about it."

"I can't think off-hand of anything obvious that I share with Holly," said Charles. "Unless it's…"

"Don't tell me you're pregnant as well," said Ben. "Tell you what. Why not come round tomorrow night?" He picked up the meteorite. "By then, I should be able to tell you something about this. You'll be able to compare notes with Holly, too."

12

Holly stroked Daisy's head as the dog settled down in her basket for the night. "There's nothing to worry about, Daisy, darling," she said. "It's all quiet here now and you can have nice doggy dreams."

She turned off the kitchen light, half-closed the door and went back to join Ben, who was lying on the sofa reading a scientific journal. "Move over," she said and snuggled up beside him. "So, tell me again. What exactly did Charles say happened to him in the States?"

"He said nothing like it had happened to him before," said Ben, and he related again what Charles had told him. "He said that he was embarrassed by it all."

"Did you tell him about my experiences?"

"Yes, he was very sympathetic. What you two have got in common, I've no idea."

"What about the meteorite he brought in for you to have a look at?"

"He was rather coy about it. He just said it was found in Ohio. All very mysterious." He looked over at the meteorite sitting on the mantelpiece. "At first glance, it's very similar to that one – the one they found in the Antarctic."

"But do you have to have it up there?" said Holly.

"Why, what's wrong with it?"

"Well, it's ugly. Haven't you got anything else? A nice vase, perhaps?"

Ben shrugged his shoulders. "Okay, I'll put it away in a drawer if you really don't like it. All right?"

Holly nodded.

Ben put his arm around her and hugged her. "Listen, you need to rest if you're going to get over this morning sickness. I've got a heavy day tomorrow, too – another departmental meeting. And I want to finish off checking Charles's meteorite."

He went over and picked up the Antarctic Meteorite. "To think that this has come all the way from Mars," he said. "It's hard to believe."

As usual, once in bed, Ben was soon in a deep sleep.

Holly tried to sleep, but she couldn't help dwelling on Charles's experiences. She knew very well that her own experiences had nothing to do with morning sickness and she tried to work out what they had in common, apart from them both living near the Rollrights. There was nothing she could think of.

Thirty minutes later, still unable to sleep, she sensed that something was wrong. The temperature in the room was dropping.

She heard nothing, but gradually became aware of a presence. She forced herself to raise her head. Whatever it was, it was at the end of the bed. Well over Ben's height, there was a dark, blurred, featureless shape, through which she could faintly discern the nearly closed bedroom door.

She tried to scream, to shake Ben awake, but somehow was unable to move. She sensed that it was studying her, possibly deciding its next move. It slowly advanced down the side of the bed and stopped beside her. Paralysed with terror, she tried to look away, but couldn't help making out from the corner of her eye a sort of vaporous tendril snaking out towards her, until it was about a foot from her face.

Holly closed her eyes and waited, petrified. She was aware of something like static electricity around her, which made her skin tingle, and she knew that whatever it was, it was about to touch her face.

Then everything seemed to happen at once. Daisy started barking in the kitchen, Holly screamed, the apparition instantly disappeared and Ben woke up with a start. "What the bloody hell!" he yelled, sitting bolt upright in bed.

"There was something in the room," Holly stuttered as Daisy burst through the door and leapt up on to the bed.

"What on earth…?" said Ben, blearily looking around. "I can't see anything wrong. There's been nobody here."

"It wasn't a person, Ben. It was like a shapeless ghost. Like a moving mist – I could see right through it. It was just about to touch me."

"Jesus," muttered Ben to himself, and he wearily got out of bed. "I'd better go and check."

Within five minutes he was back. "All the doors and windows are locked," he said. "Nobody could have got in – or out."

"I told you it wasn't a person, Ben," Holly said, quietly. "I don't know what it was, but Daisy knew something was here. She started barking and it disappeared. It was horrible, Ben. Horrible, horrible…"

He patted Daisy. "Maybe she sensed you were having another nightmare, or whatever it was. Come on, Daisy – back to your basket." The dog looked at Holly as if checking she was all right before following Ben downstairs.

When he came back, Ben got into bed and drew Holly close to him. "Charles is coming around tomorrow evening to hear about his meteorite. Let's talk to him about what's happening to you both."

13

The following evening, Holly opened the front door of the cottage to find Charles standing outside. Much to his surprise and delight, she threw her arms around him.

"I do believe congratulations are in order," he said, and kissed her on the cheek.

She flushed, then grabbed his hand and pulled him into the hall. "Ben," she called. "It's Charles."

Ben immediately appeared, took Charles's arm and steered him towards the sitting room. "I've got something to show you. Something quite amazing…"

"Can I take my coat off first, please?"

Ben took his coat, half-threw it on to the back of a chair and handed him the meteorite found at the Serpent Mound. "This is your one. I've just finished categorising it."

Charles looked at it, bemused.

"Now look at this," Ben called out as he fetched the Antarctic Meteorite from the drawer in which he had placed it. He gave it to Charles. "Tell me what you think about them both. Something they might have in common, perhaps."

Charles studied his own meteorite first, noting the cut surface from which Ben had taken a small slice. Picking up the Antarctic Meteorite, he again noticed that a small slice had been removed.

Ben went and rummaged around in the drawer again before returning with a large magnifying glass. "Use this," he said. "You'll see it more clearly."

Charles carefully examined the cut surfaces of both meteorites. "Well, I'm no expert, but they both look the same to me," he said.

"Exactly," said Ben. "It's remarkable, isn't it? I'm practically certain they came from the same geological rock structure on Mars."

"But your meteorite – where was it found?" asked Charles.

"The Antarctic. It's a recent fall sent to me for categorisation." He took back Charles's meteorite. "It's a pity you won't say where you found this one," he said. "You're being very cagey. What are you hiding?"

"There is a reason," replied Charles. "I can't tell you the details yet, but I can tell you my meteorite fell thousands of years ago."

"An amazing coincidence, but not impossible," said Ben. "It could be they were both smashed off the same geological feature at the same time by an asteroid or by another meteorite, but were sent in different directions. Maybe it just took much longer for the Antarctic one to arrive here. There are all sorts of possibilities. There could be others out there in space or even somewhere here on Earth. But for them to end up here together! You have to admit, it's quite a coincidence."

"I don't like the Antarctic one," said Holly, bluntly.

Charles looked at her quizzically. "Why?"

"It just gives me the creeps. Sometimes when I look at it, I see a face. It's just like a horrible face, Charles. There's something malign about it."

"That's a bit melodramatic, Holly," said Ben. "It's just a stone, after all."

Holly took Charles's meteorite from Ben. "This may be the same, but to me it's different. I don't sense anything bad about it. If anything, it's benign. It feels friendly."

"What about you, Ben?" asked Charles. "Do you sense anything different about them?"

"To me they are just meteorites like all the others I've been involved with – probably over a hundred by now."

Ben looked at Holly and then turned to Charles. "I should tell you that Holly has just had another nasty experience. She says she saw a ghost or whatever—"

"It was real and it was terrifying," she said emphatically. "Ben thinks it's to do with my pregnancy, but it's not. There's something about this place and it has something to do with the Rollright Stones. And that meteorite they found in the Antarctic is involved as well. I know it."

Ben looked out of the window and said nothing as Holly told Charles the details of her frightening experience with the apparition. "And that wasn't all," she said, and went on to tell him about how, first of all, she had heard music on the radio when it was not switched on. After that, she had had an experience at the Rollright Stones with Daisy. She lowered her voice as she recounted the details of her nightmare. "It's getting worse, Charles," she said.

He listened patiently, and then nodded. "Ben did tell me, Holly. I expect he told you as well about what happened to me at the Serpent Mound and at Newgrange?"

"He did. But I'm not sure how seriously he took your experiences, either."

Before Ben could say anything, the door opened and Daisy walked in, wagged her tail at the sight of Charles, and sat in the corner of the room, as if listening to the conversation.

"Daisy sensed things the same as me," said Holly. "So why Charles, me and Daisy, but not you, Ben?" she asked, pointedly.

"And not Warren, either – my friend who was with me at the Serpent Mound," said Charles. "I told him it was probably jet lag, but I know it wasn't. But then I've witnessed nothing nasty. And certainly nothing as unpleasant as your apparition, Holly. Seeing the Serpent Mound as if it were coming alive was disturbing, but I didn't sense it was a manifestation of something malign."

"What I saw in the bedroom last night was definitely evil," said Holly. "I'm frightened of sleeping there now."

Ben turned back from gazing out of the window. "Let's try and look at it scientifically," he said. "There must be a rational explanation for what's going on."

Holly looked at him as if he had no idea of the emotional turmoil she was going through. "It's all right for you," she snapped. "Nothing has happened to you."

"No, Ben's right," Charles said calmly. "We need to take a rational approach, or we'll all go mad. What were you thinking, Ben?"

"Well," said Ben, "the only thing we've got to go on at the moment is that the Rollright Stones, the Serpent Mound and Newgrange are all sacred sites. If we take the Rollright Stones, for instance, there's a long history of reports of strange experiences – such as other reports of time slips and tales of the stones going down to a spring in Little Rollright Spinney on saints' days for a drink. Local farmers are said to have taken some of the stones for making bridges and the like, only to find they've been moved back overnight. Most people would say it's just folklore, though. But now, for Holly at least, it looks as if the stones could be involved in disturbing experiences."

"What do you mean, 'could be'?" said Holly. "And don't forget the Dragon Project."

"What's the Dragon Project?" asked Charles.

"It was a scientific attempt in the 1970s and '80s to measure so-called earth energies using scientific equipment," explained Ben. "They also explored the human element using psychics and dowsers. A lot of the work was done here at the Rollright Stones."

"Did they find anything?"

"Yes, I know that they got some exciting leads," said Ben, "but they ran out of money and the project has been wound down."

"Could we do anything like that?" asked Holly.

Ben looked doubtful. "I'd find it very difficult to get hold of the right equipment. And anyway, I don't really have the time. I could check out the details of the Dragon Project, though."

"Charles – do you know if there have been any studies like that at the Serpent Mound?" asked Holly.

"Warren didn't mention any, but I know they've done geomagnetic surveys and picked up anomalies. We could have a look at that."

"I might have a better idea," said Ben. "I've got a friend – Dan Gallagher – who works at NASA in Houston. He's a bit bored at the moment and he would have access to all the necessary equipment. I could try and get him up to Ohio for a couple of days."

"Why on earth would he be interested in something so speculative?" asked Charles.

"Oh, he's definitely that way inclined," said Ben, and he laughed. "He's never really got over seeing the Rolling Stones live and indulging in certain substances. He still likes to walk on the wild side occasionally. Thinking about it, though, it would be very useful if we could have a representative there – especially somebody who has had an actual mystical experience."

Charles looked wary.

"If I could tell Dan you would be there, Charles, I'm sure that would swing it," Ben said, with a twinkle in his eye.

"But I've just got back," he protested. "I'm supposed to be semi-retired. Anyway, who's going to pay?"

"How about your friend Warren, again?" said Ben. "You could take your meteorite back and show him the cut surface. I'm sure he'll want to hear all about what we've found out. All the work was done free of charge – but a total pleasure, of course," he added, smiling.

"Why not do it properly and take the other meteorite to show him?" said Holly. "He'd be fascinated to see them both together." She looked at Charles imploringly.

"But…" said Charles.

"I'll speak to Dan right now," said Ben, picking up his phone.

"What?" exclaimed Charles, looking very disconcerted.

Holly touched his hand. "Charles – if there is any possibility that the Antarctic Meteorite is affecting me, taking it a long way from here could prove it one way or another."

Charles felt Holly's little finger entwine around his. He rubbed his jaw as he thought. Then he nodded. "I'll speak to Warren," he said.

"I'd go myself," said Ben, "but you're a man of leisure."

"Not anymore," he replied.

14

It was late afternoon and the Serpent Mound site was about to close to visitors for the day. Charles and Warren were standing by Warren's car in the nearly empty car park.

Charles shivered and did up a button on his jacket. "Getting quite nippy," he said.

"It's officially springtime now and summer's not too far away," replied Warren, cheerfully. "As long as the only sensation you encounter here is being a bit cold. How are you feeling now? You rather scared me the last time we were here – I was quite worried about you."

"I feel fine now," said Charles. "I really don't know what it was. This time I've made sure I've taken a couple of days to get over any jet lag. Did you get shot of that skeleton okay?"

"Yes, no problem at all. I boxed it up myself and had it shipped to the university with instructions to put it into a locked store." He checked the time on his watch; it said four-thirty. "What time did you say the NASA fellow is going to arrive?"

"Dr Gallagher, you mean," said Charles. "He texted saying he'd be here by four o'clock. Perhaps he ran into traffic."

Warren looked doubtful, but said nothing.

"I do feel rather apologetic," said Charles. "I mean, being over here again so soon."

Warren laughed loudly. "Well, don't be. I'm delighted, Charles. I never knew I could have such an exciting time at this stage of life. It's almost as much fun as when we went out with those twin girls. Do you remember? Valerie and Janice who worked in the Egyptology Department at the Museum? They even dressed the same."

"How could I forget," said Charles. "I think it was Valerie I went out with. Never was sure though."

Warren laughed again. "Double trouble, indeed. They remind me of those two meteorites. Can I have another look?"

Charles retrieved his shoulder bag from the car, unfolded the cloth the meteorites were wrapped in and handed them to Warren.

Warren held one in each hand, felt their weight and examined them. "Even I can see they're from the same place. Your friend Ben says it was on Mars? What are the chances? They must be millions to one? It's almost too much of a coincidence."

He handed them back to Charles, who wrapped them up again, put them back in his bag and opened the boot of the car. "They should be safe enough there," he said, closing the lid.

"You say your friend's girlfriend doesn't like the one they found in the Antarctic," said Warren. "Why on earth…?"

"She thinks there's something rather malign about it – something primaeval."

"You know her, of course. Would you say she was quite stable?"

"Well, she is pregnant and suffering from morning sickness," said Charles. "I don't think that's the reason, though. Her dog is behaving strangely as well. The experiences she says she's had – they really were very scary. They're as if her sensory range has been increased. As though something that was latent in her brain has been switched on."

"And you say the site of the Rollright Stones has a reputation for strange experiences?"

"Yes – at least there's lots of folklore. It's the same with many other stone circles in Western Europe. I've made a point myself of talking to locals around the British Isles. It was a common belief that the stones were people who had been turned into stone – literally petrified – for indulging in pagan behaviour like dancing and playing music on the Sabbath. The Rollrights are particularly rich in folklore. There's even a legend of a black dog which scares people to death."

"Are you trying to scare me?" said Warren.

Charles laughed. "There'll be four of us, so we should be okay."

"Not if the other two are like you."

"I doubt if they are," said Charles. "Scientists are normally very down to earth."

Warren didn't look convinced. "But the investigations that were done at the Rollright Stones – the so-called Dragon Project? You said they were designed to investigate why sites like that affect people? And why they are still treated as sacred places?"

"Yes – it took place towards the end of the last century. Ben checked it out and told me all about it. It seems they did a lot of the scientific work at the Rollright Stones and some other sites as well. It was all done on a shoestring – the project was too speculative to attract mainstream funding. It did attract some excellent hard-nosed scientists and technicians though – but also psychics, dowsers and the like to check out the mystical side. It was a dual approach."

"What did they find out?"

"It was rather inconclusive, I'm afraid, but they did get some good leads. Unfortunately they ran out of money, so they couldn't follow them up."

"Sounds familiar," said Warren. "Researchers always want more money to do more work. But what sort of leads did they get?"

"One particularly interesting observation was made at the King Stone – the solitary standing stone at the Rollrights. Ultrasonic pulses were detected there at sunrise, especially around the equinoxes. The pulses faded as the sun began to rise. Another researcher took some infrared photos of the King Stone around sunrise. One photo actually showed a glow around the stone at the point of sunrise itself. It never has been satisfactorily explained. They also found some magnetic anomalies at one of the stones in the circle. Anomalies such as shifts in magnetic north have been reported at lots of sacred sites."

"Not that conclusive, then," said Warren.

"No, but three people involved in the project – all very sound apparently – had similar experiences along the road which runs past the stones. Coincidence or not, they independently reported seeing things which then just disappeared into thin air – a huge dog, a cart or an old gypsy caravan. You remember I told you about the time slip experience Holly had at the stones. They also picked up high levels of radioactivity around the road where it runs past the stones. Some researchers thought that could be the cause of the sightings."

"It all sounds rather speculative to me," said Warren. "And what is Dr Gallagher proposing to bring to the act here?"

"Ben and Dan are more interested in the scientific side. I think I'm supposed to represent the psychic side of things. Ben says as a starter they've agreed to repeat the experiments the Dragon Project did at Rollright – the ones that produced leads, that is. Dan's got hold of the same type of equipment they used. That's why we've got to be ready, all set up by sunrise tomorrow."

"What?" said Warren. "I don't think I've ever got up before eight o'clock."

"Don't worry, I'll slip some whiskey in the coffee flask."

"And who exactly is this man, Dr Gallagher, who proposes to get me out of bed in the middle of the night?"

"Ben says he's an outstanding scientist, but someone who's not averse to upsetting mainstream scientific thinking. Apparently he likes a spot of adventure. He worked in the Antarctic and then on the meteorite from Mars which was thought to contain the first evidence of extraterrestrial life. The majority view is against all that now, but Dan's not convinced. He's sympathetic to the idea of panspermia – the idea that life on Earth was seeded by something from outer space. He's got Francis Crick with him there – the man who discovered the structure of DNA with James Watson. Even Ben is not averse to the idea – he showed me a meteorite in the Natural History Museum that contains organic material. It actually smelled of sulphur. Apparently Dan's bored stiff with just curating meteorites and Ben had no problem at all with getting him involved here at the Serpent Mound…"

At that moment there was the loud rumble of a car exhaust system and a red Ford Mustang screeched into the car park. As it hurtled towards them, Warren and Charles both instinctively leapt back behind their own car.

The Mustang pulled up with a jolt and Dan Gallagher clambered out, his knees jutting out of the holes in his faded jeans. His long, grey-streaked hair hung down around his face, matching a generous growth of stubble.

Warren and Charles glanced at each other with a mixture of shock and surprise as Dan strode over to them, arm outstretched. "Dan Gallagher at your service," he said. His grip as he shook hands was enough to make them both wince. Charles was instantly reminded of a brilliant but rebellious student he had taught when he was a lecturer in the 1980s.

They were both so taken aback that they didn't notice movement in the passenger seat, as someone struggled to open the door. A large dent in it was obviously jamming the mechanism. Dan went over and yanked it open.

Mary MacDougall pursed her lips, grimaced and eased herself up from the low seat, taking care not to knock off her bobble hat.

"May I introduce Dr Mary MacDougall, who I have the rare privilege of working with," announced Dan.

Mary shook hands, looking embarrassed but managing a thin smile.

"Nice car," said Warren.

"Yeah," said Dan, and smacked the hood. "A friend of mine in Cincinnati lent it to me. We were in the army together. He lives in a trailer park now."

"Have you got everything for tomorrow morning?" asked Warren. "An early start, I've just been told."

"Yep," said Dan, opening the boot of the Mustang. "Here we are – a magnetometer, a Geiger counter, an ultrasound detector and a camera with infrared film – just as Ben requested. And good to see you here, Charles. Ben told me you're the weirdo element of the project."

"I don't know about that," observed Charles.

"Is everything okay with the admin here?" asked Dan.

"Yes, all sorted," said Warren. "I handled it myself – I spoke to the site director. We've even got permission to walk on the Serpent itself, provided we're finished well before opening time."

"Splendid, old boy," said Dan. "Where are you guys staying?"

"Harper's hotel in Hillsboro," answered Charles.

"Excellent," said Dan. "That's where we're staying. Do you guys know where we can get a beer and sort out the details for tomorrow?"

Warren groaned inwardly. "There's a place in Hillsboro I think you might like. I've driven past it a few times myself, but it looks a bit rough."

"Sounds fine to me," said Dan. "Ready, Mary?"

Charles opened the passenger door for Mary and held her arm as she sank down into the seat. He forced the door closed and a few seconds later the car started with a growl.

The Mustang had almost reached the exit from the car park when it skidded to a halt and Dan wound down the window. "Where did you say this bar is?" he yelled.

15

"Have a dram of this," said Charles, offering a hip flask to Warren.

"What, at this godforsaken hour?" said Warren. He checked his watch. "A quarter past three." He sighed. "Not even the birds are awake."

"Go on," urged Charles, holding the flask in front of Warren's face. "I've just had a drop myself."

"I suppose I might as well," he said, accepting the flask and taking a sip. "Not bad, not bad at all. Mind if I have a little more?"

"Go ahead," said Charles. "It's an Irish whiskey – makes a change from Scotch. Save a drop for me, though."

"Don't overdo it, you two," said Dan, opening the boot of the Mustang. "We've got work to do and you need to be on the ball." He fished around and passed Warren a camera. "You're in charge of this. It's got infrared film in it."

"But I don't even know how to use a can opener," he protested.

"I'm sure you know how to use a corkscrew," said Dan. "Weren't you listening last night when I explained it all?

Look, it's just an old-fashioned film camera, except that the film registers the infrared end of the spectrum. I'm sure even you can press a shutter."

"Isn't there anything more up to date?" asked Warren.

"Of course there is," said Dan. "There's a whole range of infrared detectors now – they use them for creative photography. But, first of all, we're going to see if we can pick up anything with the type of equipment they used in the Dragon Project. If we do detect anything, we'll take it further with modern equipment."

Dan reached into the boot again and passed the magnetometer to Charles. "Are you feeling okay? I understand you threw a wobbly the last time you were here."

Charles drew himself up to his full height. "I feel fine, thanks, Dan."

"Good," he said, "because you're responsible for the magnetic readings. Do you want me to explain again how to work it?"

"No, no," said Charles. "You explained it all very well last night."

"Excellent," said Dan. "Now, I want you both to walk the length of the Serpent taking photos and readings at regular intervals, before the sunrise, then when the sun is coming up over the horizon and again when the sun has risen. Okay?"

"What?" said Warren. "Walk that distance at my age? It's at least a quarter of a mile long."

Dan rolled his eyes. "Just do your best and take good notes," he said. "I'll be with you taking readings with the Geiger counter."

Warren smirked at Charles. "Another sip of that whiskey and the Serpent will look dead straight."

Dan ignored them both. "Mary, here's the ultrasound recorder. At least you know what you're doing and the ultrasound readings could be the most important. From what Ben said, that's where the most interesting results were obtained in the Dragon Project."

He looked over to Warren and Charles who were chatting with each other, took Mary's arm and steered her to one side. "Help me keep an eye on those two," he said. "They're acting like two schoolboys on a day trip. Ben's going to get a real earful when I speak to him next."

Mary shivered and pulled her bobble hat firmly down over her forehead. "I could do with a drop of whiskey, myself," she said. "You've really got the bit between your teeth with this project, haven't you, Dan?"

"It's just the sort of thing I need," he replied, picking up the Geiger counter and closing the boot.

"What's the weather forecast?" Charles called over.

"Just fine," Dan called back. "Not a cloud in the sky. Perfect for what we're trying to do. And it's three-thirty – time to get started. We'll walk to the tail, checking that everything's okay, and then work back towards the egg-shaped enclosure at the head, taking measurements."

By the time they reached the tail, the eastern horizon was just beginning to lighten.

As Charles stood on the tail, he could feel the effect of the whiskey starting to kick in. Far from worrying about a repetition of his previous disturbing experience, he was now enjoying a pleasant inner glow. He checked the magnetometer again. Everything was normal; north was north and the strength of the magnetic field was exactly as Dan said it should be.

With Dan in the lead, the four walked slowly along the undulations of the Mound. At regular intervals, Dan asked for the readings or for Warren to take a photograph. About halfway along to the head, he went back to Charles. "Anything at all?" he asked.

"Nothing. Absolutely nothing. As far as I can tell, the magnetic field is entirely as it should be." He held out the magnetometer for him to check.

"You're right – definitely nothing funny going on at the moment," he said. "What about you, Mary?"

"All quiet, Dan."

By the time they reached the gaping mouth of the Serpent, there was an air of despondency. The horizon was distinctly brighter and the birds had started up the dawn chorus.

"We'll try the enclosure and then walk back to the tail as the sun comes up," said Dan, looking distinctly disconsolate.

Warren stayed back outside the enclosure to take photos while the others stepped inside it, went to the centre and studied their instruments.

Mary was the first to react. "It's pulsing, Dan. I'm definitely picking up pulsing."

He rushed over to her and grabbed the ultrasound detector. "And it's getting stronger." He studied the second hand on his watch. "The pulses are dead regular. Make notes on the intervals and the strength." He turned to Charles. "What's with the magnetometer?"

"It's going crazy. It's all over the place."

"Let me see," said Dan. He studied the dial in amazement. "Jeez – there's a major magnetic disturbance going on here. Warren!" he yelled out. "Take photos! Now! Use the film up if necessary."

Just then, Dan noticed Charles swaying to one side. "Are you all right, Charles?" he asked.

"Just a bit dizzy. Probably the whiskey."

Dan put his arm around Charles's shoulders to steady him. "Concentrate on the magnetometer. Take notes of the deviations if you can." He glanced at the Geiger counter. "The Geiger's still clicking normally. At least there's no increase in radiation."

It was Warren who noticed it first. "Have you seen what's going on at the Serpent's tail," he said, quietly.

The other three looked to where Warren was pointing. What appeared to be a mist had risen above the trees and was clearly thickening. Even at a distance it was obvious that it was creeping towards them.

"I really don't like the look of that," said Warren. "Do you think we should call it a day?"

"Probably caused by a pocket of cold air," said Dan.

Warren took two quick photos of the mist before he wrapped his arms around his body. "I don't know how cold it is where the mist is, but it's getting damned cold here," he said. "The temperature must have just dropped ten degrees. I thought you said it was going to be fine weather, Dr Gallagher?"

Dan ignored him. "What's the ultrasound doing, Mary?"

"The pulses are still getting stronger. And they're increasing in frequency."

"Charles?" asked Dan.

Charles's hands were shaking and he was making a visible effort to hold the magnetometer still and study the screen. "It's fluctuating even more," he said, and staggered sideways.

Dan grabbed his elbow. "Stay with it, Charles. Stay focused on the dial."

The mist had now expanded sideways and upwards, completely blocking out anything behind it.

Warren stared at it, wide-eyed. He looked briefly towards the site exit, took one last photo of the mist and ran into the enclosure to join the others.

"Bloody fine mess you've got us into, Charles," he exclaimed.

Charles didn't say anything, his eyes glued on the magnetometer, and Dan took no notice.

He was staring at the mist.

As it reached a point halfway along the Mound, the mist suddenly accelerated in their direction. Now, like a full-blown desert sandstorm driven by some determined force, it came on rolling remorselessly towards them.

Within a minute the mist had reached the gaping mouth of the Serpent and, like a wave about to break, the upper edge began to curl over.

Mary stood in front of Dan. "For crying out loud, Dan – this just isn't right. God knows what's going on. Let's get out of here."

Everybody turned to Dan, desperately seeking guidance as to what to do next.

"Dan, let's go. Before it's too late. Please..." implored Mary. "It really isn't worth it."

Dan faced the mist, four-square and stone-faced, holding the Geiger counter out in front of him like a weapon, as if he were facing a charging enemy. "Keep taking readings," he commanded.

The mist reared over them, the edges curling inwards so that it resembled some gigantic claw. For a moment it seemed to freeze, creating the impression of some unearthly monster pausing, before taking a perverse pleasure in trapping its prey and devouring it.

Then, as the four stood there, half in wonder, half in terror, the claw closed and the mist silently engulfed them.

Unable to see anything beyond their own faces, they instinctively reached out to touch each other and huddled together.

They were all looking around trying to get some sort of bearing, when Dan suddenly jumped sideways. "What the...?" he exclaimed.

As if some invisible hand in the ground had switched on a light, a patch of grass beside him had started to glow. He jumped to the side again as the grass lit up directly under his feet.

In an instant, the whole area inside the enclosure came alive and columns of light stretched up into the mist.

The first ball of light emerged from the ground close to Dan. About the size of a football, it rose up slowly to about four feet above the ground and hovered briefly, before rising up into the mist to slowly fade away. A second sphere of light popped out of the ground near Warren.

He edged away from it as it drifted around the group and again floated upwards to disappear.

Suddenly, the ground around them seemed to boil and balls of light of different sizes erupted from the ground. Initially, they seemed to dance haphazardly around the group. After a while, the odd sphere came to a halt and appeared to inspect them, before moving backwards, sideways and shooting upwards to burst like a bubble. Others continued to circle around them, sometimes singly, sometimes in groups.

Two approached Charles and floated, immobile, directly in front of his face, giving the impression that he was of particular interest.

Now they moved over to Mary, and two others joined them. Slowly at first and then rapidly, they spun around her in an apparent state of excitement.

"It's as though they're alive," Charles said under his breath.

"No, they're just earthlights. They're balls of plasma," replied Dan. "There must be a major geological disturbance going on right beneath us. Take a photo, Warren. Take a photo…"

Warren cursed under his breath, fumbled for the camera hanging from his neck and pointed it haphazardly at the balls of light, not even trying to focus as he repeatedly pressed the shutter.

It was at that point that one sphere shot sideways right out of the enclosure and disappeared into the mist. Others followed, some almost touching them before darting away. Mostly they shot upwards like rockets, but a few floated motionless, before popping out of existence or merely dissolving away.

Mary watched the spectacle, turning slowly around and around, as if entranced.

Unlike a firework display, there was no grand finale. The glow in the ground gradually faded and the last spheres of light rapidly disappeared, until only one remained. Like a guest reluctant to leave a party, it floated aimlessly around the enclosure. Finally, it moved towards Mary and stopped about two feet in front of her face, so that her face was lit up.

Mary stared, unblinking, at the sphere as if they were somehow communicating with each other. Her eyes widened and she lifted her hand to touch it. Instantly, the sphere moved backwards and again floated, stationary. After a few seconds, it rose silently upwards to stop once more. It seemed to waver, but as if being drawn irresistibly into another world, it rapidly ascended, until the mist closed around it.

For a while nothing happened. Nobody spoke, knowing that whatever was going to happen next was outside their control.

Dan's mind was in turmoil as he sought a rational explanation for the dramatic phenomena they were witnessing. Had a minor earthquake induced the earthlights? But that didn't explain the dramatic appearance of the mist. Could that have been due to the sudden drop in temperature? But what could have caused that? In any case, he had never witnessed the formation of a mist like this. And why did he somehow feel from its behaviour that it was alive and even malign. Should they try to walk out of it now, before something worse happened? But it was impossible to know how far it had spread.

When he sensed a slight movement of the air, he dared to hope that the mist was going to lift and go away. As the mist started to swirl and eddy, a thought flashed through his mind that it was the mist itself that had made the decision to lift.

But a sheer sense of relief overwhelmed the thought when he saw the faint glow of the sun, warm, friendly and comforting, over a barely discernible horizon. Within another minute the last wisps of the mist had wafted away and the Serpent was lit up with bright sunlight.

"Are all your experiments like this, Dr Gallagher?" said Warren, turning to him.

Dan was about to respond, when something lying on the grass caught his eye. "Mary!" he cried, rushing over and kneeling down beside her. To his horror, she was motionless and her eyes were closed.

16

Dan rubbed her hand gently. "Mary, Mary…" he whispered. "It's all right, it's gone."

Mary's eyes remained closed, but Dan was relieved that, although the movement was barely perceptible, he could see that she was breathing. He clasped her wrist. "Her pulse is fine, thank God," he said, without looking up.

Charles eased himself down on to his knees on the other side of her. "I didn't see her fall. I must have been hypnotised by those balls of light."

It was a shaft of brilliant sunlight that shot in over Dan's shoulder onto her face that brought her round. Her eyelids fluttered and opened in surprise. She was clearly disorientated, looking first at Dan, then at Charles and finally up at Warren, who was standing there, very obviously worried. "Where am I?" she whispered.

"We're at the Serpent Mound, Mary. Do you remember?" said Dan quietly. "A mist came out of nowhere. Then there were earthlights – balls of plasma. You must have fainted with the shock of it all."

Dan and Charles helped her to sit up. She looked around and blinked. The sun, now well over the horizon, was so bright that Mary instinctively put a hand to her face to shield her eyes. The Serpent Mound stretched into the distance as if nothing had happened, but a chorus of birdsong gave the impression that all of nature was celebrating a return to normality after the bizarre aberration.

"What happened to you, Mary?" asked Dan.

"I don't know, I really don't know," she said, shaking her head. "It started with that mist closing in on us. But it wasn't just a mist, was it?" She looked questioningly at Dan. "It seemed to be alive. It was horrible. It was trying to get control of my mind – like it was trying to drag me away somewhere. Then I saw the balls of light. It was as if they were wanting to save me. They were fighting the mist. They were fighting to save me – I know it. My mind was in turmoil – it was a battleground. That's when I must have passed out."

"You're okay now," said Dan, making to get up. "Do you think you can stand?"

Mary ignored him. "That's not all. Something else happened."

Dan sank down again.

"I had a vision, Dan. A terrible vision. Except it wasn't me. I don't know – perhaps it was my ancestor."

"What?" exclaimed Dan, clearly not knowing how to respond. He tried to pull himself together. "What sort of vision?"

"It was as if I were there. It was real."

"Where were you?"

"In a boat. I was in a boat." She paused. "It was horrible, Dan. I drowned."

He put his arm around her. "How? What happened?"

"The boat hit some rocks. I was in the sea. It was freezing and I couldn't swim. My clothes dragged me down. I tried so hard to hold my breath. And suddenly there was nothing – nothing at all – until I came round – just now. It was the sunlight…"

Charles caught Dan's eye, making it clear that he wanted to ask Mary questions. "It's all okay, Mary," he said. "Everything is back to normal now. But you need to tell us a little more about what happened to you."

"Let me think," said Mary. "It wasn't that straightforward, you see. I had a series of flashbacks – like a fluorescent light that needs replacing and goes on and off. It was as if something wanted to switch on in my brain, but couldn't quite make it. Something in my subconscious. It was then that it happened – the vision started."

Dan glanced at Charles, looking concerned. Warren very carefully sank down on his haunches.

"Tell us in detail," said Charles. "You said you were in a boat?"

"Yes. The first thing I remember was a splash of water on my face and I was cold and wet. I was shivering. And when I opened my eyes, I was in a boat."

"Were you in a storm?" asked Charles.

Mary shook her head. "No – the sea was calm. But it was raining, and the sea was cold and grey – the same colour as the sky."

At that moment there was the sound of car doors slamming, coming from the car park. "Sounds like the site must have opened," said Dan. "We shouldn't stay around here much longer."

Warren looked around, but nobody had appeared. "Can you describe the boat?"

"Funnily enough," said Mary, "it seemed quite ancient – like one of those ancient Greek boats you sometimes see on pots. It had a sort of platform at the front. But I was on a platform at the back with a man – I knew he was my son. There was one mast with a sail on it. It was just hanging loose. There was no wind, I remember that. And there were other boats like ours, as if we were part of a fleet. Maybe twelve other boats."

"Were there other people in the boat?" asked Warren.

"Yes, eight men who were rowing."

"What did they look like? How were they dressed?"

"Pretty rough-looking," said Mary. "Very unkempt. They had cloaks – or mantles – wrapped round themselves. Browny colour. They must have been wearing some sort of tunic underneath – I couldn't see. Bare legs, though."

Warren placed a hand on the grass to steady himself. "And what were you wearing?"

"I was wearing a woollen shawl and a long woollen dress. But it was my hair that I remember very clearly. It was red – really red – and worn loose, down to my shoulders. I knew that I was beautiful. And I knew as well that I was important – I could tell that the men respected me."

Charles eyes lit up. "Do you know who you were?"

"No idea! Yet I somehow knew the woman was me, though I couldn't really relate to her. It was as if our senses overlapped. I could see what she saw and hear what she heard, but I wasn't inside her mind, her memory."

"Do you know where the boats were heading? Where they were trying to get to?"

"No, no idea. But there is one thing that I do remember very clearly."

Mary hesitated before she spoke again, lowering her voice. "We were carrying something very precious with us. It was in the bottom of the boat…"

"What was it?" jumped in Charles.

"It was a stone. It was our sacred stone. Something that we always had with us. We believed we would always survive on our travels as long as we had 'The Stone.'"

"Can you describe it?"

"Oh, I knew what it was straight away – it was a meteorite."

Mary felt Dan's arm around her shoulder stiffen. "A meteorite?" he repeated. "What was it like?"

"It was large – a good two foot long – black, and very pitted. Typical teardrop shape. God knows how it was moved around. I'd love to have classified it."

Charles could barely contain his excitement. "Do you know where it came from? How you got hold of it?"

"No, I've no idea. All I do know is that it had always been with us and that it exerted some sort of benevolent power over us. I knew that if we lost it, for whatever reason, it would mean the end of our tribe."

Dan quickly turned and checked the site entrance again, but still nobody had appeared.

"How about the man with you on the platform? You say he was your son?" asked Warren.

"Yes, any mother knows her son. He had straggly red hair."

"It could be that you are recollecting emotions, rather than facts," Charles said. "Whoever this woman was, you seemed to be sharing her feelings."

Mary nodded.

"You can't remember the name of your son, I suppose?" asked Warren.

"No, I can't. But something happened that may have given away his name."

"What do you mean?" asked Dan, brushing his hair away from his face.

"I blacked out, like somebody had briefly switched off the light. The next thing I knew was that I could hear somebody yelling – like someone yelling right into my ear. Except they weren't, because when the vision flashed back on, I was in the boat again. Somebody was at the top of the mast, calling out and pointing to the horizon."

Warren had clearly become uncomfortable squatting down. "Could you understand what he was saying?" he said, as he eased himself upright.

Mary looked up at him. "No, not a clue. It was a language I didn't know. But the man was calling out to my son, as if he was trying to attract his attention. I think he was calling out his name."

"What was it?" asked Charles.

"It sounded like 'Eremon'. I think that's what I heard. He said it a couple of times and my son looked towards where he was pointing."

"Does the name mean anything to you?" Dan asked Charles.

"No, not at the moment, but it's definitely a start. Any idea, Warren?"

Warren looked blank. "If the boat was Greek, the name doesn't sound Greek. It would be useful if we knew the language that was being spoken."

Dan instinctively turned again and saw a young couple in the distance, walking towards them from the direction of the entrance.

"What happened then, Mary?" he asked, quickly.

"A great cheer went up and I could see it – a coastline in the far distance. I could just make it out. Everybody was very excited, I know that. But then my mind started to flash again."

"You blacked out again?" said Charles.

"Completely. And I wish I hadn't come round this time. Because that's when I drowned. I was in the sea and there was a thick sea mist. But I caught a glimpse of our boat smashed up on the rocks. Other boats as well. There were lots of people in the sea – struggling, drowning. All I could think about was 'The Stone' – that we mustn't lose 'The Stone'. That was my last thought."

Dan stood up and nodded towards the couple who were now getting closer. "I think that's enough for now. We need to get you back to the hotel."

The men helped her to her feet.

Mary stood there unsteadily, breathing deeply. The sight of the sun shining in a cloudless sky and the already warm air seemed to have a calming effect on her. She noticed a group of starlings pecking for insects in the grass on the head of the Serpent. "It's all right," she said. "I can walk."

Other visitors were now starting to appear, but took no notice of the four as they walked to the car park.

Charles grimaced as he tugged at the passenger door of Dan's car. It sprang open and he carefully helped Mary to ease into the seat. "Just one more question," he said, noting Dan and Warren were out of earshot. "A personal question, I know, but what's your ancestry, Mary? Where does your family come from?"

"My father was very proud of his Scottish ancestry. His family emigrated here during the Highland Clearances. They came from the west of Scotland, near Oban, I think. My mother's family were Irish. They came over during the Great Famine. Oh, and there's red hair on both sides of my family."

"Thanks," said Charles, thoughtfully.

17

Dan pulled up slowly outside Harper's hotel in Hillsboro, got out and wrenched open the passenger door of the Mustang just as Warren drew up alongside.

Charles immediately strode over to see if Mary needed help.

"I'm fine," she said. "I just need to go and lie down for a while."

The receptionist made no comment beyond greeting them and Dan went with Mary to her room. He took the key card from her, opened the door, and watched her anxiously as she went over and sat on the bed.

"Thanks, Dan," she said. "Give me an hour or so. I'll call you – don't worry."

"You're sure? Would you like one of the rolls we bought? You haven't eaten all day."

"I'm fine, really," replied Mary. "I just need to rest."

Dan nodded and pulled the door closed as he left.

Warren and Charles were in a small seating area close to the reception, talking and eating the filled rolls. Dan sat down with them.

"How is Mary?" asked Charles.

"I'm not sure," replied Dan. "There must be a rational explanation for what happened, but I've never known anything like it. That mist, the earthlights, those strange magnetic anomalies, Mary's reaction… It's an incredible coincidence that it all happened just when we were there."

"Did you feel anything? Anything unusual?" Charles asked Warren.

"No, nothing really. I was scared, of course. That mist came down incredibly quickly and it was very thick. And the earthlights – well, that was a completely new experience for me. But perhaps it wasn't a one-off – I've heard reports of other people seeing them. Perhaps geological disturbances at the Mound aren't that rare. Maybe it was just our luck that we happened to be there at the right time. Or the wrong time, perhaps."

"I've heard reports about earthlights appearing before earthquakes occur," said Dan, "but, as far as I know, they've not been reported as affecting people mentally." He looked enquiringly at Charles.

Charles hesitated for a moment. "Okay – I did feel something rather unusual. I felt a bit faint – I thought I was going to pass out. But that mist was not right. I sensed it was almost alive in some way – as if it possessed a mind. And it was decidedly not friendly. But somehow I knew the earthlights were the opposite – I felt they were benign. Two actually came right up to me. It's difficult to explain, but in some strange way I felt I had something in common with them. It was as if we were on the verge of communicating with each other. But it was Mary they were really interested in. Several kept moving around her and I had the impression that they were trying to protect her. Did you feel that, Dan?"

"They certainly didn't seem to worry about me," said Warren.

"Me neither," said Dan. "But it begs the question then, doesn't it?" he continued. "What's special about Mary? And maybe you to some extent, Charles?"

Charles was about to reply, when he noticed Dan was looking over his shoulder.

"Mary – are you all right?" asked Dan.

"No, not really," she said.

Dan immediately jumped up and fetched a chair. "Sit down," he said. "What's up?"

"I'm scared, Dan. I was too frightened to be by myself. I can still sense that mist, and it's not far away. I'm sure it's still around."

Charles looked worried and glanced over at Warren. "I'm going to have to tell them, Warren." He didn't wait for a response. "Ben had two meteorites in his house," he said, and he told them how Ben had classified them as being exactly the same type and that they both must have come from the same location on Mars.

"Yeah, he told me about them," said Dan. "Quite a coincidence, but not impossible. He had already told me about one – that it was found by the Brits in the Antarctic. He said you, Charles, had asked him to classify the other one and that you were rather cagey about where it came from."

Charles ignored a warning look from Warren. "What

he maybe didn't tell you was that Holly, his girlfriend, was scared out of her wits by a weird experience she had in Ben's house. She swears something insubstantial – a mist, if you like – appeared when she was in bed."

He explained to Dan what Holly had told him. "He probably didn't tell you either that Holly thought that the one from the Antarctic was evil somehow and that the apparition she saw was associated with that meteorite. And also that she thought the other meteorite was benign – rather like good and bad meteorite twins."

"No, he didn't tell me that," replied Dan. "He told me about the Rollright Stones and the Dragon Project. But he didn't tell me anything about his girlfriend having weird experiences. Anyway, the two meteorites are over in the UK near Oxford, aren't they?"

Charles stared meaningfully at Warren, who rolled his eyes and looked out of the window.

"I just need to have a word with Warren," said Charles, standing up.

Warren didn't say anything and followed Charles out of the hotel and into the car park.

"I know what you're going to say," said Warren, as they stood next to their car.

"We have no choice," replied Charles. "What's going on here is too important. Poor Mary – look at the state she's in. We have to tell them everything now."

Warren leaned against the car. "Look," he said, "I'm with Dan. There'll be a perfectly rational explanation for all of this. We just haven't had the opportunity to investigate properly."

Charles shook his head. "You haven't met Holly – she was frantic with worry. She was so relieved when I said I would bring that bloody meteorite over here."

"But if we show them the Antarctic one, we'll have to show them the one we found here."

Charles checked the hotel windows to make sure nobody was watching them. "I believe it would be irresponsible not to now. Anyway, Dan and Mary are both meteorite experts. We could need their help if we are going to get to the bottom of all this."

"On the other hand, we could be opening a huge can of worms," said Warren. "As I explained before, the discovery of the redhead giant is a dynamite story. And Dan is bound to ask where our meteorite was found."

"Then we'll just have to ask both of them to respect our side of things and not let it go beyond the six of us."

Warren stepped away from the car towards Charles. "If they don't agree and they start to talk about what happened today, we could have half the world on our backs."

"Look, we both agree there's something really strange going on. Shouldn't we at least be completely open with Dan and Mary?"

Warren put a hand to the back of his head and looked up at the sky. He slowly lowered his head and sighed. "This is all going in a direction I didn't anticipate, Charles. I mean, how trustworthy are they? And what about your friends in the UK? What's to stop them spilling the beans to all and sundry?"

"We'll just have to take our chances," said Charles firmly. "Anyway, they're all good scientists and they'll be keen to find out what's going on as well. Besides, there's something else I want to explore."

"Do we really need anything else?" said Warren wearily.

But Charles's eyes were twinkling. "It's the red hair link. That's one of the reasons you wanted me involved in all this, remember?" He checked the hotel windows again and lowered his voice, almost conspiratorially. "Not only does Mary have red hair. I didn't tell you that Holly is a redhead, too. And remember in that vision Mary had – the woman and her son in the boat both had red hair. Then, of course, the skeleton of the giant man you found here not only has tufts of red hair still attached to it, but it was holding our meteorite. And Mary said the sacred stone they were carrying in the boat was a meteorite. Why was it so special to those people in the boats? Who were they? Where were they trying to get to? And who was the woman? Could she really have been an ancestor of Mary?"

Warren shook his head slowly.

"Listen, Warren," Charles went on. "We have a good lead here. We know the woman in Mary's vision had a son who was called something like 'Eremon'. That's not all – Mary may have given me another lead. There's red hair on both sides of her family. She told me her mother's side had Irish ancestry and her father's family came from Scotland. Ireland and Scotland have the highest percentages of redheads in the world. Did I tell you I recently met somebody in Ireland who I think might be able to help us?"

Warren shook his head again and groaned. "We

don't even know Dan and Mary that well. We only met them yesterday. And Dan seems to me to be a bit of a tearaway."

"Well, Ben rates them both highly. I think I trust Ben's judgement."

"Okay," said Warren. "But be it on your head. And if it all goes wrong, you can go on television and tell everyone what happened."

"More likely I'd tell everyone how special redheads are," said Charles. "Could be quite amusing."

Warren opened the boot of the hire car. He handed the two meteorites to Charles. "Now you can do the explaining," he said.

"What have you two been up to?" asked Dan, as they both came back into the hotel. "Been having a sly smoke, have you?"

"We've got something to show you," said Charles, carefully unwrapping the two meteorites and placing them on a small table.

"What the…?" said Dan. "Are these the two meteorites Ben was telling me about? The ones you were just talking about?"

Charles nodded.

"Which one's the Antarctic one?"

Charles touched it.

Dan carefully examined it and put it down. "And what about the other one?" he asked, picking up the Serpent Meteorite. "Yes, they certainly look identical. Where was this one found?"

Warren feigned a lack of interest.

"Here," said Charles. "It was found near the Serpent Mound."

"What?" exclaimed Dan. He glanced at Mary in disbelief. Mary said nothing, looking perplexed.

"Why on earth didn't you say so before?" asked Dan.

Charles didn't reply.

"There's a good reason," said Warren eventually, and he launched into the story of the giant skeleton with red hair, the discovery of the meteorite and his concern about not making the findings public.

Dan listened, fascinated, looking frequently at Mary. She said nothing.

"We've told you all this in the hope that we can work together and keep everything quiet, for obvious reasons," said Warren.

Dan didn't hesitate. "Of course, of course. No problem. I quite understand where you're coming from. Now this sounds really fun." He beamed at Mary. "All right with you, Mary?"

She pointed to the Antarctic Meteorite. "Would you take that one away, please? I'm sure it's watching me – it's giving me the creeps. I'm sure it had something to do with that mist at the Mound. It's giving me the same feeling."

Nobody said anything for a while, wondering how to respond.

Charles spoke first. "There's something else," he said. He went on to tell Mary and Dan about Holly's extrasensory experiences, first with the radio and afterwards at the Rollright Stones. "When she had a nightmare and then saw the apparition in Ben's house, it was all too much for her. She asked me to take the meteorite away. That's why I brought it here with me. I had no idea it might affect you, Mary."

"I suppose you might expand on your red-hair theory," said Warren.

Charles went on, "Well, there's a redhead link running all through this, isn't there? Holly's a redhead, like you, Mary. Also, the woman you identified with in your vision was a redhead, as was her son. And now we've told you about the skeleton of the giant with red hair."

"Why not tell Mary about your own history, Charles?" said Warren.

Charles sighed. "Even before I had white hair, I wasn't exactly a redhead, but my mother was, which probably makes me a carrier of the gene in its recessive form. That might explain why I was affected this morning as well, but not so dramatically as you, Mary."

"Charles also had his own strange experience at the Mound when we went there together," said Warren.

Charles twitched with embarrassment. "Ben must have told you I 'threw a wobbly'. What he obviously didn't tell you is that when I visited the Mound for the first time, I thought I saw the Serpent move. I'm almost sure it did. I put it down to jet lag at the time."

"This is getting more and more interesting," said Dan, enthusiastically. "Has anything like that happened to you before?"

Charles held back for a moment and then told them about the vision he had had at Newgrange. "I have the occasional bad dream like anybody else, but a vision like that was a first for me."

"Have you been having nightmares or visions before today, Mary?" Dan asked.

"No, no, of course not. I certainly would have told you if I had. And I don't want it to happen again."

"Okay, so where do we go from here?" said Warren, abruptly, and he yawned. "Listen, I'm exhausted. After that three o'clock start I need a nap."

"I could do with some shut-eye myself," said Charles. "Why don't we meet here again at, say, six and go out for dinner? We can decide then what to do next."

"Good idea," replied Dan. "It'll give me time to write up all the notes and collect my thoughts."

"But what should we do with the meteorites?" said Charles. "Let's at least get the Antarctic one right away from Mary. It's not fair on her."

Warren picked up both meteorites and started to wrap them up again in the cloth. "Why don't I just take them back to my room for now?" he said. "I can't think of any redhead connections that I have, so I should be okay," he added sardonically.

Mary smiled appealingly at him. "Warren – would you mind if I kept the one from the Serpent Mound for a while? I don't know why, but I feel it's sort of protecting me."

"Of course," he said, handing it to her.

"Just be careful with that other meteorite," Charles said to Warren.

"Oh, for God's sake, Charles. I'm not sure I can take any more at the moment," replied Warren, getting up.

After returning to his room, Warren carefully placed the

meteorite, wrapped in the cloth, on the glass-topped set of drawers alongside the usual hotel do-it-yourself coffee kit and small packet of biscuits. He eased off his shoes, wiggled his toes, set the alarm on his phone and fell back onto the bed.

He thought briefly about the day's events, but was too tired to analyse them in any depth – it was all too much. Within minutes he had dozed off into a light sleep.

Just before two o'clock, the hairs on his arms involuntarily stood up. He twitched in his sleep and turned on his side, facing away from the door.

He was unaware of a thin translucent mist spreading silently over the floor of the room. Perhaps it was the sudden drop in temperature, but somehow Warren sensed something was wrong. He tossed and turned a few times and opened his eyes.

At first, he didn't believe what he was seeing. Then the reality hit him and he sat bolt upright, shaking. A large, lean and muscular black dog was standing in the middle of the room, panting lightly with its tongue hanging out and wagging its tail, as if in friendly greeting.

Very slowly, he turned towards the dog. It woofed and wagged its tail harder.

It was at this point that Warren noticed the door was closed. "How on earth did you get in?" he said. The dog watched him as he carefully got up off the bed and checked the door. It was firmly shut and locked.

Shaking his head, Warren unlocked and opened the door. "Somebody must have let you in here by mistake," he said. "Phew! What a stench!" He held his nose. "My God, you pong a bit. It's about time somebody gave you a bath. Were you under the bed? Do you belong to the cleaner? If so, they'll be looking for you now, boy. Let's put you out, shall we?"

The dog instantly moved towards him. Its tail stopped wagging and it growled softly.

Warren opened the door wider. "Come on, boy," he said firmly. "Out you go."

By now the dog was edging towards him, its growls stronger. Warren let go of the door as the dog snarled and forced him back into the room. Behind the dog, the door slowly swung back and closed with an ominous *click*.

Holding out his hand in front of him, Warren retreated towards the bed. "You don't belong here, you know. Just go," he ordered.

As if in answer, the dog bared its yellow teeth and its eyes seemed to light up with an unearthly red fire. Warren backed further away until he felt his legs touch the bottom of the bed.

When the dog crouched as if to leap, Warren fell back on to the bed and raised a leg in self-defence. "Come on, boy – that's enough," he whispered, feverishly glancing around for something to protect himself. His eyes fell on the meteorite and he slowly reached out to pick it up.

Now, as if tormenting its prey, the dog crept forwards. Warren drew his knees up to his chest, simultaneously pulling his arm back to throw the meteorite. He didn't even manage to scream. When the dog sprang at him, he dropped the meteorite. The only sound anyone in the room would have heard was him whimpering, "No, no, no…"

Charles was the first to arrive in the reception area, shortly before six, freshly shaved and smartly dressed. Mary joined him shortly afterwards and Charles noticed that she had changed into a dress and put on make-up. He consciously stopped himself from complimenting her. "Did you manage to rest?" he asked.

"Yes, I did, thank you. I thought I'd never be able to relax, but I went out like a light."

"I was the same," said Charles. "Exhaustion, I suppose."

Dan breezed in wearing the same clothes that he had been wearing earlier. "Well, I've written everything up," he announced. "But it's all beginning to sound a bit like a fairy story. It's not really very credible." He checked his watch. "Shall we give Warren another five minutes?" He went over to the receptionist to ask about suitable places to eat and returned looking pleased. "He recommends a place round the corner. It's walkable, so we can have a drink." He checked his watch again and looked at Charles, raising his eyebrows.

"I'll go and see what's up," said Charles. He quickly found Warren's room and knocked on the door. When there was no response, he knocked again and waited patiently. Finally, he got out his phone, called Warren, and heard a phone ringing inside the room, unanswered.

Now concerned, he went back to the others. Within a minute the receptionist accompanied Charles and Dan to Warren's room and put a card into the slot. Charles didn't wait. As soon as he heard the door unclick, he pushed it open.

Warren was pressed up against the back of the bed.

His knees were drawn up to his chest and his arms reached out in front of him, as if he had desperately tried to push something away. But it was his face that shocked the three men. Warren's lifeless eyes were wide open with the unmistakable look of pure terror in them.

It was Charles who noticed it. The cloth in which the meteorite had been wrapped was lying flat on the set of drawers. He checked around the room, even quickly looking under the bed, but the meteorite was nowhere to be seen.

18

The police investigation was thorough and explored every possible motive and reason for the death of Warren, but eventually the inquest returned an open verdict. Crucially, there was no evidence of Warren having been attacked. There were no wounds, no signs of physical violence. Neither was there any evidence of a break-in. The door had been locked and was undamaged, as were the windows, and it seemed that nothing had been stolen. The receptionist in the hotel, the cleaners and anyone else who could have accessed Warren's room were grilled, but all had good alibis.

Those, though, who first saw Warren's corpse would never forget its face. Frozen into the image of some monstrous gargoyle, the wide-open eyes spoke of witnessing some unknown horror and his mouth hung open as if emitting a silent scream. The pathologist reported the death as caused by an adrenalin surge, but he commented to colleagues that Warren had simply died of fright and he was flummoxed as to what on earth he could have witnessed.

Warren's academic status and reputation ensured that his death received extensive news coverage. Over the years he had attracted attention through contentious theories relating to the early settlement of North America, but the constraints imposed by academic tradition ensured that any debate concerning his theories had remained relatively civilised. The giant skeleton was securely locked in a container in a storeroom at the university along with hundreds of other finds. As there was no reason for anyone to suspect the controversial nature of the contents, the subject was not raised with the police. In short, Warren appeared to have had no enemies.

Out of a general respect, the details of Warren's death were downplayed. Rather, it was felt that he deserved to be remembered for his academic achievements and popular lectures and tutorials. For Mary, Charles, Dan, Holly and Ben, though, the experience was to have a profound effect on their lives.

Immediately after the discovery of Warren's body and while they waited for the police to arrive, Charles, Dan and Mary had convened in Charles's room in the hotel for privacy.

Mary was pale and distressed. "What on earth could have happened?"

Charles looked bewildered. "I don't know. I just don't know. He was clearly absolutely terrified by someone or something. And that someone or something must have taken the meteorite. The cloth it was wrapped in was lying near the bed and I checked everywhere – even under the bed. Nothing. I didn't say anything because the receptionist was there."

"Perhaps he had put it in a drawer or in his case," said Mary.

"Oh, I doubt it," said Charles. "He would have kept it wrapped up in the cloth, surely. If it's in his case or whatever, the police will find it, and if they do, sooner or later they'll come back and start asking questions. May I suggest we just keep quiet about it for now?"

Mary looked worried. "I don't like this. He's dead, Charles, and now we have to collaborate fully with the police. Shouldn't we tell them all we know? In any case, I think we could be tampering with something that should be left alone. I feel something very nasty is happening and I don't want anything to do with it."

"Listen, Warren died horribly," said Charles. "You didn't see him, Mary. It was still in his eyes – he was petrified by something. I believe we owe it to him to find out what killed him."

Dan turned to her. "Charles is right. We have to resolve this ourselves. To be honest, if we tell the police everything, they will think we're all talking a load of mumbo-jumbo. We've got involved in something we don't understand and we need to find out what's happening. If somebody or something has got that meteorite, we need to know why. Whoever or whatever it was, was desperate to get hold of it. And yes, Charles is correct when he says we owe it to Warren. I didn't know him that well, but I don't want to live with the knowledge that we just walked away from it all. And from the science viewpoint, it is quite fascinating. Something really way-out is happening, and I for one want to know what it is."

"When you say that, Dan, it scares me silly," said Mary.

"But you're crucial to it all, Mary. You are already involved," replied Charles. "That vision of yours has given us some leads. There's the red-hair link and there's the meteorite that's somehow very important to the people in the boats. We've even got the name of somebody important called 'Eremon'. It shouldn't be too difficult to find out exactly who he was."

Mary looked doubtful. "This whole thing terrifies me. I truly want nothing to do with it. It will all end badly."

"You're not alone in this," Charles persisted. "Holly experienced something similar to you. She's a redhead as well and, believe me, she's as scared as you are. But you both feel you have some protection with this other meteorite."

"I still don't like the way this is going," said Mary. "Perhaps I'll dye my hair and become a brunette. You haven't been through what I've been through, Charles."

"Well, I haven't been exactly unaffected," replied Charles. "My experiences haven't been as profound and disturbing as yours, but they were still quite scary. And Warren was my friend. Warren and I started on something together – and I'm going to see it through, for his sake."

Mary didn't reply.

"I'm going to get started and at least try to find out who 'Eremon' was," continued Charles. "Then we might find out who his mother was. That might help us discover what the meteorite was doing in the boat, and maybe even what happened to it. I believe you had that vision for a purpose, Mary."

The sound of a siren and a car screeching to a halt outside stopped the conversation.

"That'll be the police," said Dan. "Can we at least agree not to mention the meteorite?" Both the men looked at Mary.

She didn't respond immediately, but as they heard car doors slamming, she nodded.

"I think we should go to the lobby," said Charles.

As two police officers, one plain-clothes, burst in through the hotel entrance, the receptionist stepped out from behind the desk.

The plain-clothes officer flashed a badge. "Captain Patrick Glancy. Okay, where is he?"

"Follow me," said the receptionist.

Charles, Dan and Mary were standing together in the lobby when the receptionist and the officers returned. The receptionist pointed them out to the police.

Captain Glancy strode over to them. "Dr Gallagher and Professor Gresham, I believe. I understand you were also present when the deceased was discovered. Perhaps I could have a word with you first, Dr Gallagher. Let's sit over there." He indicated a quiet corner.

"Of course," said Dan.

Dan didn't say a word to Charles when he and Glancy got up and walked back to Charles and Mary.

"Shall we?" said Glancy to Charles, pointing back to the corner.

"You're British, I gather?" said Glancy, as they sat down.

Charles pulled himself up straight. "For my sins," he said.

It was clear to Charles that the officer was completely baffled.

"I didn't notice anything missing," offered Charles. "There was no sign of his case having been searched and I noticed his wallet was still on the bedside table."

"Just answer my questions, please, sir," said the officer and he proceeded to interrogate Charles about his relationship with Warren. Charles emphasised their long professional relationship, their friendship and his bafflement at the nature of Warren's death.

Queried about the reasons for his visit, Charles explained that Warren had wanted to meet up to chat about their lives and work, seeing that they were both "getting on a bit". He mentioned that his own wife had died and that he was only too pleased to have something "to take his mind off things".

Glancy grunted. "Dr Gallagher says you've been working at the Serpent Mound?"

"Yes, we've been checking out magnetic anomalies and the like – it was one of Professor Treadwell's interests. I expect Dr Gallagher told you all about it?"

"Yeah, he tried to explain it to me," replied Glancy. "I look forward to hearing the results."

"We'll publish some time, no doubt," said Charles.

"You're a professor at Oxford University, I understand – so we'll know where to find you in the future. But we'd be grateful if you would stay on here for a couple of days."

"Emeritus professor, actually. But of course. In any case, we need to talk to Professor Treadwell's friends and family."

Glancy nodded and stood up. "Thanks for your help. Forensics and a pathologist will be here shortly." He beckoned to Mary to join him.

The interview was short as he soon established that she was working with Dan and had little to add to Dan's evidence. Though she felt uncomfortable withholding the whole story about events at the Serpent Mound, Glancy didn't raise the subject and she didn't have to blatantly lie.

As soon as Glancy walked away with his colleague, Mary returned to Dan and Charles. They were both discussing their interviews with Glancy.

"I think they're as mystified as we are," said Dan.

"Did he say anything to you about something missing?" asked Charles.

"No. He mentioned the cloth and I said I didn't know anything about it. I said that perhaps he used it to clean his shoes."

Charles turned to Mary. "How did you get on, Mary?"

"Fine, but I still don't like withholding information. It's all been too much for me. I just want to get out of this place."

Dan checked his watch. "Let's try and get dinner round the corner," he said.

"Just give me five minutes to go and freshen up," said Mary.

"Fine," said Charles, fetching out his phone. "I need to look something up."

Charles could hardly contain himself when Mary returned. "It only took me a couple of minutes," he said. "I acted on a hunch. Wherever it was in your vision, Mary, it was raining. There's one place where it always seems to be raining, and that's Ireland. So I just searched the ancient history of Ireland. Eremon was one of the first High Kings of Ireland. Interestingly, he was rumoured to have had a twin brother. There's a legend that his mother drowned when she was trying to land at Bantry Bay. Her name was Scota…"

19

"Just a salad and some fizzy water, please," said Mary to the waitress in the restaurant.

"Sir?" the waitress asked Charles, and went on to take his order of the mullet and a small beer.

The waitress turned to Dan. He looked up from studying the drinks list on the menu card and did a double-take. She was a very attractive redhead, probably in her mid-twenties. She wore her hair – more copper-coloured than fiery red – long, hanging down over her shoulders in waves, and her fringe almost reached her blue eyes. He noticed she had a few freckles scattered around her nose.

Mary watched Dan's face intently, observing his reaction, while Charles just sat there, studiously polishing his glasses with a handkerchief.

The waitress brushed her fringe away from her eyes and looked, smiling, at Dan to take his order.

"Nearly there," he said, flustered.

"The food menu's on the other side, sir," she said.

Dan self-consciously turned the menu over and ran his finger down it.

"The steak's excellent today," said the waitress.

Dan put down the menu. "Enough said," he replied. "The steak, please – well done – with a stack of fries. And a large beer."

"Of course," said the waitress, reaching over his shoulder to pick up the menu so that her arm brushed his shoulder.

Dan watched her as she disappeared into the kitchen, unaware that Mary was still watching him, her face registering a mixture of disapproval and concern.

If Dan had looked towards the bar instead of the kitchen, he would have noticed a solitary man perched on a bar stool and eyeing him. The man clearly hadn't shaved for a couple of days and the pushed-up sleeves of his shirt revealed the powerful heavily tattooed arms of a man who was used to manual labour. Turning back to the bar, he sank the remains of the amber liquid in his glass and beckoned to the barman for a refill.

Dan was drumming his fingers on the table, when Charles abruptly said, "We need to plan what we're going to do."

Dan stopped drumming and he and Mary looked at Charles expectantly.

"I'll deal with anybody who approaches us about Warren," said Charles. "His family, friends and colleagues will want to know the details of his death. I'm going to downplay the horrible side, and if what happened at the Serpent Mound comes up, I'll downplay that as well."

"You don't know the press here," observed Dan. "Word will be out already and the police will issue a statement soon. There'll already be reporters at the hotel."

"Then I'll just do my best to keep us out of it," replied Charles. "But what do we actually do next?"

Mary didn't say anything. Instead she picked up her fork and started rubbing it with a paper napkin, although the fork didn't need cleaning.

Dan glanced at Mary, before he leant forwards with a glint in his eye. "I think we're on the edge of something so profound, we would regret it forever if we didn't take it further."

"I agree," said Charles. "And, as I said before, it would be the right thing to do by Warren. It's a question of principle."

Mary put down her fork. "I've had another weird vision," she said, quietly.

Dan and Charles stared at her.

"I was studying the meteorite in my room, when everything seemed to catch up with me. I suddenly felt so tired and must have dozed off."

"What did you see?" asked Charles immediately.

Mary took a deep breath. "It seemed like a continuation of the first vision I had. There was a ceremony happening on top of a grassy hill with tents everywhere. The tents had banners flying from them, all with different designs. It was damp and cold, I remember that. People were shivering."

"What sort of ceremony was it?" asked Charles.

"Somebody was being crowned in a large tent – it was a coronation. I actually saw somebody being crowned."

"Have you any idea who it was?" asked Dan.

"Yes, I knew exactly who it was. It was Eremon, the same man I saw on the ship in my first vision – the son of the woman who was somehow me. You said her name was Scota, Charles?"

"From what I've been reading, that all seems to fit," he replied. "And now you say you actually had a vision of Eremon being crowned?"

"It was the same as in my first vision – I knew he was my son. His hair was much longer, right down to his shoulders, but it was still red. And I saw somebody putting a gold crown on his head. It was a very simple crown – basically a gold band. It must have been a priest who was conducting the ceremony."

"What did the priest look like?" asked Charles.

"Very old – long white hair and a long white beard. He was wearing a whitish cloak and a beautiful gold torc around his neck."

"Interesting," said Charles. "Is there anything else you remember?"

"Yes. The throne. I will never forget the throne."

"What about it?" asked Dan.

"It was quite plain. It was made of wood with a high back and armrests. But there was something underneath the seat. I could see it quite clearly – it was on a platform."

Dan rolled his eyes. "For crying out loud, Mary, what was it?"

"It was the same stone that I saw on the ship in my first vision. It was the meteorite."

Dan shook his head. "My God, this is getting truly weird. What next, Mary? What happened next?"

"I started to feel the same sensation that I experienced at the Mound this morning. I sensed something was fighting for control of my mind – something was wanting to stop me having the vision. And I think I know what it was. I had the distinct impression of something evil again. Wherever it is now, it's the other meteorite – the Antarctic Meteorite. My mind must have dealt with it by just switching off. I blanked. I didn't realise until I woke up."

Nobody said anything as the waitress appeared with the drinks. She caught Dan's eye. "Food's on its way," she said cheerfully. "I'll just give you a steak knife." Again she leant over him so that her arm brushed his shoulder. She adjusted the position of the knife three times, ignoring Mary's frown.

The man at the bar was watching the scene intently, his hand visibly tightening around his glass, so that his knuckles turned white. He started to ease himself up from the bar stool, but sat down again when the waitress returned to the kitchen. He watched Dan for a while, before turning round to stare intently at the range of liquor bottles on display.

Dan took a deep swig of his beer. "Let's just try and summarise where we are…"

Charles raised his hand to stop him continuing. "There's something I should tell you. I've done some quick research to try and find out who Scota might be. The problem is that there are so many myths and legends about the ancient history of Ireland – and I'm no expert."

"Well, what did you find out?" asked Dan.

"Okay, there's one story that might fit in with your visions, Mary." Charles took a sip of his beer. "Very simply, legend has it that Scota was the daughter of an Egyptian pharaoh who married a Greek prince called Gathylos. They got friendly with the Israelites who were in Egypt at the time. When the Israelites were forced out of Egypt and went on their Exodus, they gave the couple guardianship of a sacred stone which the Israelites had always carried around with them. Because Gathylos had become too close to the Israelites, he had to flee Egypt as well, together with Scota and their children. They took the sacred stone with them and eventually ended up in the Iberian Peninsula, now Spain and Portugal. Gathylos died there." He stopped to make sure the others were still following him.

"Go on," said Dan.

"Well," continued Charles, "for various reasons the widowed Scota and her eight sons decided to invade Ireland. They got together a fleet of ships and took the sacred stone with them. And that's where Mary's visions seem to take over."

He breathed in deeply. "The really fascinating part of the legend, though, is – wait for it – the sacred stone we're talking about is reputed to be the same stone Jacob was using as a pillow when he had his famous dream. You remember it says in the Bible that he saw angels going up and down on a ladder to heaven, with God at the top. It's even been claimed that the stone was a meteorite."

"But, as far as I know, Jacob wasn't a redhead," said Mary.

"Probably not," replied Charles, "but based on descriptions in the Bible, some people say that Esau, his twin brother, did have red hair. So, like me, Jacob could have been a carrier of the gene for red hair. Also, the place where Jacob had his dream was clearly a very powerful sacred place. He called it 'Bethel', which means 'House of God'."

Before he could continue, the waitress returned with his and Mary's meals.

"Yours is just coming, sir," the waitress said to Dan. "Another beer?"

"Please," said Dan, flashing his best smile at her. "You just start," he said to the others. "So what happened to the sacred stone – the meteorite?"

"I don't know, it's a mystery," replied Charles. "This is where it all gets very confusing. Mary's visions featured a sacred stone – a meteorite – arriving in Ireland and being used in the coronation of an ancient king called Eremon. Thereafter, we know that a sacred stone was used in the coronations of subsequent kings and queens of Ireland, followed by Scottish kings and then British monarchs from the Middle Ages right up to the present day. It's been variously known as Jacob's Pillow Stone, the Lia Fáil, the Stone of Scone, the Coronation Stone and the Stone of Destiny. Even Elizabeth II was crowned, in Westminster Abbey, sitting on a throne with the so-called Stone of Destiny placed beneath the seat."

"But the stone used in the coronations of British monarchs since the Middle Ages is not a meteorite. Even I know that," said Mary. "It's a block of sandstone."

Charles nodded in agreement. "But perhaps that's not the real Stone of Destiny. Perhaps the real Stone of Destiny is a meteorite and nobody knows where it is. Or if they do, they're keeping very quiet about it. Now, it could be that your visions, Mary, have given us a starting point to find out."

Dan sat back in his seat as the waitress returned and placed his meal in front of him.

"Anything else, sir?" she said. "Mustard, perhaps?"

"Maybe some ketchup," Dan replied.

The waitress repositioned his steak knife yet again. "I haven't seen you here before," she said to him.

"If this steak tastes as good as it looks, I might come back again," he said.

"I'm here every evening," the waitress replied. "Except Wednesdays. That's my free night. Tomorrow," she added, and returned to the kitchen again.

Conscious that Mary was eyeing him, Dan didn't say anything and started cutting his steak. "Very good," he said, without looking up.

If he had looked up, he might have seen a man ease himself off a bar stool and walk rather unsteadily towards him. He didn't notice the man until he was standing beside the table.

"The girl's not free," the man slurred.

Dan carved off a morsel of meat and chewed it for a while, nodding his head in appreciation, before looking up. "Free? In my experience women never come free," he said. "There's always a price to pay."

"What I mean is – she's not available."

"Neither are we," said Dan, stabbing the steak with his fork. "In fact, as you can see, we're rather busy."

Mary reached out and touched Dan's hand. "Please, Dan. Please don't…"

Charles looked on with interest, as if he were watching a scene from a Wild West movie.

"Not too busy for the girl, though," said the man, pushing his shirt sleeves up to display the tattoos on his arms.

"Nice tattoos," said Dan. "Are they real or are they just painted on?" He eased himself from his seat and stood up. "I think you're just leaving."

Charles noted that the other diners had fallen silent. Their table had suddenly become the centre of attention. He noticed the redhead peering round the kitchen door.

Ponderously, the man drew back his arm and threw a wild haymaker at Dan.

Dan casually leant backwards so that the punch missed by a mile. As the man fell forwards, Dan neatly twisted his other arm up behind his back and almost effortlessly started to frogmarch him towards the exit. "Charles, old boy," he called over his shoulder, "the gentleman is just leaving. Would you kindly open the door for him?"

"Certainly," said Charles, getting up. He walked through the restaurant and pulled the door open. "After you, sir," he said, as Dan shoved the man out on to the pavement.

Dan stood there as the man stumbled and nearly tripped over himself. Raising his fist, he glared briefly at Dan, before staggering away.

There was a ripple of applause as Dan and Charles returned to their table.

"Is it always like this with Dan?" asked Charles.

"Yes," said Mary.

Dan sat down, as if nothing had happened. "So who's up for a trip to Ireland?" he said, beaming.

He and Charles both looked at Mary.

Mary's worried expression said it all. "I'm not at all sure that would be a good idea. Whatever's going on, it could get even worse – and dangerous, too. One of us is dead already."

"Do we have any choice?" asked Charles. "Dan and I both agree that we can't just leave Warren's death unresolved. Now the Antarctic Meteorite has disappeared and we have no idea where it is. The evidence suggests – we don't understand why – that it's somehow connected with something that manifests itself as a mist. And that the mist is positively malevolent. On the other hand, the Serpent Meteorite may be associated with earthlights and seems to be benign. What's more, all of this seems to be happening at, or close to, sacred sites."

He carefully separated the flesh away from the bones of his fish as he continued, "At least two people with red hair, you Mary, and Holly as well, have had visions which seem to be connected with two meteorites that came from Mars and have the same physical characteristics. Your visions, Mary, seem to have a fit with historical legends."

Dan was ignoring his meal as he listened, sipping at his beer.

"For instance," Charles went on, "the legend is that the stone Jacob used as a pillow when he had his dream was a sacred meteorite which was later used in the coronations of monarchs. We don't know where it is now, but if your visions have anything to do with historical reality, you may have given us an excellent lead.

"If we're going to follow it up, you're central to all this. You can't give up now."

"Well, I'm scared," said Mary.

Charles looked at her, imploringly. "We need you, Mary. You never know, you may discover you've got royal blood."

"If I have, I suspect it's very dilute by now," she replied.

"Don't forget we've still got the meteorite that Warren found – the Serpent Meteorite – to take with us," said Charles. "And there's something else we haven't discussed, isn't there? Something rather important." He put down his knife and fork. "Well, the Serpent Meteorite and the Antarctic Meteorite are both from Mars, aren't they?"

Dan smiled at him.

Charles lowered his voice. "It seems to me that they could be somehow alive. Doesn't that mean we've discovered possible evidence of life on Mars?"

Dan continued smiling and raised his beer glass.

Mary said nothing. She looked down and carefully poured dressing over her salad. "I think I'm going to regret this," she said, eventually.

"Excellent," said Charles. "I'll phone my contact in Dublin straight away. Her name's Gráinne O'Connor. I'll get Ben and Holly up-to-date on everything as well. They're going to find it difficult to take this all in, but I think we're going to need their help."

"Jolly good," said Dan. "I could do with a decent pint of Guinness."

20

On Saturday night, O'Casey's bar in Temple, Dublin, was rocking and Dan Gallagher was in seventh heaven. The band was blasting out "Whiskey in the Jar" and he was well into his third pint of Guinness.

Charles was trying his best to get into the swing of things with a whiskey. There was a thin smile on his face and he couldn't resist frequently looking furtively at his watch, wondering if Gráinne O'Connor would accept his invitation to join them.

Mary sipped a tomato juice and, judging by her occasional glances at Dan, seemed to be happy that Dan was enjoying himself.

It was when the band was taking a break that Gráinne arrived. She was drenched. Throwing off the hood of her cagoule, she stood immediately inside the entrance, dripping water. Charles jumped up and waved to her. She waved back enthusiastically and threaded her way through the crowd to their table. Even before he was introduced, Dan, smiling broadly, asked her what she would like to drink.

"I'll just take this off first," she replied, tugging at her cagoule.

"Raining again?" said Charles.

"Really heavy – quite a storm. I'm absolutely soaked. Welcome to Dublin."

"Thanks so much for joining us," said Charles, taking his coat off the chair he had saved for her. He introduced Dan and Mary.

"A pint of Guinness, please, Dan," she said as she sat down.

Dan returned a couple of minutes later with a glass in each hand.

The warm atmosphere of the bar was conducive to easy conversation and, inevitably, Dan and Mary talked about their work with meteorites. Charles took the line that their visit was a holiday, revolving around their joint interest in prehistoric sites.

It was Charles who casually introduced the subject of sacred stones, alluding to their importance in Irish folklore.

Gráinne's eyes lit up. "Oh, we've got them all here – walking stones, talking stones, screaming stones, oracular stones, healing stones, stones you swear an oath on, stones associated with giants – even stones associated with the Devil. Tradition says that long, long ago, stones were alive and had souls. Some were actually worshipped. And there are people here who still believe some stones are alive."

"Really?" said Dan.

"Of course," replied Gráinne. "Often you have to undergo some sort of trial before a stone will bestow its favours. Take the Blarney Stone, for instance. Nowadays the trial is just being bent over backwards to kiss the stone. And then, as if by magic, you have the gift of the gab."

"According to the Bible story, Jacob's Pillow Stone was worshipped," said Charles. "After his dream, Jacob is supposed to have anointed it in recognition of its holiness – a 'house of God', as Jacob claimed. But you mentioned screaming stones, Gráinne. Wasn't the Stone of Destiny – the Lia Fáil – supposed to shout out when a rightful High King of Ireland sat on it?"

"So the legend goes…" said Gráinne. She was about to continue when the band reappeared. She waved to a man with a violin under his arm and caught his eye. His face broke into a broad smile and he threw her a kiss.

"I'll tell you what," she said to Charles. "I'm free tomorrow. If you like, we can go to the Hill of Tara and see the Lia Fáil. It'll be easier to talk, as well."

"Okay with you?" Charles asked Dan and Mary.

"Definitely," said Dan, draining his glass.

"Mary?" asked Charles.

She simply nodded, but without much enthusiasm.

Gráinne made a note of their hotel. "I'll pick you up at ten," she said, turning back towards the band.

To Dan's delight the band swung straight into "The Irish Rover". He raised his arm in the air and whooped.

Gráinne laughed and took a sip of her Guinness.

It was Charles who noticed Mary was sitting with her eyes closed, her tomato juice practically untouched.

He touched her arm. "Is everything okay?" he whispered in her ear.

Her eyes sprang open and she shook her head. "I'm not quite sure," she said. "Something funny's happening."

Charles looked worried.

"No, it's not another vision. It's weird, but I think it's the music that's affecting me. I'll tell you later, Charles." At this point the band finished the number to much applause and cheering.

Gráinne checked her watch. "Listen, I have to make a move now – there are things I need to do." She stood up and Charles immediately got to his feet as well. "See you all tomorrow, then," Gráinne said. She patted Dan on the arm. "Thanks for the drink, Dan."

Mary was just starting to stand up. "Don't worry, Mary. Enjoy the rest of the evening," Gráinne said, and, waving to the band, she made her way to the exit.

"She seems to know plenty about the sacred stones here," ventured Charles.

"Nice girl," replied Dan. "Anybody for another one?"

Both Charles and Mary declined and Dan made his way to the bar again.

Charles turned to Mary. "What's up, Mary?"

"It's all okay. It's just that I started seeing different coloured balls of light dancing around – all over the place. They were moving in time to the music and kept changing colours. They were a bit like written notes on a stave. High notes were red and low notes were blue. The ones in between were green and yellow."

Charles looked intrigued. "But that's classic synaesthesia. It's like an extra sense some people have. Has it ever happened to you before?"

"No, never. It wasn't unpleasant – just a bit disturbing. I'm getting worried, Charles. What with the visions – and now this. Do you think I'm starting to lose my mind?"

"Would you like to go back to the hotel?" he asked, just as Dan returned with another full glass.

Mary ignored the question. "Don't say anything to Dan," she said, quietly. "Let him finish his drink first."

It was just as Dan was sitting down that it happened. The clap of thunder was so loud and forceful that it shook the windows. There was the tinkle of breaking glass as two glasses hit the floor. The bar fell silent and people looked around apprehensively. Reassured it was only thunder, they quickly resumed their conversations and the band launched into a new number.

"Some storm out there…" said Charles, and then he stopped as he looked at Dan.

Dan was obviously badly affected by the loud bang. His hands were shaking and his unblinking eyes were looking straight ahead.

Mary jumped up and went round to him. "It's only thunder, Dan. Everything is okay. You're safe, Dan – you're safe."

Dan blinked, and slowly looked around. "I need to get some fresh air. Please excuse me." Pushing the table away, he stood up, made his way unsteadily to the exit and went outside.

"Should I go after him?" asked Charles, getting up.

"No, leave him alone. He'll be all right."

Charles sat down again, concerned.

"He'll be back in a couple of minutes. Maybe we should

be going then," said Mary. She hesitated before speaking again. "I should tell you, Charles. Dan served with the army in Afghanistan. He saw some terrible things. The worst was a suicide bombing. He witnessed a blast that killed over fifty people, nearly all civilians, including women and children. He's never got over it."

21

Gráinne O'Connor was sitting in her car outside the Fitzgerald Hotel, indifferent to the rain rattling on the roof, talking animatedly into her phone.

"I think I'm onto something," she said. "The old guy I met at Newgrange is here – the one I told you about. You know, he had a vision of the priest. He's over here with two Americans, and they're both meteorite experts. One of them happens to be a woman with red hair. I don't think she likes me."

Gráinne listened to the man she was speaking to, before replying, "I don't know exactly, but I've been told by our stone that we have to find the Stone of Destiny."

She listened again.

"It seems that the red-haired woman is being directed to it as well and the other two are helping her. I think they could lead us to it. Then it would have to be destroyed."

She paused. "I need you to conduct a ceremony tomorrow night. A Black Dog will bring something to you, but it won't be the usual Black Dog. You'll need a different spell – I'll send it to you in a voicemail with a few more details."

She shook her head as the man spoke. "All I know is that the Black Dog will be bringing a special stone. Meanwhile, I have to get the red-haired woman over to Tara. That's where we're going tomorrow."

She reached out with her free hand and turned on the windscreen wipers, noting the rain was lighter, before speaking again. "Let's talk again Monday morning. There's something else I need to do now." After slipping the phone into her pocket and pulling the hood of her cagoule over her head, she got out of the car and headed towards the hotel entrance.

There was a quiet knock on the door of Dan's room. Wondering who on earth it could be, he opened it to see Gráinne standing there, smiling.

"Do you mind if I come in?" she said.

"No, no, not at all. Is everything okay?"

"Absolutely," she said, and walked straight in. "It's just that I noticed you were really enjoying the music tonight. And with a name like Gallagher, I thought I'd like to get to know you better."

Dan was clearly taken aback. Then he pushed the door shut. He turned off the television, opened the minibar and fumbled around inside. "There's red or white wine or…" He reached in further. "Or even a whiskey. Irish, I see," he said, knocking the bottles over. He looked over to her.

She was staring at him, her green eyes wide open and a faint smile playing over her face. "A whiskey would be just fine," she said softly, before taking off her cagoule, placing it over the back of a chair and sitting down on the bed.

22

Her companions were highly relieved when Gráinne finally parked her small yellow car and pulled on the handbrake. Charles struggled out of the front seat and then pulled it forwards, allowing Dan and Mary to struggle out from the back.

Bleary-eyed, Dan stretched out his arms above his head, put his hand to his forehead, closed his eyes and breathed in deeply.

"Serves you right, Dan," said Mary. "I gave up counting the number of Guinnesses you had last night."

Dan gave her a guilty smile and glanced over to Gráinne, who was taking her backpack out of the boot. During the car journey, she had acted as if nothing had happened between them the night before. In fact, she looked as if she had slept well all night and was bright as a button. *Jeez, she really is cool*, he thought.

"So this is the Hill of Tara," announced Gráinne cheerfully, pointing ahead. "And right at the top is the Lia Fáil."

After the rainfall of the night before, the air was clean and fresh and the grass glistened with sunlight reflected from myriad water droplets.

"Tara is what the ancient Celts called a 'thin place,'" explained Gráinne, as they started to climb the hill. "It's where the seen and the unseen worlds come together. Sometimes, especially at certain times of the year, the other world breaks through. It's very mystical here – you can feel it."

She ran after Dan as he started to stride away. "Dan, last night you were talking about your work with meteorites?"

Dan stopped, perplexed and still hurt at her apparent indifference to their night together. "Yep, anything you want to know about meteorites, I'm your man. Mary's pretty good as well."

Gráinne flicked her hair away from her face. "Last night we talked a little about meteorites being worshipped?"

Dan nodded.

"Well, if in the ancient world certain stones were considered to be sacred, wouldn't you say meteorites were the most sacred?" She smiled at him, waiting for an answer.

"Yes, you find written records and folk memories of meteorite worship all over the world, but I'm more up to speed on sacred meteorites in North America."

"I don't know much about that," said Gráinne.

"Did you get home okay, last night?" he asked, abruptly.

"Sorry? After O'Casey's, you mean? Yes, fine. The traffic had died down…" She waited for Dan to respond.

"Okay," said Dan finally, shaking his head as if collecting his thoughts. "The rituals associated with them are not so well documented in North America as they are with the Old World meteorites, but they were certainly venerated by Native Americans. In some cases you can still find trails leading to them, showing that they were regularly visited, and gifts – beads and the like – have been found. But it was the Greeks and Romans who really took them seriously. You should talk to Charles. He's the authority there."

He stopped and they waited for Charles to catch up. "Charles, we were just talking about meteorite mythology – how meteorites were worshipped."

"Oh, don't get me going," said Charles.

Mary came up behind them, listening carefully to the conversation.

"The Temple of Diana in Ephesus is one of my favourite places," Charles began enthusiastically. "You probably know it was one of the Seven Wonders of the Ancient World. The original temple had a sacred stone in it which was worshipped and was said to have fallen from Jupiter. Definitely sounds like a meteorite, doesn't it? It's even mentioned in the Bible. Oh, but what would I have given to have taken part in the excavations. It was a team funded by the British Museum which found it, you know."

He paused for breath. "But the best-known example of meteorite worship is probably Magna Mater, the Mother Goddess of ancient Rome where she was worshipped in the form of a meteorite. She was celebrated with a festival and games – it must have been quite a show. That meteorite is lost now, though. I often wonder where it is…" He stopped talking and looked up to the top of the hill, breathing deeply.

"Are you all right?" Mary asked.

"Fine," he said. "But there was a time when I could

have run up this hill. Let's go, shall we?" he muttered, starting to plod upwards again.

Dan and Gráinne had already reached the top of the hill and were standing by the side of the Lia Fáil, waiting for the others.

Gráinne took out her phone and started checking her messages. "You must feel at home here, Dan?" she said, without looking up. "With your Irish background, I mean?"

Dan nodded, apparently absorbed in studying the various landmarks, while Gráinne was obviously texting. He turned around as Mary and Charles arrived.

The three of them stood together and admired the view, taking in Ireland in all its green glory, stretching out into the distance under a pale blue sky dotted with white clouds.

The group was alone, the only other visitors wandering in the distance around the so-called Mound of the Hostages, in reality a Neolithic tomb.

"Well, this is it," Gráinne said, putting her phone back in a pocket. "The Lia Fáil or the so-called Stone of Destiny."

The monument was about four feet in height, phallic in shape and had no visible carvings. Charles had visited it before and was aware that, considering its reputation, the standing stone didn't look particularly remarkable.

"You probably know as much about it as me, Charles," said Gráinne.

"I doubt it," he said. "And I'm always willing to learn. But is this really the actual stone the High Kings were crowned on? I mean, it's just a regular standing stone, isn't it? There doesn't seem anything special about it?"

"Well, you probably know there are quite a few stories about it," said Gráinne. "Some academics believe it used to stand by the Mound of the Hostages and that it was moved here after the Battle of Tara, to commemorate the Irish fighters who died fighting the British. In other words, it is just a regular standing stone. But that doesn't stop it from being special, does it? Maybe it really was used in coronations and cried out when a worthy king was seated on it."

"I wonder what sort of stone it is?" said Charles, casually touching it. "My God," he exclaimed. "I felt a distinct tingle. Mary, you touch it. See if you feel anything."

Mary apprehensively placed one finger on the stone. Instantly, she cried out, staggered backwards, and fell right into Charles's arms.

As Charles struggled to hold her upright, Dan leapt over to help and together they gently lowered her on to the ground.

Her eyes immediately flickered open. "I'm so sorry," she said, shaking her head. "I seem to be making a habit of this."

Gráinne knelt down beside her. "What happened, Mary?"

"I got a shock. Like an electric shock."

Dan looked mystified and got to his feet. Very tentatively, he placed a finger on the stone, ready to immediately pull it back. Then he placed his hand on it. "Nothing," he said "Absolutely nothing."

"It's not unusual to feel a tingle or a shock when you touch a standing stone," said Gráinne. "I've met a lot of people who've had a similar experience with different stones. But you must be very sensitive, Mary, to react like that."

"So what's different about me?" asked Dan. "Why didn't I feel anything?"

"Maybe the stone discharged itself when Mary touched it," said Gráinne. "Or perhaps some people are just different."

"What about you, Gráinne?" asked Charles.

"No, it's never happened to me and I've touched a lot of standing stones."

Charles and Dan helped Mary to her feet.

"I'm okay now. Really," she said.

"You didn't have another vision, did you?" Charles asked, looking worried.

Mary looked guardedly at Gráinne. "Yes, yes I did. Well, a sort of vision. The stone seemed to emit a sudden whoosh of energy and then an image flashed into my mind."

"What was it?" asked Charles.

"It was like a photograph. It was an image of four standing stones in a row."

Charles glanced at Dan, shaking his head. "Did you recognise them, Mary?" he asked.

"No. No idea. But it was as if the stone here was communicating with them. As if they were sort of talking to each other and I could listen in."

Gráinne was searching for something on her phone.

"Here we are," she said, suddenly. "Are these the stones you saw, Mary?" She showed her the photograph.

Mary responded instantly. "Yes, yes, that's them. How did you know?"

"Oh, it was just a guess." She showed the picture to Dan and Charles. "There's another legend about the Lia Fáil that I haven't told you about. It's said one of the Irish kings lent the Lia Fáil, or at least a part of it, to a relative, called Fergus, son of Erc. He was the king of a branch of the Irish Gaels who had settled in the west of Scotland. They settled in the Kilmartin Glen in what's now Argyll and he wanted the Lia Fáil to be used in his coronation to underpin his authority. The Kilmartin Glen is famous for its Neolithic monuments. These are the Ballymeanoch Stones, which are there."

"I'm still amazed you knew what Mary had seen," said Charles, intrigued.

"Oh, there's more," said Gráinne. "The Irish Gaels who settled in that part of Scotland were known as the Scotti. That was the name given by the Romans to the inhabitants of Ireland, maybe after the legendary Queen Scota. And that's how Scotland is supposed to have got its name."

She turned to Mary. "The kingdom they founded in Scotland was called Dál Riada. The name Dál Riada comes from a redheaded Irish warrior called Cairbre Ruadh, who had previously invaded that part of Scotland. Ruadh means 'red' in Gaelic and he was nicknamed 'Red'. Dál Riada means 'Land of Red'. You'd probably feel quite at home there, Mary..."

23

At two o'clock in the morning on the Monday, the lights of the public bar in The Black Dog pub in Long Compton were casting a pale glow over the deserted street when the latch of the front door clicked open and the landlord appeared. But this time he was not there to greet local farmers keen for a beer or two with convivial company, or a Londoner up for the weekend. Satan, the black Labrador, padded up behind Dave Taylor and stood behind his master to welcome visitors with a more serious purpose.

A rattle of jewellery announced the first arrival. "Come in, come in, Delia," Dave said, opening the door wide for a middle-aged lady in a long green cloak. He quietly pushed the door closed behind her.

"Don't mind me," said Greta the Goth girl, pushing the door open again. Her fascinator and veil had been replaced by an authentic black cloche hat. "Hello, Satan," she said, patting the dog.

William Dobson and Jake Shepherd arrived together. "Bloody cold," moaned William. "Any chance of a lift up to the Stones?"

"Sure, sure," said Dave. "Just go through to the bar. And keep your bloody hands off the booze. Where's Ernest?"

"He's on his way," said Jake. "He's getting so old, we'll probably have to carry him."

"But he's still got the gift," said Dave.

"Got the gift for not paying his workers, that's for sure," said Jake.

"But he did find water on old Jenkins' farm, first time," answered Dave firmly. "They dug down ten feet and then it gushed. Right where he said it was."

"S'pose so," said Jake. "Anyway, here he is."

At that point an ancient Land Rover drew up in the pub car park and an elderly man eased himself out. After reaching back inside for a walking stick, he made his way slowly to the entrance. He pushed the door open with his stick. "Morning, gentlemen," he said. "Oh, and ladies, of course."

They all sat in front of the bar as Dave instinctively went behind it. Satan lay down in his favourite place in front of the bar.

"So what's it all about?" asked Ernest.

"Hang on," said Dave. "Let's do this properly." He stood to attention behind the bar. "I hereby declare this an official meeting of The Order of the Black Dog," he announced solemnly.

"The Order of the Black Dog," the others intoned.

"So what's it all about?" asked Ernest, again.

"It's Gráinne," replied Dave. "She must have been having visions again – the stone's been in contact with her and giving her instructions. She says something is happening and she wants us to do the dog ceremony. But this time a bit different."

"What's she mean by 'different'?" asked William.

"Same, but with a different spell and a different dog," said Dave. "She sent the words to my phone by voicemail. It's some language I don't know – no idea. She said I had to learn it off by heart. Wasn't easy, I tell you."

"So, what's going to happen?" asked Ernest.

"Apparently this dog's special. It'll be a dog all right but not the usual Black Dog. She says it's got something for us."

"The Black Dog we called up last time was pretty good. Worked a treat with that banker bloke," said William. "He saw it on Meon Hill and had a stroke two days later when he was taking an evening constitutional."

"What's this one got for us?" asked Jake.

"Some special stone. She says to keep it safe until she gets here to pick it up."

"Shouldn't she be here herself then, if it's so bloody important?" said Jake.

"She says she's onto something she has to check out. Something to do with some old guy who had a bit of a vision at Newgrange. She was going to go with him and a couple of his friends to Tara. Then she'll be over here later this week to pick up the stone and take it up to Scotland for a ceremony with the coven at Bandirran. And no, I've got no idea what it's all about."

Jake shrugged his shoulders. "We'd better get a move on, then. It'll be getting light in a couple of hours. Can me and William go with you, Ernest?"

Ernest nodded. "Just hope there's no one at the Stones."

"What about Satan?" asked Greta.

"We leave him here," said Dave. "If we take him, he'll run a mile like the last time we called up the Dog."

"So what ceremony are we going to do?" asked Delia.

"Same as usual," replied Dave. "Widdershins around the Whispering Knights, but this time I have to call out Gráinne's spell. And you can keep your clothes on this time, Delia."

Delia eyeballed him. "Too cold, anyway…"

"I'm not sure I like this," said Ernest. "You don't muck around with spells that have worked for centuries. Never know what's going to happen."

Dave came round from behind the bar. "Okay, let's go. I'll take the ladies. Jacob and William, you go with Ernest."

Within five minutes, the two vehicles pulled quietly into a deserted lay-by next to the Rollright Stones.

Dave got out of his car. "Let me just go and check first. Stay here," he said to Delia and Greta.

He looked up at the sky. Dark clouds were scudding across the full moon, so that it appeared only intermittently to light up the landscape. It was as if nature was sensing something alien was about to happen and the clouds were trying to block the moon from fulfilling its supporting role.

Dave felt apprehensive as he walked down the track until he could see the King's Men stone circle. The moonlight played on the stones so that they lit up and then faded into the gloom only to reappear, like ghosts recalling the ancient ceremonies that once took place there. Dave forced himself to walk around the circle, although it was obvious that the place was deserted.

In the distance he could just make out the stone slabs of the Whispering Knights burial chamber. He started as a barn owl hooted somewhere in a distant wood, then he shivered and walked back quickly to the lay-by.

Delia and Greta were chatting and didn't notice Dave returning. They jumped when he tapped on the roof of his car. "All clear," he said, and waved to Ernest, Jake and William.

Keeping close together, the group was walking down the track towards the Whispering Knights when the moon disappeared behind the clouds.

"I don't like this," said Jake. "It's too different. I just hope Gráinne knows what she's doing."

"She's never let us down yet as High Priestess," said Dave.

"But there's only six of us," said William. "Not enough to hold hands around the Stones."

"We've been okay with six before," said Dave. "No choice, anyway. It's all been at short notice. No way could I get thirteen of us together."

When they reached the ancient burial chamber, Ernest reached out and grasped the surrounding railings. "Energy's very strong tonight," he said.

"Ready, then," said Dave.

They positioned themselves at intervals around the monument.

"Widdershins," Dave said, and they started to walk anticlockwise.

The clouds parted briefly, but closed back over the moon once more, as though trying to give a final warning. Now, seeming to surrender to the inevitable, they cleared so that the moon shone brightly down on the scene below.

Ernest stumbled and practically fell, but hauled himself upright with his stick. Slowly, they continued their circular route.

Dave took a deep breath and started chanting in a language none of them had heard before. After chanting what he had learned off by heart three times, he said, "Stop."

They stood stationary and waited. As Dave looked at his watch, they heard the owl hoot again. He could just make out the dial. "That's five minutes," he said, finally.

"Nothing," said Jake. "I knew it wouldn't work."

"We'll do it once more, and if nothing happens, we go back home," said Dave. They started walking and Dave began to chant again.

In the graveyard of the Church of St Peter and St Paul in Long Compton, the tombstones seemed to stand more upright, like guardians sensing an enemy was about to invade the sanctity of their church.

For a split second, the porch of the church lit up with a strange blue light that emanated from the stone animal at the foot of the effigy of the woman in the horned headdress. A moment later, the light flickered again and the whole animal started to glow with an electric blue light. Just a wisp of mist rose above it.

The mist poured silently from the stone animal and eddied and swirled until it filled the porch, blocking out the effigy. For a minute nothing happened. Then, as if it had made up its mind, the mist drifted out of the porch and moved across the graveyard as a small, discreet cloud. Unhindered by the powerless tombstones, it rolled on towards the main street and gained speed.

The mist slowed momentarily in front of Ben's house, but picked up speed again and continued towards The Black Dog. As it passed the pub, Satan sensed its presence, whining and lying down as flat as he could.

At the edge of the village, it left the road and rolled quickly over fields and through hedges. In less than five minutes it had reached the King's Men stone circle. There it halted and grew smaller and thicker.

In the distance, Ernest leant against the railings of the Whispering Knights. "Let's just call it a night," he said.

"Third time lucky," replied Dave, and once more they reluctantly started walking around the railings.

It was Greta who saw it first. "Look, over there – by the King's Men," she said, pointing. "I can see something. It's blocking out one of the stones. Whatever it is, it's coming this way."

"Dammit, I don't like this," said Ernest.

The mist avoided the path and rolled across a field directly towards them.

The group scattered as it neared them. "This isn't right," cried out Jake. "Let's just get out of here." He edged away from the burial chamber, before standing still, frozen in place.

Not knowing what to do, William joined him.

For his part, Ernest hadn't realised he could move so

fast as he put the burial chamber between himself and the approaching cloud, hoping that the monument would somehow protect him.

Greta grasped Delia's arm hard. "I'm scared," she whispered, and they both edged towards Dave.

Only Dave stood firm. "Wait…" he ordered.

Now, as they watched, the mist came to a stop in front of the monument. There was a faint crackling sound and tiny blue sparks flashed inside it, like some nebulous brain firing off signals.

Ernest felt his hands tingling and the hairs on the back of his hands stood straight up. "Energy level's rising," he muttered. "My body's fairly buzzing."

"Just wait," said Dave.

The mist slowly moved forwards through the railings and into the burial chamber. The stone slabs seemed to absorb it, so that in a few seconds the mist had completely disappeared.

The first they saw of the dog was two red eyes glowing deep inside the burial chamber between two upright stone slabs. Without warning, it leapt out, cleared the railings and landed on the track. It turned around and stood still, staring at them, the eyes like burning coals in its enormous head. The ears stood upright like those of a jackal and its sleek black coat glistened in the moonlight.

"It's huge," whispered Greta, turning away and burying her head in Delia's cloak.

Jake coughed violently and put his hand over his nose and mouth as the stench of rotting flesh overwhelmed him. William could barely stop himself from retching.

The dog ignored them, as if it were there only to fulfil a duty.

"It's got something in its mouth," Dave said, under his breath. "Just stand still. Don't move."

The glow of the dog's eyes faded slightly and, very purposefully, it lowered its head to drop the Antarctic Meteorite.

As if knowing its task had been completed, the dog raised its head to the moon and howled. Even after the dog had lowered its head again, the sound continued as faint echoes bouncing around the King's Men stone circle.

In a second the dog seemed to dissolve and the mist reappeared. Very slowly it drifted into the burial chamber to be absorbed again into the stone slabs.

High in the sky, the moon disappeared again behind the clouds, and in the far distance the lights of a car flashed through the trees.

Dave picked up the meteorite, weighed it in his hand and inspected it. The cut surface where Ben had taken a sample was clearly visible. He showed it to the others. "This isn't any old stone. It's a meteorite," he said. "I wonder what's so special about it."

"Knowing Gráinne, it won't be pleasant," said Jake.

"I'll tell her we've got it," said Dave.

24

Like sentinels still performing their duty of guarding the Kilmartin Glen after 5,000 years, the four standing Ballymeanoch Stones stood in line, the taller at one end and the shorter at the other.

Dan was rubbing his hand over the lichen-covered surface of the tallest stone. More than twice his height, it soared into the sky. "Well, I haven't had a shock," he said. "What's supposed to happen now? I'm still not sure why we're here."

"I don't know either," replied Mary. "I didn't feel anything either when I touched it. But I do believe that the Lia Fáil told me to come here to the Ballymeanoch Stones. And I also believe that we've been sent here for a reason."

Dan didn't look entirely convinced. "Well, okay then. We've made it. What now?"

"I've no idea," said Mary. "We'll just have to wait and see."

Charles was relaxed and obviously in his element. "I've only been here once before and that was for a brief visit when I was a student. This whole glen is a cemetery and a centre of ritual over a mile long—"

"Can you be sure that these really are the stones you saw in your vision, Mary?" asked Dan.

"Exactly the same. But I didn't see those other two, though." She motioned to two stones a short distance away, standing parallel to the four stones. "If you really use your imagination, I suppose you could see them as some kind of prehistoric radio receivers," she said.

"Apparently they might be the remains of an avenue which was marked out by a lot more stones," said Charles, getting into his stride again. "I wonder what sort of ceremonies were held here? I've read they could be aligned to mark important solar and lunar events. It's a pity Gráinne's not here. She probably knows this place inside out."

"Do you know where she is?" asked Dan, looking innocent.

"Didn't she tell you?" said Charles. "She told me she had to go from Dublin to England for an urgent meeting. She said she had to pick something up. But she also asked us to let her know how we get on here."

"It still worries me," said Mary, suddenly. "How exactly did Gráinne know these are the stones I saw in my vision? It's downright weird that Gráinne knew what I'd seen, isn't it? I mean, there are standing stones all over the British Isles. And not just the British Isles – they're all over the world. There must be other standing stones just like these around somewhere."

"But she knew all about the Dál Riada connection, didn't she?" said Charles. "Maybe she just put two and two together. She's quite bright."

"I'm sorry to say this, but I really don't trust her," said Mary. "Put it down to female intuition, if you like. I mean, is it by accident we went with her to the Lia Fáil where I had a vision and now we've ended up here?"

"I was the one who made contact with her in the first place," said Charles. "And she does know an awful lot about the Neolithic period. Especially sacred stones…"

He turned and gazed northwards up the glen. "There really is something very magical about this place, isn't there? Even I can sense it crackles with some sort of positive energy. I'm sure that's what made it sacred to the ancients. It's all here, isn't it? Burial cairns, standing stones, a stone circle and some of the finest rock art in the British Isles."

He turned and pointed in the opposite direction. "To cap it all, a couple of miles away, there's the hill fort of Dunadd, the ancient capital of Dál Riada. If ever there was a sacred hill, that's it."

Going over to the second-tallest stone, he ran his hand over the side. "See here. If you look carefully you can see the whole surface of the rock is covered with depressions. They're called cup marks. I wouldn't be surprised if these stones were cut from rocks in the ground that already had cup marks carved into them. This is the simplest form of rock art, but around here I could show you quite remarkable carvings – cup marks with rings around them, sometimes with channels coming out of them that link up with other cup and ring carvings. Then there are rosettes, spirals – you name it." He caught sight of Dan ostentatiously stifling a yawn.

"Sorry," said Dan. "I didn't sleep too well last night."

Mary frowned at him. "Any idea what they're about?" she asked Charles.

Charles shook his head. "Nobody really knows – it's one of the great archaeological mysteries. Take these simple cup marks, for instance," he said, touching a depression in the stone. "They're not just found here. They're found carved into rocks literally all over the world. There are loads of theories about their function – I've read there could be over a hundred. Some of them are quite reasonable, such as they indicated safe routes through the landscape…"

"I get the idea," said Dan.

Charles ignored him. "Personally, I think the people who carved them believed that the rocks were alive. Perhaps they collected rainwater from the cup marks for ceremonial purposes, like using holy water for modern-day baptisms. It could be that women used the rock dust ground out of the depressions in the belief it would make them pregnant. Or, once they knew they were pregnant, maybe they believed they could use the dust to impregnate themselves with a spirit that dwelt in the rock. There are lots of traditions and folk tales around here in Scotland about people putting food and drink – milk, butter and the like – into the cups in the belief that they were caring for the rock spirits."

He stepped away from the stone and swept his arm around. "It's obvious to me that the people who built these monuments were profoundly in touch with nature. To me, it's all part of a universal belief system that was once found throughout the prehistoric world. These days we still haven't come to grips with it. Unlike us nowadays, they weren't destroying the planet. They sensed that everything is alive – everything – the Earth, the Sun, the Moon, the Stars…"

Mary glared at Dan who was smirking, but Charles seemed not to notice him.

"Just look at these stones here," he said. "They're a bit like antennae, aren't they? Perhaps they were built to communicate with each other and Mary has tapped into the process. Maybe the people who built them could sense these earth energies. Could it be that some people still have that sense? Perhaps it's latent in us all…"

"Phew," said Dan. "And I thought that I was a bit on the edge."

"Sorry," said Charles. "I do sometimes get carried away. It's just that this place is very special."

"Don't worry," replied Dan. "I'm inclined the same way. But it's a bit early in the day for me."

Mary had remained silent until now. "It's because of the meteorites that we're here," she said, bluntly.

Charles and Dan stared at each other, taken aback.

"Do you have the Serpent Meteorite with you, now?" asked Charles.

She patted her backpack. "In here. I felt we should keep it with us. It's the other one I worry about – and I know it's not far away. Someone, something's got it. And that someone or something is not nice."

Not knowing what to say, Charles and Dan checked around, looking for something strange or significant.

A light morning mist was still hanging on around the trees and in odd pockets where the land dipped. In the far distance, the hills were just discernible through low clouds.

Charles broke the silence. "Not every mist is evil, Mary. And I'm sure there's nothing evil about this place." He clasped his hand to his forehead as he looked at the sun, which was already well clear of the hills and the clouds. "The warmth of the sun will soon drive the mist away, you'll see." He noted the time. "Shall we go and look at some of the other monuments? There's one quite near that will definitely interest you, Mary. It's the last burial cairn to the south of the glen. It's called Ri Cruin."

When they reached the cairn, Mary seemed to relax. Even though it had been desecrated many times over the millennia and was essentially nothing more than a low pile of stones, there was a peaceful air about it. Perhaps it was because it was in a woodland setting, guarded by watchful trees.

"Come over here," said Charles, and he stood in front of the information board. "It's only an artist's impression of one of the burial chambers they found here, but just look." He stepped aside so that Mary could see it.

She turned to Charles, laughing. "I see what you mean. He's a real ginger, isn't he?"

The board displayed a large illustration of a burial chamber lined with stone slabs. The incumbent was depicted as if he had just been placed in the tomb. He was in the foetal position with a pot by his head and a bunch of flowers placed by his clasped hands. His red-coloured hair was braided and swept back from his bearded face into a ponytail.

"Perhaps the artist knew something," said Charles.

Mary nodded and smiled. "Somehow I do feel at home here," she said, and started to read the description of the cairn.

Charles stood alongside her for a while, before going over to Dan, who was taking photographs. "Shall we take a walk up the glen?" he suggested.

"Sure," said Dan. "Let me just take a couple more shots."

"Are you coming, Mary?" Charles called out.

She didn't respond but stood there, staring, transfixed, at the information board.

Charles went back to her. "Shall we take a look at some of the other monuments?"

Mary shook her head a few times as if coming out of some sort of daydream.

"Are you all right?" he asked.

She turned to him. "Very all right." She paused as if trying to find the right words. "I've just seen my son."

"Sorry?"

"My son, Charles. Bryan. Bryan just came to me and smiled at me. I actually saw him. And I feel so happy."

He didn't reply.

"I saw my son, Charles. Bryan was killed in a climbing accident sixteen years ago – not far from here, on Ben Nevis. He was just twenty-one. He looked just the same as he was then."

"I'm so sorry. I didn't realise," said Charles.

"He loved adventure. He loved mountains and climbing. He was studying English at Berkeley. Every vacation he was off somewhere – the Rockies, the Alps, even one trip to the Himalayas. But Scotland was the place he loved most. I suppose it was because that was where his grandfather came from – it was in his blood. And, do you know, Bryan had ginger hair as well."

Charles seemed to be struggling to find the right words.

Mary looked hard at him. "He's still with us, Charles. He wanted me to know he was all right. He didn't stay long, but just before he faded away, he pointed in that direction." She turned and gestured south.

"That's towards Dunadd hill fort," he said. "The sacred place where the kings of Dál Riada were crowned."

"Let's go there," said Mary. "Now I know what I have to do."

25

"Looks like a mist up there," said Mary, pointing to the site of the ancient hill fort of Dunadd at the top of the rock-strewn hill.

"Just low cloud – perfectly normal," replied Charles. He gestured into the distance. "Look, there are clouds on all the hills around here. Anyway, the sun is already breaking through – you can see it reflected from a rock right at the top."

Dan opened the boot of the car, took out his bag and slung it over his shoulder. "I'm going to have a look at that information board over there."

Mary watched him as he walked away, until he was well out of earshot. Then she stood in front of Charles. "I really did see my son, Charles," she said. "You don't believe me, do you?"

"I don't know what to believe any longer," he said. "What with Warren's horrible death, magic meteorites, evil mists, weird earthlights and your visions, Mary. And there's Holly as well, with her experiences. Even I have had my odd moments. I really don't know what's going on here, or even whether I want to know, or be involved in it any longer. I have a feeling Dan, too, has his doubts."

"But you're the one who felt we owed it to Warren to find out what's going on – what really caused his death," she insisted. "I saw my son, Charles, and I know he wants me to push on. I'll go it alone if I have to." She took a bottle of water out of her bag. "This is really all I can manage," she said. "Would you mind carrying the meteorite this time? It's just too heavy for me to carry up there and we really should keep it with us."

"Of course," said Charles, picking up the meteorite and putting it in his own backpack. He retrieved his climbing boots from the car and glanced towards the top of the hill. "I'm not quite sure I'm up to another climb – I'm still recovering from the Hill of Tara. Still, at least that cloud's disappeared. The sun's probably put paid to it."

Mary looked relieved. "Guess I'm getting rather paranoid. Do you mind if I go ahead?"

Charles was putting his boots on when Dan returned. "You probably know all about this place, Charles. Apparently there's a flat outcrop of rock near the top with a footprint carved into it and a basin which collects water. They are supposed to have been used in coronation rituals."

"Yes, I came here during my visit as a student," replied Charles. "I suspect I found it easier to climb then." He smiled. "You never know, perhaps there really was an unearthly cry when a rightful monarch placed his foot in the depression. And maybe the rock basin collected water that was deemed holy and used to anoint the monarch." He finished tying his bootlaces, swung his bag over his shoulder and locked the boot of the car. "Just about ready, Dan."

Dan turned and watched Mary striding out towards the bottom of the hill.

"Mary's very enthusiastic all of a sudden," he observed. "It's not like her to pound on ahead like that."

"There's a reason," said Charles, watching her as she reached the rocks at the bottom of the pathway and started to scramble upwards. "I'm sure she won't mind me telling you, Dan." He took a deep breath. "She had another vision – at the Ri Cruin cairn we've just been to. She says she saw her son. She told me he was killed in a climbing accident on Ben Nevis, not far from here."

Dan looked baffled. "She didn't mention anything to me about another vision."

"I think she only told me about it because I was there with her when it happened. She must have felt rather overwhelmed. She'll probably tell you about it later. That's really why we've come here. She says her son pointed towards here – Dunadd. She's changed, Dan. She's really got a purpose now. It's fired her up to find out what on earth is happening."

Dan still looked confused, but didn't say anything.

"Do you know anything about her son?" Charles asked, as they started walking. He immediately stepped on a patch of mud and skidded.

Dan grabbed his arm to steady him and studied the pathway leading to the summit. "It's not that high and the climb seems easy enough. Look, I can see a man near the top."

It was not until Mary was out of sight and they reached a level piece of track that Dan seemed to brace himself to answer Charles's question. "Her son Bryan was killed climbing the North Face of Ben Nevis with a friend. At the time, apparently, it attracted a lot of attention in the media. You probably know, but it seems every year thousands of people go up the mountain on the Mountain Track from the south – but the North Face is something else. They were climbing an ice gully in March. It was after a mild February and there had been a fresh snowfall. That's when the avalanche happened – a couple of other climbers witnessed it. It must have caught Bryan and his friend completely unawares. They never stood a chance. It took two days to find their bodies."

"She didn't tell me that," said Charles. "But what's her background? How did she cope?"

"Was she married, do you mean?" Dan said. He stopped and leant against a rock. "She was a California dropout. You know – sex, drugs and rock 'n' roll. She was shacked up with some rock guitarist – she told me he was very good. Anyway, she got pregnant. The guitarist denied it was anything to do with him and drifted away. I'm told he died of a drug overdose soon afterwards. It was a turning point for Mary, because she threw herself into doing a degree in physics at Berkeley and went on to do a doctorate in meteorology. She funded her studies by waitressing – that sort of thing. And, no, she never married. She dedicated her life to bringing up her son – it was very tough. She's very independent, Charles. And a very strong lady."

They climbed on in silence, Dan waiting at intervals for Charles to catch up.

Mary was waiting for them, alone at the summit. "You two took your time, didn't you," she mocked. "I've already tried it," she announced, indicating the footprint in the rock. "Yes, my foot does fit. And here's the rock basin, but there's no water in it."

"So, this is the actual place where the kings of Dál Riada were supposed to have been crowned," said Charles. "And they could have used the Stone of Destiny as well. Did you hear a roar of approval, Mary? That's what's supposed to have happened when a rightful monarch put his foot in the depression and it fitted exactly."

"No, nothing. But I think we're here for another reason." She hesitated before she spoke again. "There's something I should tell you, Dan…"

"It's okay, Charles has already told me," he cut in. "Bryan didn't say exactly why we should come here, then?"

"No," she replied. "But we'll find out, I'm sure of that."

Dan idly put his foot in the depression in the rock. "See, even my foot fits in it. On your knees, you two." He passed the camera to Charles. "A moment to immortalise, don't you think?"

Charles fiddled with the camera, took a couple of shots of Dan posing and passed the camera back.

"Thanks," said Dan, and he proceeded to take numerous shots of the rock platform and the magnificent views. "So, where do we go now?"

"Back to Kilmartin, perhaps," said Charles. "I wouldn't mind looking around the museum there."

As the three started to climb down again, Mary went on ahead. "By the way, did you see a man coming down when you were coming up?" she called back.

"No, nobody," said Dan.

Mary stopped and waited. "That's odd," she said. "When I was getting close to the top, I saw a man standing on the rock platform. He was standing still, taking in the view. I didn't see his face but he was wearing a jacket a bit like yours, Charles. In fact, for a second I thought it *was* you. But when I reached the top, he had gone. There was nobody there at all. I was completely alone until you two arrived."

"Yes, we saw him as well," said Dan. "Perhaps he went down another way."

"I didn't notice another route down," said Mary. "It is a bit odd."

For a while they were concentrating too hard on the demanding descent to be able to talk. Only when they reached the bottom of the pathway did they stop to take stock.

It was Charles who saw him first, standing with his back to them, apparently studying the information board. He was indeed wearing a tweed jacket similar to the one Charles was wearing. His unkempt dark brown hair reached down to the collar, but it was his jeans with extravagantly flared bottoms that attracted attention.

"Is that the same man you saw at the top?" asked Charles.

"Yes," said Mary. "That's definitely him."

Charles looked intrigued. "I wonder how he came down. Perhaps I'll just go and say hello."

"Can I have the car key?" asked Dan. "I want to put my things back in the trunk."

"I'll come with you, Dan," said Mary.

As Charles reached the figure, he stopped, confused. *I had a jacket just like that*, he thought. *And those jeans…* The man didn't acknowledge his presence as Charles stood behind him.

"Fascinating place," Charles said, amiably.

When the figure turned around, Charles froze, before shuddering with disbelief. He knew instantly that he was looking at himself as a young man. For a while the figure looked at Charles, impassively. Then its face broke into a shy, boyish smile.

Charles emotions swung wildly between bewilderment, wonderment and fear. "Hello," he spluttered.

The figure continued to smile, but even as it did so, it started to fade, so that Charles could see the information board through its body. It was only then that the figure raised its arm, turned and pointed in a northerly direction. Within seconds the apparition had faded into nothingness, leaving no trace that it had actually been there.

Charles stood, shaking his head, his thoughts in turmoil. Feeling very old and confused, he walked slowly back to the car.

Mary looked up from putting her water back in her bag and noticed that Charles was looking distraught.

"Charles? Are you okay?" she asked.

"I don't know," he replied, quietly. "You're not going to believe this…"

26

"I tell you, Dan," Charles said. "I'm sure that was me. He even had the spots on his chin that used to come up every time just before a party." He pushed his coffee cup away and glanced around the pleasant outdoor café attached to the museum at Kilmartin. Everybody seemed to be relaxing and enjoying the late morning sunshine, taking no notice of them.

Dan groaned. "This is all getting a bit much for me. But at least you say the figure you saw seemed friendly."

"He seemed friendly enough – he smiled at me just before he faded away."

"Well, I certainly saw him," said Mary. "I saw him on top of Dunadd and when he was looking at the information board as well. How could anyone forget those flared jeans?"

"They were the fashion then," replied Charles, curtly.

"And you say you've been to Dunadd before, Charles?" said Mary.

"Yes, when I was a student at Oxford. We had an archaeological field trip to the Kilmartin Glen here."

"So, suppose you somehow left an imprint in another

dimension," suggested Mary. "And somehow you managed to access it."

Dan looked unconvinced. "Putting it frankly, Charles, I'm wondering if you, Mary and Holly are having some sort of effect on each other – some sort of joint paranoia. Nobody else seems to be having visions, so what's so special about you three? What about me, for instance? Why am I not affected? No visions, nothing."

"Two things, I'd say," said Charles. "Firstly, we've all been in close contact with the meteorites – you included, of course. But the other obvious thing is that Mary, Holly and I all carry the genes for red hair." He took a sip of his coffee. "Perhaps someone in the genetics department at Oxford might be able to help. Perhaps the genes associated with red hair do something that makes the carriers susceptible to whatever's special about the meteorites."

Dan looked around at the people in the café. They were behaving perfectly normally. "Listen, it's all right for you two – you seem to be on a mission. But I'm beginning to wonder what I'm doing here. It's as if our lives have been taken over by those two meteorites. They're alive, somehow, aren't they? And we seem to be involved in some ancient battle between whatever powers the meteorites manifest. We're being used, aren't we? They're manipulating us – and I don't like it. I don't like being out of control of my own life."

Mary looked thoughtful and patted her bag. "This one here is the good one. And it's something to do with the real Stone of Destiny – I know it. Maybe it wants us to find the Stone of Destiny. And it is using me, protecting me, because somehow I'm tied up with it. It's all to do with my ancestry, isn't it? It's to do with my ancestral tribe, whatever it is. And I feel that the other meteorite, wherever it is, is trying to stop us."

"I know your idea seems outrageous, Mary," said Charles, "but I'm beginning to think that you could be right. Somehow the Serpent Meteorite could indeed be connected to the Stone of Destiny. I think it knows you're special in some way. And you're right, it is using you."

"But I'm very ordinary, Charles, I can assure you," she said.

Dan laughed. "Much as I admire you, Mary, it does sound like a long shot to me."

"You may laugh, Dan," said Charles, "but I'm going to settle down tonight and do some real research on the Stone of Destiny. I'm wondering where we will be sent next."

"Wherever it is, we'll have to get a move on," said Dan. "I'm rapidly using up all my annual leave. Look, I do care about what's happening, but I have a career to pursue as well. Maybe you two should continue by yourselves?"

"I understand how you must feel – I do really," said Mary, "but I have to go on with this and I really need you with me. I've no idea what's happening, but I did see Bryan. He came to me, Dan, and he did direct me to Dunadd. Then Charles saw his younger self. They must have been giving us instructions. That's right, isn't it, Charles?"

"That's right," he replied. "As I said, judging by the position of the sun at the time, my younger self pointed northwards. But that doesn't mean that much. Are we talking one mile, ten miles, a hundred miles…? I don't know."

Dan sat there silently brooding. He idly picked up his camera, switched it on and started to check through the shots he had taken that morning. He pressed a button several times and then frowned. "Charles, did you do anything funny to my camera when you were taking those photos on Dunadd?"

"I don't think so," said Charles. "I only took a couple of shots, as you asked. Even I can work a camera."

Dan looked disturbed and checked the camera again. "Charles, you took a couple of photos there. I also took a few of the rock slab with the footprint in it and a whole lot of the views. Do you remember?"

"Yes, I remember," he said. "The views were superb. Can I have a look at them?"

"I wish you could," said Dan, "but every photo I took at Dunadd has disappeared. They're not on the camera."

"Has it happened before?" asked Charles.

"No, never. And all the photos I took before and all the ones I took in the museum just now, they're all here. It's just the photos I took at Dunadd that are missing. How can that have happened?"

"Could it be you're being affected as well?" said Charles.

Dan checked his camera yet again. "There's definitely something very odd about this place, Kilmartin." He took a couple of photos of the café and played with the camera. "There we are – it's working fine now," he said, shaking his head in bewilderment.

"Welcome to the club," said Charles.

It was a full minute before Dan spoke again. "Okay, I

wonder what's north of Dunadd that could be of possible interest to us?"

Charles reached into his bag and retrieved a map. "Excuse me," he said, pushing the coffee cups to one side and spreading the map out on the table. He ran his finger up from Dunadd. "Dunstaffnage Castle!" he said suddenly. "It's just north of Oban. And it's another place where the Stone of Destiny is supposed to have been kept." He folded up the map, put it back into his bag and smiled at Dan. "Let's go there tomorrow. Your turn to drive, Dan…"

27

As Charles and Dan stood at the edge of Dunstaffnage Bay first thing the next morning, there seemed to be an air of foreboding about the place. Apart from their car, the car park was deserted, and they were the only people around. Small boats were moored off-shore, but the forecast of bad weather and the grey overcast sky had clearly discouraged anyone from making a pleasure trip to explore Loch Etive, visible in the distance.

Charles contemplated the calm grey waters, deep in his own thoughts about the tragedy that had befallen Warren and the strange path his life was now taking.

Dan stood beside Charles, playing with his camera. He took a shot of the boats in the bay and inspected the picture. "It's still working fine," he said. "I've no idea what could have happened at Dunadd. Perhaps the memory card slipped out of position when we were climbing up to the fort."

"Perhaps," said Charles, looking straight ahead. He felt a spot of rain and glanced impatiently over to Mary, who was busy sorting out, in the boot of the car, what she would need for the day. "Are you ready, Mary?" he called over. "It's starting to rain. Can we get a move on, please?"

"Ready," she called back. She shoved a few things into her bag, completely forgetting to pick up the Serpent Meteorite at the back of the boot. After grabbing her umbrella, she slammed the boot closed. Waving at them, she yelled, "Let's go," and strode out ahead down the long driveway towards Dunstaffnage Castle.

Charles and Dan had to run to catch up with her, cursing that, unlike her, they hadn't thought to bring umbrellas. None of them had any reason to look back, but if they had, they would have seen a small yellow car arrive and park unobtrusively on the opposite side of the car park to their own car.

As the castle came into view, the three of them stopped simultaneously and stared, without saying a word. Dark, brooding and built squarely on a massive outcrop of rock, the castle seemed to be defying anybody who would dare to try to enter against its will.

It was Charles who eventually broke the silence. "It does look rather forbidding."

"There's bound to be some sort of ghost in a place like this," said Dan.

"Yes, and no doubt I'll be the one to see it," replied Mary.

As they walked over to the visitor centre, they realised that much of the castle was in a state of ruin and it no longer seemed so daunting. On closer inspection, they saw it was surrounded by well-tended lawns and peaceful woodland, rightfully assuming its status as an impressive tourist attraction.

The attendant in the visitor centre beamed a welcome

and after they had exchanged pleasantries about the weather, Charles put on his best innocent expression and plunged straight in. "I've read somewhere that the Stone of Destiny is supposed to have been here. Is that true?"

The attendant laughed. "Perhaps it could still be buried somewhere in the castle grounds."

Charles smiled indulgently.

"We don't really know," continued the attendant. "It is said that when Kenneth MacAlpin united Scotland in the ninth century, he took the Stone to the abbey at Scone for his coronation. The thing is, we don't know where he actually took it from. He might have taken it from Dunadd, where it could have been used for coronations there. No real evidence, though. Or perhaps it was sent from Dunadd to here at Dunstaffnage for safekeeping – there was a lot of warfare at the time. It could then have been sent from here to the abbey at Scone. For me, though, the most plausible theory is that it was on the island of Iona for some time, because we know from actual records that coronations took place on Iona. Somehow, Kenneth MacAlpin then got hold of it." She shrugged her shoulders. "But who knows, really?"

"Who knows, indeed?" said Charles.

Dan obviously had something else on his mind and couldn't resist the temptation. "Do you know if there's a ghost that haunts the castle?" he asked.

Mary gave him a warning look. "Not every castle has to have a ghost, Dan."

The attendant laughed again. "Actually, there is supposed to be a ghost here. But I can't say I've seen it, personally. It's claimed to be a woman in a green dress, known as the Ell-maid of Dunstaffnage. She's said to make an appearance whenever something sad or happy happens to the Campbell family. It was the Campbells who used to own the castle, before it was placed in the care of the state."

At this point the attendant smiled at Mary. "There is a more interesting paranormal phenomenon, though – especially if you're a MacDougall with red hair."

Mary flushed as Dan and Charles smirked. "How do you know that I'm a MacDougall?" she asked.

"Oh, we get a lot of American MacDougalls here, checking out their heritage. You must know that it was a Duncan MacDougall who built the castle. He was a grandson of Somerled, the great sea lord who ruled this part of Scotland when the Norsemen were here. He had a Norwegian background and was very much a redhead. There's a picture of him in a stained-glass window upstairs in the information display – you can go and have a look. And in fact there are still a lot of redheaded MacDougalls around." She reached under the counter. "Hang on a minute," she said as she pulled out a file. "This might be of interest to you." She flicked through the pages.

"Here we are," she said, unclipping a sheet of paper. She held it up and started reading. "'If a true descendant of the MacDougalls with red hair and without freckles should stand in the ancient chapel of Dunstaffnage and shout the battle cry of the Scots: "Strike for the Silver Lion!", instead of an echo he will hear a ghostly voice say, "Where is the Stone?"'"

"Hmm… Very interesting," said Charles. "And I can't see any freckles on your face, Mary."

Mary flushed a deeper pink. "I used to have freckles," she said, "but they disappeared as I got older."

"Where's the chapel?" asked Dan, rather impatiently.

"It's just a short walk from the castle through the wood," said the attendant. "But do check out the information centre and have a look around the castle first. It's quiet now, but it'll get very busy later."

"Thank you, good idea," said Charles. "Let's check out the information centre. Are you coming, you two?"

Reading about the chequered history of the castle, its central role in Scotland's tumultuous past of savage, internecine warfare became clear. There was even a display about the Stone of Destiny. "Just like she said downstairs," said Dan, "there's nothing to prove it was ever here."

"In that case why did my younger self seem to direct us here?" said Charles. "There must be some reason."

"Perhaps we were directed here to rule out the possibility that the Stone of Destiny is here at Dunstaffnage," said Mary. "I think we should go to Scone next. At least we know that a stone actually called the Stone of Destiny was used at Scone for ceremonial purposes."

"But we're here now," Dan said. "Shall we have a look around the castle? It looks as if the rain's stopped."

They toured the deserted castle in silence. For the tourist, everything was clearly described on information boards: the ruins of the kitchen, the great hall and the donjon. The gatehouse had been restored, although there was little of interest inside. It all seemed strangely impersonal, perhaps because nobody was actually living there, and there was not even a single suit of armour to remind the visitor of previous occupants.

"Does anybody want to take a look at the chapel?" said Charles, eventually.

Mary nodded apprehensively.

"Are you coming, Dan?" asked Charles.

"I just want to take a walk around again," Dan said. "The views from the top of the battlements over the bay are fantastic. I'll see you there in a minute."

"We'll wait for you at the chapel," said Mary.

Dodging water droplets showering down from the trees, Mary and Charles walked down the woodland path until the chapel came into view. Ruined and deserted, there was an air of deep sadness about it. Built with great care, and even love, the ruins still reflected the robustness of a building designed to keep out the worst excesses of the Scottish weather.

They stood together in the centre of the chapel, inspecting the ruins.

Charles pointed out the fine, well-preserved lancet windows. "I read that sunlight would have streamed in to light up the altar," he said. "Clearly not on a day like today, though."

They walked around the outside of the chapel and stopped to peer through an iron grille and inspect the burial ground built by the Campbell family in the eighteenth century, at a time when the chapel itself was already in ruins. Proud but deserted, the fine monuments were a reminder of the once-thriving dynasty that had lived in the castle until it slowly fell into disuse.

Having now read the inscriptions and wondering about the lives of the people associated with the castle, Charles looked at Mary. "Well, are you going to do it?" he ventured.

"Do what?"

"You know. Do what the woman said – stand in the chapel and say the magic words. You are a redheaded MacDougall with no freckles, after all."

"I've forgotten the words," said Mary.

"I haven't," said Charles. "I'll whisper them to you. Then you can say them out loud."

"Surely we've had enough weird things happening to us, without inviting more?"

"Oh, come on!" he said, beckoning and starting to walk around the chapel, back towards the entrance. Mary sighed and followed him until they stood together in the centre again.

"Ready?" asked Charles.

Mary looked around warily, then nodded.

"If a true descendant…" he began.

Mary quietly repeated the words.

"Say it louder," said Charles, and he continued the incantation.

Mary repeated the words, raising her voice and speaking as clearly as she could.

"Now, say this as loudly as you can," said Charles, and spoke the battle cry of the Scots.

"Be it on your head," Mary whispered to him. Then she stepped forwards and raised her arms in the air. "Strike for the Silver Lion!" she yelled.

The words briefly echoed around and then there was complete silence.

"See," said Mary. "Nothing – and this place is starting to give me the creeps. Shall we go now?"

She had started walking out of the building when they heard it. A low voice, almost like a whisper, seemed to come out of nowhere. "Where is the Stone?"

Charles was clearly shocked, but Mary just looked suspicious. When she heard a cackle, her green eyes flashed. "That's probably the first ever Scottish ghost to have an American accent," she said. "That's enough, Dan."

There was another drawn-out cackle and Dan appeared through the entrance, grinning.

"Very funny. Not," said Mary.

"Well, I thought we needed to lighten up a bit," said Dan.

"Ha, ha," said Charles, sheepishly. "Shall we go to the loch?"

"Good idea," said Mary, firmly. "Dan?"

"All right, all right. Just a joke," he replied. "I'm coming."

They had walked barely twenty paces away from the chapel when they heard it. The voice was male and decidedly Scottish.

"Go to the Hill of Dunsinane," it boomed.

Dan spun around. "That wasn't me!"

They stood there, staring at each other, not knowing what to do.

Mary shook her head. "You two can go back, if you want to. I'm staying here."

"What about you, Dan?" asked Charles.

"Well…"

"Oh, for crying out loud, Dan. It's probably somebody playing a prank like you," Charles said, and he started to walk back to the chapel.

Dan looked hard at Mary, then gritted his teeth and followed Charles.

He was already standing in the middle of the chapel when Dan appeared. "If anybody was here, they've gone now," Charles said. "Let's check outside, then that's it."

As they came to the entrance to the burial ground, Charles felt a strange urge to look inside. He had previously inspected the monuments and read the inscriptions, but this time was different. This time they seemed to have a presence and seemed in a funny way to be looking back at him, as if somehow alive.

He had already read the inscription on the magnificent monument to Victorian husband and wife Campbells, but now he read it again. *No way*, he thought.

Then it caught his eye, up against the wall at the back of the burial ground. It was a semicircular gravestone. Although half-covered by ferns and grass, the skull and crossbones inscribed on it were still very evident. Charles tried to avert his gaze, but found he couldn't take his eyes off it. The image of the skull and crossbones bored into his mind and he felt a faint tingle run up his spine…

28

Not far from Dunstaffnage, Gráinne O'Connor turned down a quiet country lane. She drove slowly until she saw a track that would take her well away from the road and parked her car behind a clump of trees, so that it was shielded from sight by any passing traffic.

Instinctively, she touched the bulging velvet bag on the passenger seat before fetching out her phone. She heard it ring twice before the call was answered.

"Dave Taylor. What's going on, Gráinne? Did you get to Dunstaffnage?"

"Yes," she said. "I'm still close to it now."

"Well? What happened?"

"They had a bit of a scare."

"Why? What did you do to them?"

"I'll tell you about it later. What I will tell you is that it's all going to plan, and they'll be heading for the Hill of Dunsinane."

"Do you think you scared Gresham and the American guy enough to stop them from helping the red-haired woman?"

"Mary MacDougall, you mean," said O'Connor. "I

doubt it. For some reason they both seem very close to MacDougall. I haven't worked it out yet, but I think the American could still be a problem. It's MacDougall, though, who's the real obstacle. She's being protected by another meteorite and normally I can't get near her. The others are being protected as well, provided they stay close to her. But they must have forgotten to take it with them at Dunstaffnage."

"What about Charles Gresham? The academic?" asked Taylor.

"He's an unknown quantity, but I think he's tougher than he looks and he's very supportive of MacDougall – I suspect there's something going on there. He's certainly sharp, but rather naïve. I believe he's vulnerable, though, and I'm working on him as well." She held the phone away from herself for a moment, before speaking again. "There is another way, though, to get to the Stone of Destiny."

"What do you mean?"

"That girl, Holly Fraser, who lives in Long Compton. You told me about the experience she had at the Rollrights? She's got red hair, right?"

"Yes. I told you, she's very friendly with Charles Gresham. Everybody in the village knows about her experiences. This is a village, after all, and everybody knows everybody else's business. She's shacked up with Ben Harrington. You remember he's the guy who works with meteorites at the Natural History Museum? He's very friendly with the American guy, as well." There was a silence at his end before he continued, "I have a horrible feeling I know where you're going."

"I may be thinking of going even further than you're thinking," said O'Connor. "Holly Fraser could be vulnerable. We know the meteorite that's protecting MacDougall has to be physically close to her to keep her safe – right? She's here in Scotland. Holly Fraser is in Long Compton. Their meteorite won't be able to protect her that far away." Again, there was a pause before she continued. "I'm being told we need to kidnap her. Then use her as a ransom to get hold of the meteorite that's protecting them."

Taylor didn't respond.

"Are you still there?" asked O'Connor.

"Yes. But you must be joking?"

"No joke. You told me she had an experience when she was walking her dog at the Rollrights?"

"That's right. She goes up there with it most days."

"That'll be a good opportunity. You can do it when there's nobody else around."

"Are you completely mad?"

"Probably," said O'Connor. "And when you've done that, you need to get her to Cornwall. I'll speak to the coven at Boscastle. It's on the coast and they can easily arrange a boat to take the girl to Lewis."

"Lewis? Who's Lewis?"

"I mean the Isle of Lewis in the Outer Hebrides, idiot. Off the west coast of Scotland, remember?"

"What the hell!"

"There's a cave there that we use sometimes. It's quiet. Nobody will know what's going on."

"But…"

"Don't worry – I'll set things up in Cornwall. You just need to get her down there." Taylor couldn't see O'Connor's expression harden. "Just do it. If you don't, I dread to think what the Black Dog could do to you."

For a while, there was no response from Taylor. Finally, he asked, "Where are you going next?"

"The Hill of Dunsinane. My guess is that our friends are already preparing to go there. But there's something else I need to do first."

29

In the dead of night, at one o'clock the following morning, less than a mile from the Hill of Dunsinane as the crow flies, the same yellow car drew quietly onto a farm track and parked in front of a closed gate.

Gráinne O'Connor switched off the lights, half-opened the car door and sat there, breathing in the cool air.

When a woman's voice behind her said, "Will you let us out, please," in a strong Scottish accent, she clambered out of the driver's seat and pulled it forwards.

"Give me a hand, then," wheezed the same voice. A gnarled hand reached up towards Gráinne, who stretched into the car and took the old lady by the elbow.

"Just take it easy, Agnes," she said, with a hint of irritation.

Agnes's other hand shakily grasped the inside door handle and a wizened face appeared. Wearing a woollen hat pulled well down over her head so that only a few wisps of white hair were showing, Agnes pursed her lips and shuffled to the edge of the seat. She stared at Gráinne with cold, rheumy eyes through metal-framed glasses, eased her legs out of the car and placed her feet, shod in old, mud-caked Wellington boots, onto the rutted track. "Just pull me up gently," she said tersely.

Gráinne leant forwards, put her hands under the old lady's armpits and lifted her.

Slowly, Agnes stood as upright as she could. Stooped and shaking, she turned back to the car. "Pass my stick, will you," she said to a shadowy figure in the back of the car. A gnarled walking stick appeared and the old lady grasped it.

"It's only a few yards to walk, Agnes," said Gráinne.

"I know, I know. It's not as if I haven't been here before." Agnes leant on her stick and started to walk unsteadily towards the deserted lane, before stopping. With difficulty, she wrapped her woollen coat around herself more tightly. "Can we get a move on – I'm cold," she complained.

Another figure appeared from the back of the car and eased itself up.

"Do you want a hand as well, Diana?" asked Gráinne.

"I'll manage," said an attractive middle-aged lady wearing a Puffa jacket, jeans and inappropriate sneakers. She wore no make-up and was clearly indifferent to the odd wrinkle on her face, describing them to friends as laughter lines. With her long dark hair parted in the middle and her large, hooped earrings, she would instantly have been categorised by an impartial observer as "New Age". But there was one feature that could not be missed: she was obviously heavily pregnant. "No moon, then," she observed, taking in the overcast sky.

"It doesn't matter," said Gráinne. "It's up there, isn't it, even if we can't see it." With both hands she carefully picked up the heavy bag, made of purple velvet and tied with a ribbon, from the passenger seat.

Together, the three walked slowly down the lane, the quiet *tap tap* of Agnes's stick marking their progress. The only evidence of human habitation was a cottage adjacent to the lane, a few hundred yards away. But it was in darkness, the inhabitants clearly having retired for the night. Far from the spooky atmosphere contingent with the task that lay ahead of them, for the moment everything seemed calm and relaxed, with nature at peace with itself.

When they saw car lights appear in front of them, though, they muttered a few curses and sank back into the shadows. There was a blaze of light as a car rushed past, before disappearing into the distance. Within a minute, the quiet forces of nature had reasserted themselves.

Woodland lay on the opposite side of the lane, but a fence alongside it seemed to proclaim, "No admittance". They had walked only a hundred yards or so when they reached the stile over which the woodland could be accessed. Now, as if some ancient instinct had been switched on, they sensed the deep, mysterious world of the woodland beckoning.

It was Gráinne who spoke. "Agnes, why don't I go over first, so you've got somebody to hang onto?"

Agnes looked at her with faint contempt. "Don't worry, dearie, I must have done this a hundred times before. Take my stick." She lifted her foot onto the step, then the other, and somehow seemed to roll over the stile to stand on the step the other side. "Stick, stick. Give me my stick," she demanded.

Gráinne instantly passed it over. Agnes leant on it and eased herself onto the ground. She didn't say a word but a thin smile of satisfaction spread over her face.

"Well, if she can do it," said Diana, "I guess I can." Clumsily, she climbed over the stile to join Agnes.

"Hold this," Gráinne said to Diana, passing the heavy bag over to her, and she practically leapt over the stile.

They stood silently for a while, tuning in to the woodland world around them.

"I'll take the bag, now," Gráinne said, holding out her hand to Diana. "And be careful, Agnes. Don't trip over."

There was a sharp *crack* as Diana trod on a dead branch and a disturbed pheasant, perhaps sensing something unnatural was about to happen, flapped its way to a more peaceful resting place.

When Agnes put her foot in a depression in the leaf mould and stumbled, Gráinne grabbed her. "Careful," she said. "We don't want any accidents tonight. It's too important."

Now they moved forwards, making their way into the depths of the woodland until they reached it: their sacred place. They stopped together, mesmerised.

Being in the shadow of the Hill of Dunsinane, it was difficult not to associate Bandirran Stone Circle with the three witches of *Macbeth* fame. On a clear summer's day with sunlight streaming in through trees in full leaf, it nestled in a dappled woodland glade. But at night it took on a very different aspect: a cursed place, almost inviting something untoward.

Small as stone circles go, it was once described as being

a circle of nine stones. Now only seven stones were evident, two of which were still upright, standing together and about five feet in height. Even if the stone rumoured to be buried in the centre was still there, it would be difficult to locate as the remains of an uprooted tree stretched across the circle.

Holding the bag, Gráinne stood with her back to the two upright stones and looked directly at each of her two companions in turn. "Are you ready?" she asked.

Neither Agnes nor Diana spoke.

"Just tell us again about this woman," asked Diana, eventually. "We don't even know her. What's wrong with her?"

"She's getting too close to finding out about us. And she's against everything we stand for. She's trying to take our power."

"How?" asked Diana.

"She's everything we're not," replied Gráinne. "What's more, she's getting stronger and she's got help. Two men. I'm working on them, as well."

"We've been hearing rumours about another stone," said Diana, her eyes on the bag that Gráinne was holding. "Something about the Rollright coven calling up the Black Dog, which gave them a stone. Your name has been mentioned."

"It's here," said Gráinne, holding up the bag. "This is it. I went to England and picked it up myself." She carefully untied the ribbon, reached inside the bag, and pulled out the Antarctic Meteorite. Very carefully, she placed it on the flat top of the slightly shorter upright stone. Agnes and Diana peered at it with interest.

Agnes leant on her stick. "Doesn't look very special to me," she said, and reached out to pick it up.

Gráinne quickly put her hand over the meteorite. "Best not," she said.

Agnes pulled her hand back. "What about the Black Dog? Will the Black Dog appear if we go ahead with the ceremony?"

"The Black Dog won't appear," Gráinne said, emphatically. "It's done its job."

"What's the woman's name?" asked Diana.

"Mary MacDougall. Her name's Mary MacDougall."

"Sounds harmless enough," said Agnes, dismissively. "Anyway, how do you know this Mary MacDougall is coming to the Hill of Dunsinane?"

"I've been following her around – at a distance, of course," said Gráinne. "First Kilmartin, then Dunadd and, just now, Dunstaffnage Castle. And that's when I got in quickly with the stone. While they were in the visitor centre I went to the deserted chapel. Our stone communicated with the tombstones – and one in particular. Only too pleased to oblige, it was. It's the Campbells who are buried there and there was no love lost between the Campbells and the MacDougalls."

She picked up the meteorite, held it in front of herself and glared at the others. "I want rid of her. Let's just get on with it, shall we?"

Agnes and Diana didn't say anything for a while, sensing the powerful energies of the circle that were building up.

"We do the Macbeth curse, then?" said Agnes, eventually.

"The Macbeth curse," replied Gráinne. "Don't worry, we'll take our time and do it slowly."

With that, she reached out, took the stick from Agnes, placed it against the upright stone and, with her left hand, grasped Agnes's right hand.

Diana hesitated momentarily, but then stepped over to take the free hands of the other two. Together, they stood in a circle in front of the meteorite.

Gráinne O'Connor nodded, and they began to chant:

"The weird sisters, hand in hand,

Posters of the sea and land,

Thus do go, about, about:

Thrice to thine, and thrice to mine…"

Very slowly, they went around twice in a circle. It was when they started to circle the third time that Agnes stumbled.

"Keep going, you old bitch," Gráinne spat out.

Agnes scowled and said something inaudible through gritted teeth; they went around one more time before stopping.

Gráinne now placed her hand under Agnes's arm to support her and they started circling in the opposite direction. Together Gráinne and Diana practically dragged Agnes around three more times. Stopping again, they waited till Agnes got her breath back before Gráinne nodded once more:

"And thrice again, to make up nine."

Gráinne now practically jerked Agnes off her feet and they changed direction yet again. This time, they almost had to carry Agnes round. At the end of the ninth round they came to a halt and, holding hands, raised them in the air.

"Peace! the charm's wound up.

To Dunsinane we three shall go."

Finally, they called out their victim's name:

"Mary MacDougall. Mary MacDougall. Mary MacDougall."

Gráinne abruptly let go of Agnes, Diana was unable to hold her up by herself and Agnes sagged, falling slowly to her knees. Silently, she keeled over and lay prostrate on the ground.

Gráinne and Diana didn't even look at her. Instead, their eyes were fixed on the meteorite.

As if it were being commanded, the air stilled, and the mist rose straight up above the standing stone. Now, like an atomic bomb, the mist formed a mushroom shape. Both women looked up, hypnotised, as the mist thickened and stretched over them to encompass the entire stone circle.

Diana found she was unable to move, even if she'd wanted to, and stood there like a statue. But Gráinne smiled enigmatically and raised her arms again, as if to welcome the mist.

As it engulfed them, Gráinne slowly lowered her arms. Diana disappeared from her sight first, followed by the fallen body of Agnes.

Gráinne waited, praying that the spell had worked.

Slowly, the mist eddied and disappeared, as if it had never been there.

Gráinne turned to where Diana had been standing

and then looked down to where Agnes had been lying. Slowly, she spun around on the spot, laughing out loud. Both Diana and Agnes had completely disappeared.

30

"Not another bloody climb," Charles said with a groan, noting the steep start of the pathway that led straight up to the hill fort at the top of the Hill of Dunsinane. "It's at least one thousand feet up there."

"You managed Dunadd okay," said Dan. "It's a beautiful day and I doubt if anybody else will be up there at nine o'clock in the morning."

"You seem very calm about all this," observed Charles.

"It appears we've not been given any option, have we?" he replied. "All I know is that we have to press on. In some strange way we seem to be trapped, don't we?"

"It's going to work out okay," said Mary, struggling to put her arms through the straps of her obviously heavy backpack.

"Do you want a hand with that?" asked Charles.

"I'll manage," she replied, adjusting the backpack to get it as comfortable as possible. "As long as we've got our meteorite with us, I believe we're protected. Now the meteorite stays with me all the time. Look what happened when I left it in the car at Dunstaffnage."

"Wherever it came from, the message from that voice

seemed very clear and positive," said Charles. "'Go to the Hill of Dunsinane', it said and, lo and behold, when I checked, there is indeed a Stone of Destiny connection with Dunsinane."

"But do you honestly believe it was here?" asked Dan, checking his camera.

"I don't know," replied Charles, "but *The Times* newspaper took a letter seriously enough to publish it on January 1, 1819. And it does read as being credible." He got his phone out of his pocket. "Have a look, if you like."

"Just remind us," said Dan.

"It says some workers connected with Dunsinane House near here were taking stones away from the hill fort up there at the top – the letter refers to it as 'Macbeth's Castle' – when the ground suddenly collapsed and they all fell into a vault. They found a large stone in it, described as being, quote, 'of the meteoric or semi-metallic kind'. Note the reference to it being a possible meteorite. It also says they found two metal tablets.

"One had a reference to 'Bethel' engraved on it and the letter refers to the local belief that the stone was brought from Bethel to the site of Scone Palace, down the road from here. The crucial thing about it all is that it says in the Bible that Bethel is the place where Jacob had his vision. Anyway, the letter then says the stone was hidden here, possibly by Macbeth, to keep it away from the marauding English."

"Don't you think that all sounds a bit far-fetched?" said Dan.

"Certainly questionable, I'd say. The so-called 'castle'

is actually a late Iron Age hill fort. There are still some remains of defensive earthworks and it was obviously a very impressive structure. But there's no evidence of it being occupied at the time Macbeth was around. Macbeth was much later."

Dan slipped his camera into a jacket pocket. "Does the letter say what happened to the stone?"

"It says the stone was sent to London for investigation. But, if it was, as far as I can tell all reference to it has disappeared."

"And the vault?"

"There's been some further excavation since *The Times* letter was published, but no evidence of any vault has been found."

"Perhaps it was all a false trail," Mary called over. "Perhaps the letter was published deliberately to put people off the scent as to where the Stone of Destiny really is."

"In that case, why have we been directed here to Dunsinane?" said Charles.

"I don't know, but I don't trust the situation," said Mary. "That's one reason why I'm keeping the Serpent Meteorite with me all the time."

"Anyway," said Dan, "I'm off to the top. Do you think we'll be able to see Birnam Forest from here? 'I will not be afraid of death and bane, Till Birnam forest come to Dunsinane,'" he proclaimed smugly, quoting the already doomed Macbeth. With that, he started striding up the footpath.

Charles looked impressed.

"Actually, he looked up that quotation this morning," said Mary. "I saw him at breakfast doing it on his phone."

Charles laughed as he watched Dan pounding up the hill. "I doubt if he'll see anything of Birnam Forest – there's only one tree left. Shall we follow him, Mary?"

Dan was already well up the hill, jumping over dips in the path, obviously enjoying himself and keen to get to the summit.

After only 100 yards or so of climbing, Charles came to a stop. "Listen, Mary, I'm just slowing you up," he said. "Why don't you go ahead? Try and catch up with Dan. He may need protection as well – probably from himself, the way he's leaping around."

"But what about you?"

"Don't worry about me – I'll make it eventually. I'll see you at the top."

Mary nodded and started to climb steadily at her own pace, smiling to herself at the thought of Dan's enthusiasm. The footpath initially ran alongside woodland but then progressed up onto rough grassland, where the climb became harder. Ahead, Dan had disappeared from sight, and she decided to stop and admire the scenery.

Even halfway to the top, the views were magnificent. The tiny village of Collace nestled far below, and beyond, fields and forests stretched into the distance. Far away, she could even see the River Tay, with sunlight glinting on the water.

Breathing in the fresh air slowly and deeply, on that hill and at that moment, she felt for once at peace. She knew the meteorite resting on her back was alive in some way and that it had taken over her life. Somehow it was guiding, directing her to something she didn't yet understand. She knew it was no accident that it had tracked her down and that for some reason she was special to it. She realised also that she, herself, was changing and evolving. Her senses seemed to be expanding and starting to overlap, but at the same time becoming more acute. Charles had alluded to synaesthesia, but now it was much more than that. Her visions and her contact with Bryan were all part of the change.

She was also aware that other forces – evil forces – were fighting to stop whatever was happening to her, and that those forces were connected with the Antarctic Meteorite. And, she sensed, it was not far away.

Far below, she could see Charles slowly trudging up the hill towards her. He gave the impression of being solid and reassuring, but she sensed his loneliness, his needs, and she felt for him. And Dan? Well, Dan was just Dan. Wild, unpredictable, he was a lost boy in many ways and he needed protecting. She wondered about his mother. *Did she really care about her son?* In different ways she wanted to comfort both men.

She didn't know how she knew it was there, but maybe it was some ancient animal instinct that made her look upwards and, directly above her, she saw it.

Almost stationary, a bird of prey hovered, steadied by its fanned tail, its wings twitching occasionally. Facing into the wind, it was waiting patiently, or so it seemed, to detect with its sharp eyesight the movement of some small animal.

Transfixed, Mary watched it, revelling in its freedom and oneness with nature. As if it sensed her interest, it flapped its wings and circled above her. She smiled and almost unconsciously stretched out her arm. It continued to circle, giving the impression that it was inspecting her before deciding its next move.

Mary lowered her arm, pulled the sleeve of her anorak over her hand and held out her arm again. The bird now circled lower. Encouraged, she moved her hand up and down in a gesture of friendliness.

It dropped out of the sky like a stone and swooped towards her. Mary almost pulled her arm back but steeled herself. With a flap of its wings, the bird landed with a *thump* on her wrist. She winced as its claws dug through the sleeve into her wrist, but she gritted her teeth and kept her arm held out straight.

Mary was surprised at herself. Far from being shocked and afraid, she felt a sense of wonderment and pulled her arm in closer to her body. In response, the bird loosened its grip and shifted its balance to get more comfortable. Cautiously, she reached out her other hand and stroked the rich brown feathers on its back. She winced again when the claws momentarily dug into her wrist once more, but then the bird relaxed, cocked its head to one side and stared at her without blinking. Its eyes seemed to hypnotise her; huge and black, they seemed fathomless.

It didn't need to speak. In some mysterious way it was telling her that, like itself, she was at one with nature. It was as if it were communicating with her true self, a wild creature now unencumbered by the layers of civilisation and the inhibitions that mankind had imposed on her. She couldn't help it: pure joy pulsed through her and she laughed out loud.

The bird cocked its head one more time, then spread its wings and flapped away. Mary lowered her arm and watched it, still entranced, as it caught the wind and rose high into the sky.

She jumped a mile when Charles suddenly appeared beside her, beaming. "That was a kestrel," he said. "It's quite a gift you've got, Mary. But nothing surprises me now." He leant back and watched the bird circle above them.

"Oh, to be free like that," he sighed. He pointed up towards the hill fort. "Shall we try and catch up with Dan?"

31

Dan had already reached the summit of the Hill of Dunsinane and was feeling vaguely disappointed. He was half-expecting to have come across the ruins of a medieval castle standing starkly and defiantly on top of the hill, a reminder of bloody battles fought by Macbeth against his enemies. Instead, he had clambered over a few earth terraces and was standing next to a cairn consisting of nothing more than a tall pile of stones.

Yet the views were fantastic, and they prompted him to fetch out his camera. He took a single shot, still concerned as to whether the camera was working. It was, and he was soon absorbed in taking more shots than were strictly necessary.

It was while he was holding the camera up to his face and framing a picture of the so-called Black Hill in the distance that he felt a tap on the shoulder. "So you made it, Mary," he said, turning around.

He stopped, shocked. "What the…?"

It was Gráinne who was standing there. She giggled, girlishly.

"What are you doing here?" he asked, dumbfounded.

"I could ask you the same," replied Gráinne.

"But the last time we saw you was at Tara," he said, mystified.

"This is one of my favourite places," she replied, smiling cryptically.

"But…" He didn't really know what to say.

"You are pleased to see me, aren't you?"

"Of course, but…"

"Then show it," she said, reaching up to put her arm around his neck. Pulling him towards her, she kissed him hard on the lips.

The camera dropped from Dan's hand and fell into the grass. Totally bewildered, he felt his arm moving, uncontrollably, around her waist.

Gráinne pulled away, abruptly. "Don't tell me you didn't enjoy that," she said.

Dan was about to reply, when something extraordinary stopped him and he started to shake violently.

Imperceptibly at first, but then unmistakably, Gráinne's face was changing. It was becoming plumper, the tiniest of wrinkles were forming around her eyes and mouth and her hair was growing longer. He tried to look away but couldn't; now Gráinne's stomach was undeniably swelling.

Dan staggered back, but then froze, staring at her in disbelief. It was her cagoule and her jeans all right, but now they were being stretched to the limit. He blinked, but there was no denying the reality of what he was witnessing: a different woman was appearing in front of him.

"Gráinne?" was all he could say. But standing there, smiling mysteriously, was an attractive, clearly pregnant, middle-aged woman with long black hair parted in the middle and wearing large, hooped earrings. Only Gráinne's green eyes hadn't changed. Then the woman turned completely around on the spot, so that she was facing him again.

He fell back, stumbled and just managed to stay upright. Whoever, whatever, it was, it was now changing again. Slowly, the woman was growing smaller and the pregnancy swelling was shrinking, until her stomach was flat. Finally, her whole body bent over, so that she was facing the ground.

"No, no…" Dan said to himself. He couldn't see the face, but he could see the hands. The skin had wrinkled and was covered with age-blotches. One hand was clutching a walking stick, the fingers curled tightly around it so that the knuckles showed white. Now, around this frail body, Gráinne's cagoule reached baggily to the knees and her jeans were crumpled around the ankles.

Dan couldn't take his eyes off the figure as it slowly lifted its face towards him. It was the face of an old hag, staring at him with the same green eyes through metal-rimmed glasses. Her skin was like ancient parchment and the eyes were now cold and hostile. As she leant on her stick and reached out her other hand towards him, he couldn't help taking a step backwards in disgust. Then he lost his footing and fell, stretching up his arms to ward her away.

The grotesque figure stood over him for a while, before leaning down towards him and opening her mouth, as if to say something. Instead, she hissed at him like a snake and dribbled copiously on to his trousers. She lifted her stick as if to strike him, but instead turned and hobbled towards the cairn. Reaching it, she turned again, shook her stick at him and stepped out of sight behind the pile of stones.

Dan lay there in shock, praying that she had gone. Eventually, he glimpsed his camera lying half-hidden in the grass, and reached out to pick it up. Very cautiously, he staggered to his feet and stared at the cairn. There was nothing to indicate that anything or anyone had been present.

He approached the cairn apprehensively and peered behind it. There was no sign of whatever it was that had appeared to him. Gráinne, the pregnant woman, the old hag – they had all disappeared.

He stood there a while, trying to come to terms with what he knew was impossible. Was there something supernatural about this place that had been playing tricks with his brain? Was he cracking up? All he wanted to do now was get out of the place. When he felt a tap on the shoulder, he practically fainted.

"What's happened, Dan?" he heard Mary say. "You look terrible."

32

Charles's smile of relief at reaching the top of the hill rapidly disappeared when he saw the distraught look on Dan's face.

"Dan's just had a bad experience," Mary said quickly.

"What on earth has happened?" asked Charles, looking worried.

Dan turned to him. "It's this bloody place. I just want to get out of here."

"He says he saw Gráinne O'Connor," said Mary. "Except it wasn't exactly O'Connor."

"What do you mean?" asked Charles.

"I still don't know if what I saw was real," said Dan. "Was it all in my mind? Could it really have happened? I just don't know what's going on here..."

"He says he was taking photos when she suddenly appeared beside him," continued Mary. "He doesn't know where she could have come from."

"What happened, Dan – exactly?" said Charles.

Dan stared at him, shaking his head slowly. "There was absolutely no sign of anybody else here when I got to the top. All I can think of is that she was hiding behind that pile of rocks over there."

"The cairn, you mean?" said Charles.

"Whatever you say it's called," said Dan. "There's nowhere else she could have been – I would have seen her coming. She was friendly at first. Very friendly. She asked me what I was doing here. Then it happened. She started to change, Charles. Even as I watched her, her face suddenly got older. Then she got a baby bump. I couldn't believe what I was seeing – she had suddenly turned into this pregnant middle-aged woman. It was another person – a completely different woman. But she was still wearing Gráinne's clothes."

Charles looked dumbfounded.

"But it got worse," Dan went on. "She changed again. She turned into this horrible old woman with a stick. It was disgusting – she dribbled on me." He pointed to the damp patches on his trousers.

Charles pulled a face. "That looks real enough to me."

Dan turned towards the cairn. "She went behind that and just disappeared. I went to look behind it, but there was nobody there. Nothing. Whatever it was had gone. I still can't believe it really happened."

"I told you there's something not right about her, Dan," said Mary, abruptly. "And do you think I don't know what's been going on between you and her? I could tell straight away by the way you looked at her when we were at Tara."

Dan looked shocked at first. Then his expression became decidedly sheepish.

"And there's something else," continued Mary. "You thought you were so bloody clever quoting from *Macbeth*, didn't you? But you clearly don't know the background to the quote. The quote you looked up this morning over breakfast comes from the end of the play. Macbeth was repeating what the witches told him earlier in the play." She stood back and took a deep breath.

"Macbeth shall never vanquish'd be until
Great Birnam wood to high Dunsinane hill
Shall come against him."

"So?" said Dan, taken aback.

"There aren't only the three witches in the earlier scene, Dan. Somebody else makes an appearance."

Neither Dan nor Charles said anything, wondering what on earth Mary was talking about.

"It was Hecate," she said. "Hecate, the goddess of witchcraft, was there as well."

"Of course," said Charles. "I think I'm getting there. Hecate was a triple goddess, wasn't she? She could take the form of a girl, a mother and a hag. She represented the three stages of the moon – the waxing moon, the full moon and the waning moon." He thought for a moment. "She was also associated with serpents, wasn't she? But, mostly, wasn't she associated with dogs?"

Mary placed her hands together as if praying for forgiveness for being in the company of idiots. "You're on the right track," she said. Her expression softened as she turned to Dan. "Don't you see? You saw Gráinne O'Connor as a girl, a pregnant woman and then as an old crone. Gráinne O'Connor is a witch. That's what we're up against."

Dan paled.

"How do you know all this?" asked Charles. "I didn't know you were an expert on witchcraft."

"I'm not," said Mary, "but we did *Macbeth* at school and I had to research the background to the play. I know it inside out. I even played one of the witches in a school production."

"Well, I never," said Charles, as Dan shook his head in disbelief.

"There's more," she continued. "I'm sure she's got the Antarctic Meteorite and I believe that's what's feeding her power. But she can't touch me whilst I've got the Serpent Meteorite. That's why she's working on you, Dan. And you as well, Charles." She looked at each of them in turn. "You're both going to have to stay very close to me. So long as I've got our meteorite, I believe we are protected."

"All I know," said Dan, "is that I just want to get away from this place. I don't understand what the hell is going on, and, putting it frankly, I'm ready to go back to the States. I've had enough."

"But look what happened to Warren," said Charles. "Whatever's going on doesn't seem to have any geographical barriers. You could be safer here with us, odd so that seems."

Dan looked down at his boots, before looking up again. "I don't know. I just don't know what to do."

"I don't think you've got much choice, Dan," said Mary. "You mixed it with O'Connor and now she's got a hold on you. You as well, Charles, for that matter – you heard the voice in the chapel at Dunstaffnage. I'm sure O'Connor was behind that and that's why we're here at Dunsinane. I know she's behind what's happening to us here."

Charles didn't say anything but instead walked to the

cairn and went completely around it. Then he scanned the surrounding countryside and hills as far as he could see. "Nobody," he said. "I can't see a soul. If O'Connor was here, she's certainly gone now. Can I suggest we get down to the car? We can decide there what to do next."

They made the descent easily and quickly and were relieved to see that their car was still the only car in the parking spot.

Mary took off her backpack and carefully placed it in the boot.

"So, what now?" said Dan.

Mary slammed the boot closed. "To me, it's obvious," she said. "We are being used by the Serpent Meteorite and it wants us to find the Stone of Destiny. The Antarctic Meteorite is using Gráinne O'Connor and whoever she's mixed up with to get to the Stone of Destiny first. It wants to prevent us from discovering it before her.

"And I know I'm changing, as well. First, there were the visions I had at the Serpent Mound. And I won't forget my synaesthetic experience in the Dublin pub, when I saw coloured lights dancing around to the music. At Tara, when I touched the Lia Fáil, I saw the Ballymeanoch Stones. So, we went to Kilmartin and that's where I had the vision of Bryan directing me onwards to Dunadd. And, just now, I had the strange experience with the kestrel. You witnessed it, Charles. I don't know what's going on either, but I do know I can't turn back. The Serpent Meteorite has taken me over. I'm being used, guided if you like. And so are both of you. Now you are starting to have supernatural experiences yourselves. Putting it frankly, we're all in this together."

Dan looked up at the sky for a while, as if seeking guidance. Looking down again, he saw a large black bird sitting in a nearby tree. "That's a big crow," he said. The bird emitted a *croak* in response.

"It's actually a raven," said Charles. "Ravens croak, crows caw."

Mary eyed the bird suspiciously. "Something else, Charles," she said. "The raven is well known as a witch's familiar." As if in response, the bird languidly swooped away towards Collace.

Mary continued to watch the bird until it was out of sight, before turning to the others. "Scone," she declared. "Scone Palace. It's just down the road from here – and that's where we're going next."

Later that morning, a silver Range Rover drew into the car park at Scone Palace and an obviously pregnant woman emerged from the car. She opened the passenger door, shifted over a Puffa jacket on the seat, carefully picked up a velvet bag and placed it in a shopping bag.

Checking a map, she made her way towards the palace. However, before reaching it, she turned off down a pathway known as the 3rd Earl's Walk, which led into the spacious grounds. She soon left the practically deserted pathway and walked purposefully into grassland dotted with trees.

Noting a family picnicking under a tree in the distance, she veered away in the opposite direction until she was completely alone. With some difficulty she then crouched down beneath a copper beech tree and carefully removed the Antarctic Meteorite from the shopping bag. After checking again that she was alone, she placed the meteorite against the trunk of the tree, stood up and stepped backwards. Any of the Long Compton coven who were at the Rollrights ceremony a few days previously would have recognised the spell she quietly chanted. Once she had finished, she briefly bowed her head to the meteorite and waited.

After less than a minute, a thin mist rose straight upwards through the foliage and mushroomed before descending to the ground.

33

"Let's check again," said Dan. "I'm going to walk around the car park once more, just in case. I really don't want another *experience*. That was enough for one day."

"Her car is definitely not here, I tell you," said Charles. "There isn't any yellow car here. I suppose she could've come in a coach or even a taxi. Perhaps somebody else could have brought her here in another car."

"So we'll just have to keep our eyes peeled, won't we?" said Mary. "Now we're here, at the very least I want to see the replica of what they claim is the Stone of Destiny." With that she opened the boot of the car, took out her backpack, felt the Serpent Meteorite in it for reassurance and slipped the bag over her shoulder. "I'll see you in front of the chapel where the stone is," she announced, starting to walk away.

Charles and Dan looked at each other, then quickly followed her.

"Is that really it?" said Dan, shrugging his shoulders.

He stood alongside Mary and Charles in front of the copy of the so-called Stone of Destiny. A block of sandstone no bigger than the average pillow, it sat on two low stone pedestals in front of the chapel, which itself was built on an artificial mound known as Moot Hill. One of the many peacocks that frequented the palace grounds stood beside the stone, eyeing the trio.

"I can't believe this is what all the fuss has been about over the centuries," Dan announced. "I mean, it doesn't look exactly special, does it? It hasn't even got any carving on it. It could be any old block of stone."

As if in protest at the comment, the peacock flared its magnificent tail, shook its feathers and emitted a piercing screech.

"I think the peacock must've heard that comment a few times before," said Charles. "The original is actually in the Edinburgh Castle Museum for safekeeping, until it's moved to a permanent home in Perth. It'll be taken down to Westminster Abbey in London for the next coronation of a British monarch."

"It's odd to think that we're being directed to the whereabouts of the real Stone of Destiny by something in my backpack," said Mary.

The peacock screeched again in apparent consternation, lowered its tail and strutted away.

"Wherever the real Stone of Destiny is," said Charles, "there's no doubt that Moot Hill here is the place where Scottish kings were enthroned for over five centuries – including Macbeth, incidentally. Just think – all those Scottish kings took their oaths using a stone as a witness. Odd, isn't it, to think that a stone could have that much power. Then, of course, when Edward I of England defeated the Scots in 1296, he sent his troops here to take the Stone of Destiny to Westminster Abbey."

"Except it wasn't the real Stone of Destiny that he took back to England, was it?" said Mary, firmly. "Edward I and all the successive kings and queens were crowned sitting in the Coronation Chair on top of a fake, including the present monarch. There's a story that monks here at the abbey kept the real Stone of Destiny and hid it. What Edward took back was a block of local sandstone. Like this," she said, patting the replica. "The real Stone of Destiny is still somewhere in Scotland. And the Serpent Meteorite here is going to lead us to it." She adjusted the backpack on her shoulder. "Let's go and have a look inside the chapel."

The chapel was deserted. It was built as a mausoleum dedicated to the inspirational 1st Viscount Stormont, an ancestor of the present owners of the palace, but Dan showed limited interest.

Charles noted him looking over to a grassy area in front of the palace, where tables had been set out and visitors were eating and drinking in the sunshine. "It looks very pleasant over there. A coffee, perhaps?" he suggested.

Mary didn't respond. "Can't you feel it?" she said.

"Feel what?" said Dan.

"The tingling in the air – like electricity." She pulled back the sleeve of her jacket. "Look at the hairs on my arm – they're standing on end."

"Here we go again," said Dan. "Can we just leave, please? I'm not quite sure I can take any more after what happened on top of that hill."

Charles nodded in agreement. "It has been quite an eventful day."

Mary's face showed her impatience, but with some reluctance she followed the two men towards the café. "If we're going to crack this, we can't run away from things we don't understand," she called out after them.

It was just after they left that a patch of mist formed thinly and unseen over the ground behind the chapel and sat there eddying.

"I believe places like Moot Hill were originally chosen because our ancestors sensed they were special," said Charles, as they sat down at a table laden with coffee and rolls. "I wouldn't be surprised if it's always been a sacred place, right from prehistoric times. Even I could feel that there was something in the air."

"Your earth energies again, I suppose?" said Dan.

Charles leant towards him. "Scotland's geology means that it's packed with fault lines in the rocks and fault lines mean pressure on the rocks. And the rocks are full of crystals, especially quartz. Even I know what happens if you put quartz under pressure. It produces electricity, doesn't it? And electricity's another form of energy, isn't it?"

"Piezoelectricity," said Dan, stifling a yawn. He started to explain…

Neither Dan nor Charles noticed that Mary was looking worried. "Quick! Look over there," she said.

Dan and Charles stopped talking and looked towards where she was pointing. In the distance, at the opposite end of the palace, a black dog was running around on the grass, as if chasing an invisible frisbee.

"It seems harmless enough," said Charles, taking a sip of coffee and stretching out his legs.

"Dogs are only allowed here on leashes," said Mary. "I read it on the website. And it doesn't seem to have an owner."

"The owner's probably not far away," said Charles.

"As long as it doesn't come over here," said Mary, removing her backpack from a chair and placing it firmly in the middle of the table. She eyed the dog as Dan and Charles resumed their conversation. "It's coming over here," she cut in.

The dog approached the table that was furthest from them, panting with its tongue hanging out, and went up to a middle-aged man who was chatting to a woman of a similar age. He turned idly to the dog and stroked its head while he continued to talk.

"I still can't see an owner," said Mary, looking increasingly disturbed.

The dog now walked, rather than ran, to an adjacent table and sat down. The old man sitting there reading a newspaper completely ignored it.

Mary stared at the dog intently and instinctively placed her hand on her backpack. The dog barked at the man and started walking casually towards their table. "Get that bloody dog away from me," she said.

The dog slowed down as it neared them and looked at them dolefully. It whined and pawed the grass in front of itself, as if wanting to play.

Mary turned to Dan. "Please! Just get rid of it!"

Before Dan could respond, Charles called over to the dog, "Probably not the best time, doggie."

The dog eyed him for a while, before it suddenly bounced into life and bounded away to the other end of the lawn, before disappearing behind the building.

"Thank God for that," said Mary. "There's something definitely not right about that dog, I know it."

Charles made to stand up. "Shall we go around the palace?" he said.

Mary didn't respond but sat there, as if listening to something. "Can you hear music?" she said, turning towards the palace.

"It's coming from somewhere inside the building," replied Dan. "Perhaps it's a rehearsal for a concert."

Charles listened appreciatively for a while. "It's a choir singing sacred music, isn't it? It's beautiful. Shall we check it out?"

Dan was looking around at people sitting at adjacent tables. "Something's wrong here," he said. "You'd think other people would be showing some interest in the music."

Judging by the lack of response to the music that was now becoming louder and clearer, it seemed that somehow nobody else could hear it.

Charles shrugged his shoulders. "Well, I wouldn't mind going to have a listen. Who's got the tickets to visit the palace?"

"I have," said Dan. "I paid, remember?"

"Well, I paid for the coffee and rolls," replied Charles, cheerfully.

Mary glanced around, mystified, then shook her head, picked up her backpack and without saying a word followed Dan and Charles.

Just inside the public entrance to the palace, a smiling middle-aged woman held out her hand. "Can I see your tickets, please?"

Dan retrieved them from a pocket and passed them over.

"Can you tell us where the music is being played, please?" asked Charles. "We'd love to go and listen."

"Sorry?" said the woman.

"The music. The sacred choral music we can hear. Is it a rehearsal?"

A faint smile played over the woman's face, as if she were wondering whether a trick was being played on her. "What are you talking about? There is no music," she said.

Charles turned to Dan and Mary. "You can still hear it, can't you?"

"Sure can," said Dan.

Mary nodded in agreement.

The woman beckoned to a smartly dressed man who was sorting out a pile of information leaflets. "John, can you hear any music?"

He listened hard, before looking dumbfounded. "I can't hear anything. Perhaps one of you has a phone switched on?"

"No," said Dan, emphatically. "You must be able to hear it. It's getting louder…"

The woman and the man stared at each other, before the man finally spoke. "There's definitely no music being played here."

The woman was obviously anxious to defuse the situation. "The last time we had any sacred music being played here was when we had a group from an Edinburgh choral society going around. They gave an impromptu performance in the Drawing Room of a piece by Robert Carver. They told me afterwards that there was something about the room that almost compelled them to perform a work by Carver – they all said the same. And it wasn't an easy piece to sing, either. It was a mass written for ten voices – *Dum Sacrum Mysterium*. It was just magic…"

The man was quick to take the initiative. "Robert Carver was a composer who lived at Scone in the sixteenth century when there was an abbey here. He spent practically all his life as a monk and specialised in polyphonic music – music where multiple melody lines are sung so that they interact with each other. Carver took it to the highest levels. Tragically, most of his written music was destroyed during the Reformation. Just a few pieces survived…"

Charles abruptly turned to Dan and Mary. "It's not just me, is it?"

"No," said Dan. "For crying out loud, it can't be just us…"

"Sorry to bother you both," Charles said, quickly. "Let's go, shall we." He started to walk away in the general direction of the music, but stopped and turned back. "What's the quickest way to the Drawing Room?" he called out.

"Take the first…" the man replied, gesturing, but they were already rushing on, leaving the palace employees totally bewildered.

None of the other visitors seemed to notice the music at all, chatting among themselves and talking to the palace guides.

Just as they reached the Drawing Room the music seemed to be reaching its climax. This time, it was as if the invisible choir were in the very room. The only other people there were a young couple, completely unaware of the profound event taking place around them. Beyond the ropes placed there to prevent closer inspection of the room, the opulence of the décor on display seemed almost intimidating. A writing desk gifted by Marie Antoinette vied for attention with portraits of King George III and Queen Charlotte, against a background of silk brocade wall coverings and a royal blue and gold monogrammed carpet.

Yet to the three of them, the power and the beauty of the music transcended the more earthly delights that the room had to offer. Numerous male voices were weaving threads of rich soaring melodies, floating ethereally and entwining, until they reached a crescendo that seemed to touch the sublime.

Mary barely noticed that the music had stopped. The final ecstatic chorus continued to echo in her mind, and in front of her eyes an image of a choir slowly began to appear. The monks, delighted with their own performance, were beaming at each other and at their elated conductor. She remained entranced as a sense of wonder continued in her head until the image faded away and she realised where she was.

Both Charles and Dan seemed stunned, trying hard to come to terms with whatever they had experienced.

Only the reality of the young couple talking quietly to each other nearby gradually brought them all down to earth, and for a while they just stared at each other in silence.

It was Dan who spoke first. "I definitely think I'm going mad. I mean, what was that about? Only the three of us being able to hear the music?"

Charles didn't answer him directly. Instead, he said, "Have you ever felt you were in contact with another dimension? It's said that music can sometimes do that – take you to a higher plane. And did you notice that all the voices were male?"

"I actually saw the choir – they were all monks," said Mary, quietly. "I've just had another vision, and I believe I witnessed Robert Carver conducting the performance."

Dan and Charles looked stunned.

"This is all to do with the Serpent Meteorite," Mary continued. "The music came out of the fabric of the building itself. It was the stones that were singing. The music – the performance – was embedded in the stones and the Serpent Meteorite somehow switched it on."

"How could it do that?" said Dan.

"I don't know," replied Mary, "but I believe that somehow it can switch on whatever's locked in stones – past events, spirits of the ancestors… We're only just beginning to find out what it is capable of."

"You're not suggesting that we heard an actual performance by the monks, are you?" said Dan. "But the abbey wasn't even here on the site of the palace. It was about one hundred yards from here. I read that the abbey was burnt down and the palace we're in was built much later."

"It is possible that they could have used stones from the ruined abbey to incorporate into the palace," said Charles.

"But even so…"

"Well, you heard the music, didn't you, Dan?" said Charles. "And it was just the three of us – nobody else." He thought for a moment. "Holly told me about a similar experience she had when the Antarctic Meteorite was in her house. She said she heard *The Rite of Spring*, although the radio wasn't on. Ben didn't hear anything. *The Rite of Spring* is about a pagan ceremony in ancient Russia where a young girl is ritually sacrificed to Jarilo, a god linked to the moon. He had a twin sister…"

"But I believe what we heard was to do with the Serpent Meteorite," Mary said. "I believe the Serpent Meteorite was giving us another message. And the clue is in the music."

Charles and Dan looked blank.

"Just think about it," she said. "We heard sacred music, didn't we? Where else in the past would you have heard sacred music?"

"Loads of places. Any church, I should think," said Dan.

"But where's the most sacred place in Scotland, apart from here at Scone? Where is the favoured resting place of the old Scottish kings? Including Macbeth? Where else is the Stone of Destiny supposed to have rested?"

"Iona," said Charles.

"Precisely," said Mary. "The abbey on the Isle of Iona. And I believe that's where we're being told to go next."

Charles and Dan stood there, stunned, trying to take in the implications.

It was Charles who reacted first and checked his watch. "No way will we get there today. If we can get to Oban, though, we could get the ferry over to the Isle of Mull tomorrow and then on to Iona…"

"I don't know if I can—" started Dan.

"There's something else," said Mary. "I know that black dog we saw was to do with the Antarctic Meteorite. And I know as well that the Antarctic Meteorite must be around here somewhere. And so, somehow, is Gráinne O'Connor. Together, they will try to stop us."

"I'm sorry, but this is all getting too much for me," said Dan. "I mean, I was just leading this normal life. Then Ben rings me up about a meteorite. Next, I meet you, Charles, with another bloody meteorite. I witness a horrible death. Now, it's one weird experience after another…"

"You've got no choice," said Mary. "Move away from the Serpent Meteorite and you'll be picked off."

"I think Mary's right," said Charles. "We have to continue…"

Dan looked exasperated.

"Okay," said Charles. "Let me just remind you. I believe we're witnessing evidence of life on Mars. I believe the Serpent Meteorite and the Antarctic Meteorite are alive, even if not in a conventional sense. They contain spirits of some sort and it's likely that the rocks on Mars they come from also contain spirits. What if Mars is covered in rocks that contain spirits, and earthlights and mists are just two of their manifestations? Could that be how life exists on

Mars? Not based on organic life, but inorganic. Maybe it exists like that on other planets, other stars. And here we are as witnesses to it all. Yes, I know we're on a journey into the unknown – it may be dangerous. But do you really want to pull out, right now?"

Dan closed his eyes and gritted his teeth. "Okay, one more incident and I'm off – I'll take my chances. And if that bloody yellow car is in the car park…"

When they walked around the car park, to their immense relief they found no sign of any yellow car. If they had been looking for Diana's silver Range Rover, they wouldn't have found that either…

34

Charles was sitting with Mary and Dan in the bar of the Harbour Hotel in Oban when his phone buzzed. He looked at the screen, puzzled. "It's Ben," he said. "Excuse me a minute."

He took the call in the foyer of the hotel and sensed immediately that something was very wrong. "Are you all right, Ben?" he asked.

"Yes, yes, I'm fine. But it's Holly." He sounded distraught and seemed to be struggling to find the right words. "Charles, she's disappeared," he finally blurted out.

"What?" exclaimed Charles. "What do you mean, 'disappeared'?"

"I got a call at work late yesterday afternoon from Joanne Clayton. You know, she's a friend of Holly in Long Compton…"

"Yes, go on," said Charles.

"Holly and Joanne often take their dogs for a walk together. They sometimes meet at the Rollrights, where they can park their cars. It's normally quiet late in the day and the dogs always seem to like it there. When she arrived, Joanne saw Holly's car, but there was no sign of her and Daisy was running around, in quite a distressed state. Joanne tried phoning her, but her phone was switched off, so she phoned me. Anyway, I left work immediately and got back home as quickly as possible. When I got here, she'd obviously had a cup of tea and the washing-up was still waiting to be done. But there was no sign of her and no note saying where she was. The strange thing was, when I went up to the Rollrights, her car was still parked there and she hadn't even bothered to lock it."

"Was there anything missing?" asked Charles.

"Nothing I could think of. The glove box was closed and there was no sign of anything having been stolen. But she wouldn't normally leave anything valuable in the car. And if she did, she would have put it in the boot and locked it."

"Have you contacted the police?"

"Yes, but they're not exactly rushing around. I think they suspect it's just a domestic tiff – and pregnant women have a reputation for being rather emotional. I can hardly tell them the details of all her experiences, can I? But I know for sure that something must have happened to her, Charles. When I left yesterday morning for work, she was fine. It was her day for working from home – she's allowed to work at home one day a week and she was looking forward to it."

Charles didn't respond, but his mind was racing.

"I'm out of my mind with worry, Charles," Ben said, suddenly. "I've been spending all my time contacting her family and friends. I've spoken to half the village, but nobody knows anything. Everybody's very worried. I tell you, something truly weird is going on. I just wish she had stayed away from the Rollrights. There's something not quite right about that place. What with your experiences and Holly's experiences, I couldn't help wondering…"

"Look, Ben," said Charles, "can you give me five minutes? I'm just going to talk to Dan and Mary. Holly's disappearance may well be connected to what's happening here in Scotland at the moment. It's just possible we may be able to help. I'll call right back…"

"There's something else, Charles…"

Charles waited, wondering what could be worse than what he had just been told.

"Holly had her first baby scan last Monday."

"Is everything okay?"

"Yes. It's just that she had rather a surprise. She came home in a state of shock. They told her she's expecting twins. She could see them in the scan."

"My God…" said Charles. "Look, I'll phone back in a minute. Promise."

Charles rushed back into the bar. Mary and Dan could tell immediately that it was bad news. "That call was about Ben's girlfriend, Holly…"

When he had explained everything, Mary didn't hold back. "It's Gráinne O'Connor. Make no mistake – it's her who's behind this."

"I think so, too," said Charles. "God knows what's happened to Holly or where she is now. We've got the Serpent Meteorite here, but she's got nothing to protect her from what's going on. I don't know what to do…"

Mary responded immediately. "From what you've

told me, Holly and I must be on the same wavelength. I've never tried it before, but I'm wondering if I could invoke another vision. If I could make contact with her, I might be able to find out where she is."

"Please could you try?" He looked lost for a moment. "You know, Ben and Holly are very dear friends of mine."

"Well, I'll try…" she said. "But you know I can't promise anything."

"Could you use the Serpent Meteorite, maybe as a pillow – like Jacob did with his stone at Bethel?" suggested Charles.

"Well, I'll have a go. I'll go to my room now."

"Hang on, I'll just call back Ben," said Charles. He didn't bother to return to the foyer. "Ben, we've got an idea. It's a long shot, but we've got the Serpent Meteorite here and Mary is sitting next to me. I can't tell you everything that's been going on right now, but she's going to try to use it to get in touch with Holly. She thinks she might be able to make contact with her telepathically somehow. I'm sorry to say this, Ben, but Mary is convinced something quite nasty is going on here. It's to do with the Antarctic Meteorite. I'm afraid we think witchcraft is involved."

There was silence at Ben's end.

"Ben? Are you there?"

"Yes."

"To be quite blunt, Holly could be in real danger – and you could be as well. If you can get yourself up here, we can tackle this together."

"What? I don't even know where you are?"

"We're at the Harbour Hotel in Oban. Listen, Ben,

whatever's going on here in Scotland is coming to a head and you need to get up here quick."

Charles waited for what seemed ages before Ben spoke.

"I'll get a flight to Edinburgh first thing tomorrow morning and drive up to Oban. I'll be in touch."

"We'll be here," said Charles.

"Right, I'll just arrange for Joanne to look after Daisy. I'll tell her I think I know where Holly might be – spin her a bit of a yarn. It'll soon get around the village. See you tomorrow."

Charles ended the call and Mary picked up the bag with the Serpent Meteorite in it.

"I'm going to my room. Leave me alone – I'll let you know if anything happens." She stood up. "We're going into new territory now," she said, looking tense. "Having visions happen to me is one thing. Trying to create one on purpose is a very different matter. It may not even be possible."

An hour later Mary reappeared in the bar where Charles and Dan were deep in discussion.

"Nothing," she said, looking despondent. "I was lying there for nearly an hour. Nothing at all."

Charles went to the bar and picked up a menu. "Let's get some food before they stop serving for the evening. Perhaps something will happen to you during the night."

Mary took the menu gratefully. "This whole business is beginning to take its toll on me," she said.

"I know," said Charles, and, without thinking, he reached out to place his hand over hers.

Later, as Mary climbed into bed, an immense tiredness hit her. She knew she had reached a point where the traumatic events of the previous days had taken her to the verge of utter exhaustion. Dan and Charles's support and friendship – and perhaps with Charles it was becoming something more than that – had kept her going and she felt comforted knowing that they were close by.

She carefully placed the Serpent Meteorite behind the pillow, wedged it firmly against the bedhead and, relaxing in the knowledge of its presence, slipped gratefully between the sheets.

Her mind drifted over the events of the day. So much had happened and now her life seemed totally out of control. Even then, she couldn't help fretting about Holly. Like her, Holly was deeply involved in the strange events that were dictating their lives. And now she was in great danger.

Determined to think positively, Mary forced her mind to dwell on her vision of Bryan. It was this that finally brought her peace. Almost instinctively, she reached out, touched the meteorite and, reassured by its protective presence, fell into a deep sleep.

35

Well after midnight, Gráinne O'Connor stood alone on a sandy beach, holding a torch and studying the horizon. The air was still, the sea calm and the light from a gibbous moon was reflected intermittently in the water as clouds moved slowly across the sky.

She heard it before she saw it: the faintest *chug chug chug* that came and went. Checking around, she confirmed that the beach was still deserted and switched on the torch to ensure that it was working.

When the fishing boat came into view, just the faintest lights were visible. O'Connor switched her torch on and off and smiled with satisfaction when she saw an answering light.

The engine cut and the boat drifted silently to within a couple of hundred yards from the beach. The sound of a girl crying broke the silence, followed by a splash as a dinghy was lowered.

Over the water, O'Connor heard the bark of a man's voice and tearful protests, then the regular creak of oars as the dinghy approached the beach.

Although she knew she could now be seen, O'Connor

flashed the torch a few more times before stepping down to the water's edge.

There was a crunch as the dinghy beached, and Dave Taylor stowed the oars before jumping out and hauling it up onto the sand.

Holly Fraser sat in the back of the dinghy, her arms clasped around herself. She shrank away from Taylor when he made to grab her arm, but O'Connor had already grasped her other arm.

"Get out!" O'Connor commanded.

Together Taylor and O'Connor manhandled Holly upright and half dragged her onto the beach.

Holly put her hands up to her face as O'Connor shone the torch directly into it. "So this is her," O'Connor said.

Holly lowered her hands. She looked distressed and her face was streaked with tears. She glanced around the beach, bewildered, and then turned to O'Connor. "Who are you?" she said, shaking. "What's going on? Where am I?"

O'Connor's face was set as hard as stone. "Doesn't matter," she said, and turned to Taylor. "Was she seen?"

"No," answered Taylor. "We kept her in the back of the van for the journey and there was nobody around Boscastle at that time of night. I'm pretty sure nobody saw us get her onto the boat." He stood there, obviously waiting for instructions.

O'Connor pointed to the rocks below the low cliffs at the end of the beach. "The cave," was all she said.

Holly froze when she heard the words. Then it hit her and the memory of the nightmare she had had in

Long Compton seared into her consciousness. She knew instantly that this was the beach in her vision and "the cave" was where the red-haired girl had met her terrible fate. "No, no," she screamed and made to run, but Taylor instantly grabbed her.

"Let's go," said O'Connor, through gritted teeth.

"Get off me," Holly shouted, and struggled again.

Taylor only gripped her harder and propelled her along the beach to the rocks at the base of the cliff. They stopped in front of the boulder that guarded the entrance to the cave.

"You're not getting me in there," Holly cried. Her eyes glinted and she swung around to face Taylor. "You bastard," she spat out. "Do you really think you'll get away with this? Do you really think Ben is not desperate, trying to find me? And he will – I know it. He'll kill you when he finds you…"

Taylor seemed uneasy. "No need for that," he said, taking Holly firmly by the arm. "Just do as you're told."

He looked distinctly worried. "She knows me," he said to O'Connor. "When she's found, she'll talk."

"If her friends don't cooperate, she may not get the opportunity," said O'Connor. "Don't worry. If anybody in the Long Compton coven feels inclined to talk, the mist and the Black Dog are there, waiting. A couple of warning appearances and the whole village will be petrified. And you'll be the first to see it, Taylor."

Dave Taylor quivered and his face twitched.

O'Connor turned to Holly. "Do you remember the mist? One wrong step…" she said.

"You're just sick," said Holly, glaring at O'Connor.

O'Connor ignored her and eyeballed Taylor. "Don't just stand there. Pull the bloody boulder back."

Taylor swore under his breath, put both his hands on top of the boulder and pulled hard. It rolled back easily to reveal the entrance to the cave.

"I told you – I'm not going in there!" screamed Holly, and she started sobbing. Her voice echoed around the rocks.

O'Connor stood back. "Well, go on then," she said to Taylor.

Taylor's face set cold and hard. Then he knelt down and crawled through the entrance. At the same time, O'Connor moved behind Holly, blocking her from running away.

As O'Connor pushed Holly in the back, Taylor's arm reached out, grabbed her hand and pulled her into the cave. He hauled Holly to her feet as O'Connor crawled in behind them and stood up.

"Help me, damn you," yelled O'Connor. "Move her!"

For a moment Taylor seemed shocked, but the look on O'Connor's face forced him into action. "Best do as she says," he said to Holly.

Holly turned to him. "Don't do it," she pleaded. "Help me. Please…"

O'Connor took Holly's arm and brutally half-dragged, half-pushed her forwards.

Holly knew it would be there. The hole in the cave roof was still present, but no Milky Way was evident. Only a few stars could be seen as clouds edged over the sky. It appeared only briefly, before it disappeared behind a cloud, but Holly instantly recognised it and shivered. For a few seconds, the planet Mars looked down at the scene below. Holly didn't even have time to think before another hard push to her back propelled her further into the cave.

They stopped when they came to the rock face. Holly froze when she saw it: the large rock was still there, wedged in place with a stone.

O'Connor kicked the stone away. "Open it!" she barked at Taylor.

Taylor looked at Holly and then at O'Connor.

"Open it!" repeated O'Connor.

Taylor grasped the rock and pulled. As it fell away, the stench hit him and he clasped his hand to his face. "It's in there, isn't it?" he said. "That's where it is."

O'Connor didn't answer him. "Help me with the girl," she rasped, putting her hand on Holly's shoulder to push her down.

Taylor hesitated. "It's in there, isn't it?" he said again. "The Stone of Doom?"

O'Connor didn't answer the question. "I want her in there."

Holly tried to back away. "Let me go," she screamed. "You're both sick. Do you really think you can get away with this?"

In response, O'Connor forced Holly onto her knees. "Push her," she said, coldly.

Taylor stood there shaking, then knelt down.

Holly struggled, but didn't stand a chance. With a final shove from Taylor she disappeared through the hole in the rock face.

O'Connor grabbed the boulder herself and heaved it back into place.

Taylor stood there, stunned by what had just happened, as O'Connor kicked the wedge under the rock. "Don't worry, there's food and water in there and I've left a torch," she said. "She'll find it all eventually."

"But what else is in there?" said Taylor.

O'Connor still didn't answer. "Let's get out of here. If you say a word…" She growled at him like a dog.

Taylor turned on his heels and stumbled back down the passageway. He emerged from the cave gasping for air and ran as fast as he could back to the dinghy.

36

The vision happened early in the morning as the first rays of sunshine shone through a gap between the curtains. But this time it was different.

Mary's previous visions had related to past events, to her personal history or linked to her ancestors. Now, she found herself standing alone, dressed in her usual outdoor clothes, on a deserted beach. It stretched away in both directions to fade into a distant haze. There was no sign of life, not even a bird, to alleviate the bleakness.

She turned round to see that, behind her, there was a low cliff of reddish rock, which had crumbled in places on to the beach. Above the cliff, there was no evidence of human habitation, not even a deserted building, only patches of dull green spiky grasses.

In front of her, grey clouds scudded over the sky, threatening a storm, and the waves were breaking with ominous intermittent growls on the shingle. A cold, damp wind was gusting, and out to sea, white horses were starting to form.

She searched her memory in vain to recognise where she was and had the strange sense of not knowing why she was there. She scanned the sky and the sea hoping to see or hear anything living or moving, maybe even a small boat. But there was nothing, only the motion of a disinterested sea. She had no sense of time; was she in the present, the past, or perhaps even in the future? Now, a profound feeling of utter bewilderment and loneliness threatened to overwhelm her. Shivering, she zipped up her anorak as far as it would go.

At that moment it caught her eye: a distant speck in the sky, high above the indistinct horizon where the clouds merged with the sea. Intrigued, she watched as the speck grew in size to become a white dot. The thought that it was a plane entered her mind, but she could see that the speck was moving slightly from side to side and up and down.

Mary watched it, transfixed, as she realised that, almost imperceptibly, the object was coming straight towards her. She couldn't take her eyes away from it until, after a couple of minutes, it became obvious that it was a bird. As it came closer, it was clear that it was flying quite fast, perhaps driven by an onshore wind.

She spun around as it flew directly overhead and banked above the cliffs to approach her from the opposite direction.

Circling above, it appeared to be inspecting her, before drifting lower and fluttering its wings rapidly, as if aware that it had reached what it was looking for.

Mary could now distinguish the features of the bird. Although its head and underparts were white, the back was grey and the wings were tipped with black. She guessed that it was some sort of seagull.

Suddenly, it uttered a series of loud screams, followed by a cacophony that resembled mocking laughter.

Mary's nose wrinkled at its vulgarity, but with apparent indifference the bird continued to slowly circle above her, each time edging further over the sea and screaming again.

She knew instinctively that the bird was instructing her to follow it, and she was irritated by its persistence. In any case, she was unable to follow it, even if she wanted to.

Then something else entered her mind: could the bird have been sent by somebody, or even something? Was it a messenger? If so, who or what had sent it, and why? A response of a kind came quickly. Like an iron nail attracted to a magnet, she felt a powerful, unknown force that was emanating from the bird, trying to draw her upwards towards it.

She struggled briefly to resist it, but somehow the force took control of her and she found herself floating up towards the bird, until she was actually moving alongside it. Now, she became aware of the sheer determination, the singlemindedness of the bird and its obligation to fulfil some unknown purpose. Such was its steely resolve and concentration on its task that it seemed unaware of her.

When the bird's cold, impersonal black eye appeared to grow larger and she tried to look away, she found it was impossible. Mesmerised, she had the disturbing sensation of somehow relating to the bird, of identifying with it and sharing in its existence.

The strange force that had driven her to the bird now overwhelmed her completely. In an instant, she became aware that something was compelling her to enter into the very being of the bird. She struggled against it, but the force was so strong that the last remnants of her resistance finally snapped. She knew, in that instant, that she had become the bird itself.

She was not even conscious that she was flying. What was now driving her onwards over the shoreline and above the sea was not a bird's instinctive need to find food, nor the urge to join its fellows. She didn't know why, but only knew that she had to reach a destination somewhere over the water and that she would recognise it when she arrived.

Occasionally, with her keen eyesight, she caught sight of the flash of a shoal of fish darting close to the surface of the water and felt an urge to swoop down. But a stronger force prevailed and she drove onwards, remaining focused on the far horizon.

For a moment she relaxed and glided as, in the distance, a strip of land appeared. Summoning a final burst of energy, she forced herself to beat her wings until, below her, a shoreline took shape.

On either side of her, a beach of golden sand stretched into the distance and, at each end, there were cliffs. Here, the sea had eroded the stone to create piles of rocks and rock pools.

This time there was life: other birds were circling above the cliffs. She knew instinctively that they were not her own species and that they were looking for food and protecting their young. But the need to find her destination, whatever it was, overcame any fear of attack.

The beach below the cliffs was deserted and she sensed that it was cold and damp from recent rain. She drifted lower, so that she was below the top of the cliffs, and floated along, scanning the shoreline.

When she arrived at the end of the bay, the sand petered out into jagged rocks, and, catching the uplift of the wind in front of the cliffs, she wheeled around to return along the beach. With the wind now against her, flying was more demanding and the ache in her muscles became acute. Approaching total exhaustion, she was constantly resisting the urge to land on the beach and rest.

When she caught sight of the large boulder at the other end of the bay, there was no sense of relief or any other emotion, only the knowledge that at last she had reached her destination.

She couldn't see the cave entrance; it was blocked by the large boulder. But she knew the cave was there. Gliding in closer, she drifted downwards, checked her flight and stretched out her legs. Finally, she landed on the sand in front of the boulder. Unable even to walk, an intense weariness engulfed her and, gratefully, she sank down into the sand.

Then it hit her. Whatever it was, the impact was like a sledgehammer smashing into her head, and instantaneously, a black curtain descended. In limbo, like a helpless observer, she became conscious that behind the curtain a battle was commencing between powerful, unknown forces. And she knew that the battle was for control of her own mind.

As if they were being used as weapons in the struggle, occasionally the curtain seemed to lift and, like intermittent beams from a lighthouse, images flashed out of the blackness.

The meteorite in the bottom of the ancient boat, the sacred stone of her tribe, appeared for a second, only to be replaced again by the blackness out of which she saw a pair of blood-red eyes approaching her. She mentally shrank back as they grew ever larger and threatened to engulf her. But, instead, they dissolved into a red swirling mist.

Slowly, the red mist eddied and disappeared, so that the black curtain fell once more. Beyond it, she was conscious of the battle continuing to rage.

She was first aware that somebody was struggling to reach through from the other side of the curtain when a hand appeared, followed by another. Suddenly, as if the hands had clawed a rent in the curtain, a girl's face sprang into view, contorted with fear and silently pleading for help.

Lit by torchlight, the girl's face was streaked with tears and framed by dishevelled red hair. Mary knew instantly that it was Holly, trapped somewhere in the cave. Immediately she identified with her, as if Holly's plight could be her own. Overwhelmed with an uncontrolled concern, she knew that, somehow, she must get her out of the cave.

Perhaps it was the distressing image of Holly and the irresistible urge to rescue her that triggered Mary's mind to reassert itself, but now it was as if an ultimate weapon were being brought into action. When a blinding light flooded into her mind, she felt as if she were being bathed in sunlight.

Out of the light itself, another image came into focus. But this time her heart leapt with joy, as she saw her son Bryan standing there, smiling at her. He reached out his hand and, in her own mind, she tried desperately to reach back and touch him.

Yet she could not. The image disappeared and the black curtain fell again. But, this time, there was a sense of calm behind it.

Mary was convinced that even if the image of Bryan had been snatched away, something had managed to invoke his presence to protect her. She knew, on this occasion at least, that the battle for her mind had been won.

She gradually began to surface, becoming aware that she was cold because the duvet had nearly slipped off the bed.

She opened her eyes and blinked as sunlight poured in through the gap in the curtains and lit up her face. Wearily, she turned her head to check that the Serpent Meteorite was still there. Cold, impassive and betraying no sign of the powers it represented, it was exactly where she had placed it.

Mary sat up in the bed, trying to allow her mind to adjust to whatever had happened to her. She was aware that the Serpent Meteorite was somehow involved with the surreal journey she had endured to reach the cave.

But it was the final images of Holly in the cave and Bryan's smiling face that kept re-asserting themselves. Even then, those images were accompanied by a profound fear. She knew that deep within that cave was something malevolent, something evil, something foul beyond her imagination. She knew also, at the same moment, that if she were going to rescue Holly, she would have to confront it.

37

Dan sat in the dining room of the hotel, his fork poised over a full Scottish breakfast, wondering whether he had over-ordered. He looked up and put down the fork as Charles came over to join him. "Have you heard anything more from Ben?" he asked.

"Only that he's getting the first flight to Edinburgh out of Heathrow. Then he's hiring a car and driving here," said Charles, sitting down. "I guess he'll be here sometime after eleven. What he must be going through is beyond imagination."

Dan shook his head. "But where do we start to find out what's happened? Where Holly is?"

"Let's hope that Mary had another vision last night and found out something. A clue, even," said Charles.

Dan checked his watch. It was eight-thirty. "Do you think we should make sure she's okay?"

"Let's give her a few more minutes. She looked exhausted last night and she may not have slept too well."

As if to create a distraction, Dan prodded a small disc of something black on the plate alongside a fried egg. "What's this?" he asked.

"Black pudding," answered Charles, helping himself to a slice of Dan's toast.

"Yes, I can see that. But what's it made of?"

"Blood," replied Charles, expressionless.

Dan grimaced and moved the black pudding to the edge of his plate. He was obviously worried. "Do you think she can take much more? These visions must be taking a toll on her."

"I agree," said Charles. "And I wish we could do more to help. But we're involved in something that's beyond our understanding, aren't we? It's as if we've all been set up."

Dan poured Charles some coffee, but didn't respond.

"Well, think about it," said Charles. "It's all too neat, isn't it? Let's sum up what's happened. First, Warren, who happens to be an archaeologist, discovers the skeleton of a red-haired giant at the Serpent Mound. The skeleton is holding a meteorite. As you know, the Serpent Mound is one of the most mysterious sacred sites in America. Warren knows me of old and I know a bit about the mythology of the ancient world, including meteorites and red hair. So, at his behest, I go over to the States to visit him."

"I'm listening," said Dan, as he apprehensively poked a sausage with his fork.

"Well, I also have a particular interest in the Neolithic world, especially the stone monuments built at that time – standing stones, stone circles and the like. Remarkably, I live in the same village as Ben, who happens to be an expert on meteorites. And our village just happens to have associations with witchcraft and is situated next to the Rollright Stones – another sacred site. His girlfriend happens to be a redhead who's been having extrasensory experiences. She told me she had a terrible nightmare where she witnessed an obviously very special girl with red hair trapped in a cave and about to be sacrificed to an evil meteorite. And now Holly's disappeared. Is it all some sort of coincidence?"

"Are you going to suggest that it's no accident that I know Ben? The world of meteorite specialists isn't that big, you know."

"Granted. But you work with Mary, don't you? Isn't it odd that she's another redhead who starts to have visions? Plus she happens to have Irish and Scottish ancestry?"

"I guess you're right," said Dan.

"Okay," Charles continued, "so a meteorite falls in the Antarctic and, against the odds, it's found by a British team hunting for meteorites. Somehow, Ben gets hold of it and establishes that it comes from, quite remarkably, the same source on Mars as the meteorite found at the Serpent Mound. Then I bring the Serpent Meteorite back from the States and it ends up in Ben's house, together with the Antarctic Meteorite. So, incredibly, the two meteorites have ended up together. As we've said before, one could be forgiven for believing that they were destined to be together."

"Yeah, it is a bit weird."

"Quite," said Charles. "And now the real action starts. At this point, we become involved in a battle at the Serpent Mound between what appears to be a decidedly nasty mist with a life of its own, and strange balls of light, which seem to be benevolent. Mary has visions there that imply she has regal ancestry – an ancestry which is associated with red hair.

"By chance, or perhaps it wasn't, the Antarctic Meteorite ends up with Warren. And he dies, literally frightened to death. A warning to us, perhaps?

"Was it really by coincidence that I went to Newgrange in Ireland, and, would you believe it, I met Gráinne O'Connor who later became, er, *involved*, with you? I should have suspected from the start that it was more than a coincidence."

"I thought that might come up," said Dan. "Okay, okay – so I went a bit over the top."

"To get to the point, it seems clear to me that we're pawns in some metaphysical game of chess being played by powers we can barely comprehend. In essence, one of the powers is benevolent." He looked Dan straight in the eyes. "But I believe we now all accept the other power is profoundly evil."

"If you see it as a game of chess, that was quite a *knight* with Gráinne," said Dan.

Charles couldn't help smiling, before he checked himself. "Okay, but let's continue. The evidence suggests that the Serpent Meteorite is trying to lead us to the Stone of Destiny. We don't know why, but it seems that Mary has been chosen as the key player on our side. And, in the process, her consciousness is evolving. It's expanding, isn't it? Not only has she had profound visions relating to her ancestry and the Stone of Destiny, but, at Kilmartin, her dead red-haired son appears in a vision and becomes involved in her destiny – whatever that may be. Now it seems her evolution is moving towards an increasing empathy with nature. Witness her experience with the kestrel."

"I've not exactly been suffering from a shortage of weird experiences myself," observed Dan.

"None of us has," said Charles. "But, on the other side, there's an equally powerful force at work which, for some reason, is desperate to stop us finding the Stone of Destiny. And that agency has its own players in the game, including Gráinne O'Connor. She clearly has access to the darker powers of witchcraft, which seem to be channelled through the Antarctic Meteorite. Either way, both those powers, whatever they are, simply won't let go of us. We really are caught in a web, aren't we?"

He took another bite of toast and chewed for a while. "But now there's another factor that's come into it."

Dan sipped his coffee and eyed Charles expectantly.

"Twins," said Charles. "It all fell into place yesterday when Ben told me that Holly was expecting twins. The Serpent Meteorite and the Antarctic Meteorite are physically the same, like twins. If the Serpent Meteorite is related to the Stone of Destiny – a chip off the old block, if you like – then doesn't it suggest that somewhere there's a meteorite that is related to the Antarctic Meteorite?"

"Are you suggesting that the Stone of Destiny has a twin somewhere?" said Dan.

"Just an idea," replied Charles. "And there's something else. It's claimed that the Stone of Destiny is Jacob's Pillow Stone. In the first vision that Mary had, she saw a tribal sacred stone in the ancient boat. Furthermore, the boat was typical of a kind found in the ancient Near East. Her later vision suggests that the sacred stone was the Stone of Destiny. So, if you remember, that brings in another pair of twins."

"I say, Sherlock Holmes, you're not by any chance referring to Jacob and Esau, are you?" observed Dan.

"Exactly," Charles said. "The Biblical twins, Jacob and his brother, Esau. Not identical twins, I know, and I wouldn't necessarily claim that one was good and one was bad, but they certainly had a stormy relationship." He thought for a moment. "Mary isn't a twin by any chance, is she?"

Dan looked taken aback. "Well, if she is, she's never mentioned it to me." He smiled at Charles. "Why don't you ask her yourself? You seem to be getting on quite well with her."

Charles flushed.

"Oh, it's all right," said Dan. "She's a lovely lady. And she needs someone like you to support her, especially at the moment."

"I get the feeling she looks more to you for support," responded Charles.

"I guess I'm her surrogate son." He suddenly looked serious. "And, thinking about it, I suppose she could be my surrogate mother."

"Oh, I don't know. You don't exactly come over as a 'Mummy's boy'. You seem pretty independent, Dan, and well able to look after yourself. The way you handled that drunk in Hillsboro was quite impressive."

"Oh, that's my training in the army," he replied.

"You served in Afghanistan, I gather?" said Charles.

"How do you know that?"

"Mary told me."

Dan looked at him quizzically. "Did she say why I joined the army?"

"No," said Charles. "I didn't ask."

Dan picked up the jar of marmalade and casually inspected the label, before glancing around the room. There was now only a handful of diners. As if reassured he wouldn't be overheard, he turned purposefully to Charles. "It was basically my home life. Dad was in the navy and he was naturally away a lot. I suppose my mother got lonely. Anyway, she had affairs. There always seemed to be various *uncles* around the place and I just got in the way."

"You were an only child?"

"Yes – and quite a loner. The army offered a way out – it became my family." He fell silent, giving the impression that he was choosing his words carefully. "Except that it didn't all work out – I experienced something in Afghanistan…"

"You must have gone to college at some stage?" jumped in Charles.

"Yes – I managed to get into Penn State. I did geosciences and then a PhD in meteoritics." He sat back in his chair and laughed sardonically. "And here I am now, sitting in a hotel in the north of Scotland. I'm caught up in something I don't understand, which, putting it frankly, scares me silly."

Charles looked at him sympathetically. "But I guess there are various reasons why we're here and we both seem destined to see this through. We're both pretty well trapped together, aren't we?"

Dan didn't answer; Mary was standing at the entrance to the dining room, looking for them. He waved to her.

As she approached, both men got up and went to pull out a chair for her, but Dan was closer and she smiled wanly at him as she sat down. She pointedly placed the bag containing the Serpent Meteorite in front of herself on the table.

She looked pale and tired and it was immediately evident that something was wrong. "I had a vision – but it was horrible," she said, shaking her head.

"What on earth happened?" asked Charles.

"I saw Holly."

Charles sat bolt upright. "Where was she?"

"In a cave…"

Charles practically fell out of his seat. "In a cave!"

"Yes – for just a second an image of her flashed into my mind. There was a look of pure terror on her face. I know she was desperate and reaching out to me for help. But there was something else in that cave. Something that was blocking me from going in there. I had a sense that whatever it was didn't want me to join forces with Holly. I was an enemy."

"But that's just like the nightmare Holly told me about. I told you about it, remember? She saw a red-haired girl in a cave about to be sacrificed to a meteorite that produced a foul mist. She said she saw two red eyes approaching the girl through the mist. My God! Do you know where the cave is?"

"That's it – I've no idea. I just know it's somewhere by the seaside. Somewhere cold, windy and damp."

"Did you see a meteorite in the cave?"

"No, but whatever was in there was very powerful and seemed to be fighting to get control of my mind. It didn't win, thank God – there was another force which stopped it."

"You'd better tell us everything in detail, Mary," said Charles.

She looked down at the table in front of her, as if trying to collect her thoughts, while Charles poured a cup of coffee for her.

Mary looked up. "Thank you," she said. "This time it was all very different to my previous visions…"

The men listened intently as she related her experience, trying to remain as dispassionate as possible. "It's just that I have no idea where the cave is. And I don't know what's inside it. But I do know it's something horrible," she concluded.

"Right," said Charles. "We have to find out where this cave is."

Dan reacted immediately. "Can you describe the seagull again?"

"Well, I thought I had," said Mary, and she proceeded to repeat the description of the bird, adding as many details as she could recollect.

Charles fetched out his phone and was soon reeling through pictures of different species of seagull. "Sounds like a herring gull to me," he said, showing the image to Mary.

"That's it!" she exclaimed.

Charles checked the description. "'Very common,'" he read out. "'Found along all the shores of Western and Northern Europe – even including Iceland.'" He sighed. "Unfortunately, that doesn't help much in locating the cave."

"You're completely missing the point," said Mary.

Charles looked taken aback.

"I believe the seagull was sent to me as a messenger. It was sent to get me to that cave."

"By what?" asked Charles.

"I don't know, but I do know the Serpent Meteorite was involved. The seagull found me, and to get to that cave, I had to become the seagull myself. It was like entering into another layer of consciousness – a vision within a vision. Like when a shaman becomes another living being."

"But why a seagull?" asked Dan.

"I'm not sure, but all the time the Serpent Meteorite was next to my head. I now know it's capable of changing my level of consciousness, and yet this experience was on a completely different level. It was as if the Serpent Meteorite itself was being used by something even more powerful to get me to the cave. And whatever that thing was, it was determined that I should make contact with Holly. I believe I was meant to help her, somehow – to make her realise that she wasn't alone."

"If the Serpent Meteorite was involved in this, do you think the Antarctic Meteorite could also have been involved?" asked Dan.

"I'm sure it was, but I don't think it was actually in the cave. I think Gráinne O'Connor still has it – but I'm sure she was not in the cave. I had the feeling that whatever's in there was immensely powerful and trying to stop me from making any contact with Holly. Some force slammed into me like a whirlwind and made a heavy black curtain come down. But all the time I was aware that another force was fighting back and urging me to help Holly. My whole mind became a battleground between two strong opposing forces."

"Are we assuming that somehow Holly has been kidnapped and forced into that cave?" asked Charles. "And if so, why?"

"Well, obviously the Serpent Meteorite is guiding us towards the Stone of Destiny and something's trying to stop us finding it. Gráinne O'Connor obviously believes that if she can get hold of the Serpent Meteorite, then she can stop us. All I know is that I'm ready to believe anything of Gráinne O'Connor."

She suddenly looked exhausted. "Listen, I've told you about everything that happened last night. Do you mind if I go back to my room and lie down?"

"Of course not," said Charles. He noted that they were the only people left in the dining room. "Shall we get together again in the lounge at around eleven, to meet Ben when he arrives?"

"Good idea," said Dan, getting up. "You need to rest, Mary, and I need to check my emails – to find out what's going on in the rest of the world."

Charles watched Dan until he had left the dining room, and then turned towards Mary. "Only a thought, Mary. A personal question."

Mary looked apprehensive.

"Just by chance, you're not a twin, are you?"

"Me? No, certainly not," she exclaimed. "I think I know where you're coming from, but no. And Bryan wasn't a twin either – he was an only child. I have an elder sister, but she virtually gave up on me when I had Bryan." She looked at Charles with tired eyes. "You see, I was an unmarried mother, and my sister's very different to me. She's the very model of morality and being an unmarried mother wasn't an acceptable thing in my family. Father was a local politician – a very pillar of society in North Carolina – if you get my drift. All my family, my mother included, just wrote Bryan and me out of their lives."

"I'm so sorry, really. I shouldn't have asked," he said. "I didn't mean to pry, but when Ben told me that Holly was expecting twins, it set me thinking about the meteorites."

"It's all right," replied Mary. "I've been thinking along the same lines myself." She stood up, making to leave. "I can't prove it yet, but I believe what I witnessed in my vision was a battle for my mind between the Stone of Destiny itself and its meteorite twin. And that meteorite twin is in that cave…"

38

When Dan came back and looked for Charles and Mary in the lounge, he saw them sitting together on a sofa, deep in conversation. He went over and sank into an adjacent armchair. "Any conclusions?" he asked, genially.

"We were just talking about what to do next," replied Charles.

"And?"

"Trouble is, we still don't know where that cave could be—" He suddenly jumped up and waved.

Ben wearily lifted his arm in recognition and walked over to them. There was shock, pain and anxiety on his face. In short, he looked devastated.

Charles put an arm around his shoulder, while Dan grasped his hand at the same time. Mary and Ben just smiled at each other and then hugged, as if immediately recognising soulmates. Charles pulled up a chair for him.

"Well?" asked Ben, falling into the chair. "Have you *any* idea where Holly could be?"

Mary and Dan both looked at Charles.

"We've got so far, Ben," he said. "Mary did have a vision and we think Holly's being held in a cave up here, somewhere on the coast. Look, a lot has happened you need to know about…"

Ben listened in silence, looking distraught and shaking his head as Charles outlined all their experiences to him. When Charles had finished, Ben just sat there, crestfallen.

Mary placed her hand on his arm. "We'll find Holly, I promise," she said. Almost unconsciously, she touched the Serpent Meteorite in the bag beside her.

"So, what now?" said Ben. "I'm here and we're obviously all mixed up in this together."

He didn't receive a reply. Dan swung around as he heard his name mentioned.

"Dr Gallagher?" The hotel receptionist was standing there, holding out a letter.

"For me?" asked Dan. "Are you sure? No one knows I'm here."

"A young lady delivered it, sir. She asked me to take it to you as a matter of urgency."

"Young lady?" said Dan. "What did she look like?"

The receptionist shrugged his shoulders. "Mid-twenties, I would say, dark-haired…" He thought for a moment. "She had a strong Irish accent."

"She wasn't wearing a red cagoule, was she?"

"Yes, sir, she was."

"Where did she go?" Dan demanded, looking out of the window.

"She just left. I don't really know…" He looked over to the reception desk where another guest was waiting. "Just coming," he called out, as he walked away.

Dan looked warily at the others. "There's only one

person I know who wears a red cagoule and has an Irish accent."

Mary didn't look surprised. "You'd better open the letter, Dan."

Dan studied the address on the envelope. It just said "Dr Dan Gallagher. Harbour Hotel". Ripping it open, he found a single sheet of paper inside, without an address or a signatory. He read the letter silently, ignoring the enquiring looks from the others.

When he had finished reading, he put the letter down on the table. He was white as a sheet.

"What does it say?" asked Mary.

Hesitantly, Dan picked up the letter. He didn't look at Ben as he read the message aloud: "'You want to know what has happened to Holly Fraser. For the moment she is safe. You want the girl back, we want the meteorite. Call this number...'" He read out a phone number.

"That's straightforward blackmail," said Charles, indignantly.

"We must do what it says," said Ben. "Holly's clearly in incredible danger..."

Charles looked worried. "It's not quite as straightforward as that, Ben. We don't really understand what's going on. We don't even know where the cave is. We really need to think this over very carefully. I suppose we could now hand it all over to the police..."

"Oh, come on. They'd be completely out of their depth. We can't just..." Ben didn't finish.

"I don't trust this situation one little bit," said Mary, abruptly. "I'm sorry, Ben, but Holly's being used to set a trap. We need to play O'Connor at her own game. Make the phone call, Dan. Arrange to meet her. She'll dictate the place, but it doesn't matter, because nobody is going to turn up. Make sure *you* dictate the time for the meeting. Make it for exactly two o'clock this afternoon. If we're going to rescue Holly, we need something that can protect us from whatever's in that cave."

"And that is?" asked Ben.

"The Stone of Destiny," she replied.

Ben looked dismayed. "But you don't even know where the Stone of Destiny is."

"We're going to find it," she said. "I think the powerful force that won the battle for my mind was connected with the Stone of Destiny. And I believe this is going to guide us to it." She touched the bag with the Serpent Meteorite in it. "There's only one place left where the Stone of Destiny is supposed to have been and where we haven't already investigated."

"And where's that?" asked Ben.

"Iona. The Isle of Iona. And that's where we're going this afternoon. Two o'clock is the time the ferry leaves."

39

Charles slumped against the steering wheel. "Made it," was all he said.

Their car was at the back of the queue of vehicles waiting to embark on to the ferry from Oban to Craignure on the Isle of Mull, the stepping stone to the Isle of Iona.

"Stay here," said Dan. "I'm going to have a look around."

He walked casually down each line of cars, looking primarily for a yellow car but also checking the passengers by sight for Gráinne O'Connor, whether in her normal form or even as the middle-aged pregnant woman or the old crone. He pointedly ignored inquisitive looks from other passengers as he peered into their vehicles and was clearly relieved when he arrived back at their own car.

"Can't see her," Dan said through the window. "But it wouldn't surprise me if she was in the back of a truck. And I suppose I ought to check the café in the terminal building."

Rather self-consciously, he inspected the few people eating and drinking, but she was clearly not among them. "No sign of her," he said, as he opened the passenger door and climbed in alongside Charles.

"We'll check the ship once we're underway," said Charles.

Mary didn't say anything, but clutched the bag in her lap tightly, while Ben sat alongside her, slumped and deep in thought.

A general air of excitement spread through the passengers as an official beckoned their line of vehicles forwards to drive into the bowels of the ship. Charles slipped the car into gear. "Iona, here we come," he said.

The four initially settled into a corner of a lounge towards the bow of the ship. Charles seemed slightly embarrassed. "I suggest Dan and I check around the ship, but would you please check the, er, facilities, Mary – just in case. Then let's meet up again back here."

"I think you mean *washrooms*, Charles," replied Mary. "But yes, certainly."

She was talking quietly to Ben when Dan and Charles returned ten minutes later. "I couldn't see her," she said, shaking her head.

"We couldn't see her either," said Charles. "If she's here, she's hidden herself very well."

"Shall we go outside?" said Dan. "The deck at the stern is practically deserted. Anybody coming?"

Without a word, the others followed him.

The engine throbbed quietly as the ferry eased out of the harbour and into the open water. The sea was smooth and the sight of the wake streaming out behind the ship seemed oddly distracting and relaxing.

It was Ben who shattered the moment of calm. He

practically exploded as he released his pent-up emotions. "Look, this isn't an excuse for a bloody holiday trip! My pregnant girlfriend's been kidnapped for God's sake and we need to find her as quickly as possible. You, Mary, reckon she's in a cave with something horrible in it. We've no idea where it is, so why the hell are we spending time going to Iona? It's not exactly a short trip, is it? What's so special about Iona? And what is it about this bloody Stone of Destiny? Are you all mad?"

Charles spoke quietly. "We're wondering what it's all about ourselves, Ben. For some reason, we are being directed to the Stone of Destiny, even if other forces are trying to stop us. And those forces are very real – they've already cost one man his life. What's more, from what Holly told me about her experiences in Long Compton, hers were very real as well. She's an integral part of what's going on and that's why we think she's been kidnapped. Now you're deeply involved as well…"

Ben calmed down a little. "Yeah, yeah, I get all that. But why Iona, exactly? What's Iona got to do with the Stone of Destiny?"

"On the face of it, not much, I'm afraid – just hearsay, really," replied Charles. "Some say St Columba brought it with him from Ireland, but there's no real evidence."

"So, it's unlikely we're going to find it on Iona," said Ben, dismissively.

"I'm afraid I have to agree. The last we hear of it regarding Iona is that it might have been taken from Iona to Dunstaffnage for safekeeping, or even Scone, because of the murderous Viking raids that were starting to occur.

But there's something else, Ben. It's the fact that Iona is considered one of the most sacred places in the British Isles. And it's at sacred places where everything seems to be happening…"

"So, what's so sacred about it?" asked Ben.

"It's always been seen as sacred," answered Charles. "There's something about the place – it was originally a pagan site. St Columba, the Christian missionary, must have sensed its mystical nature when he arrived from Ireland in the sixth century, because he decided to build a monastery there. Now there's an abbey – that's the main tourist attraction. And, of course, many of the early Scottish kings are buried there – including Macbeth, apparently…"

"I still don't get why we need to go there…"

"There's something else, Ben…" said Charles. He didn't have the chance to continue.

"It's because St Columba had visions there," said Mary. "It's claimed that he saw angels. He was supposed to always be seeing angels and heavenly lights, particularly on Iona. That's why we have to go there."

"Not only that," went on Charles. "It's said he was always working miracles."

"It sounds like we're going to need a miracle," said Ben.

"Tell Ben the real reason we have to go to Iona," said Mary.

Charles took a deep breath. "St Columba's pillow stone," he said. "He was supposed to have carried it around with him. It's claimed he had visions when he rested his head on it at night. It's in the abbey and it's the one thing we have to check out."

"You're not suggesting it could be the Stone of Destiny, are you?" asked Ben.

"Oh, I doubt it very much," replied Charles. "The official view is that the stone is probably a grave marker. It was found some distance away from the abbey by a crofter, when his cart kept knocking against it. Of course, it was immediately claimed that it was St Columba's Pillow. But it's got a cross carved into it in a style that was common a couple of hundred years after Columba's death. So now it's thought that it's a grave marker of someone unknown."

"So why are you so keen on seeing it?" asked Ben.

Charles had a twinkle in his eye. "There's always the possibility that it actually is Columba's pillow stone, initially uncarved, then carved two hundred years later to disguise its real nature. And visions are one thing St Columba and Mary have in common."

"Sounds like a long shot to me," said Ben.

"It's on display in the abbey in a prime position," said Charles. "The authorities obviously value it very highly."

Not long after, the ship suddenly shuddered and the engine sound became noisier. Dan stood up and went over to the railing. "Looks like we're here," he called back.

"We'd better check the passengers again," said Mary. "If O'Connor's not here, I'll be amazed if she hasn't found out that we're on this ferry. If I know her, she'll follow us at a distance. She's not stupid."

"You seem to know the way she works very well, Mary," said Charles.

"Female intuition, again," she said.

"Even so," replied Charles. "Which way is it to the car?"

After driving carefully on to the quay, Charles came to the main road and turned left, while Dan was setting up the satnav on his phone.

"No need, Dan," said Charles. "This is the only road. If we'd turned right, we'd be heading up to Tobermory, the main town here on Mull. This is the way to the ferry terminal for Iona." He noted the time on the dashboard. "It'll take about an hour to get there. No cars are allowed on Iona, so we'll take the ferry and walk to the abbey. Last visitors to the abbey are admitted at five, so it's going to be very tight to visit it today. I was lucky to book accommodation on the island for tonight."

"Let's at least try to get to the abbey today," said Mary.

The road to the ferry terminal was mostly single track with passing places and Charles drove carefully, concentrating hard rather than talking.

Ben sat in the back with Mary, taking in the scenery without saying a word. It was when Charles pulled over to allow a car coming from the opposite direction to pass them that Ben suddenly came to life. He had clearly been thinking hard. "There's something that bothers me," he said, turning to Mary. "In the last vision you had, you say you saw a seagull, and then you became that seagull. You said it was a messenger?"

"That's right."

"Well, an obvious question. You claim that the force that eventually won control of your mind was associated with the Stone of Destiny. In that case why did it have to send a messenger to get you to the cave to comfort Holly? Maybe even to rescue her?"

Mary turned to him. "I think it could have given me a vision of Holly in the cave without the seagull being involved. But remember I told you about the kestrel at Dunsinane? I established real contact with the kestrel – for a while we were on the same wavelength. By making me become a seagull, the Stone of Destiny was taking me to an even more profound level of consciousness. I know now what it's like to actually be a seagull."

"But how does the Serpent Meteorite fit in with the Stone of Destiny?" asked Ben.

"It's as if the Serpent Meteorite is a disciple to the Stone of Destiny," replied Mary. "It must be the same relationship between the Antarctic Meteorite and whatever's in that cave. I don't know exactly what's happening to O'Connor, but it's as if we're both being prepared for something. I just don't know what."

Ben looked dumbfounded. "I still don't understand how going to Iona will help to find that cave."

"I don't know, either," said Mary. "We'll just have to trust this." She patted the Serpent Meteorite.

Ben fell silent for a while. "Do we at least know if there are any big caves on Iona?" he suddenly asked.

"There are a couple of large caves on Iona," said Charles, who had been listening carefully. "But not associated with the type of beach that Mary saw in her vision." He pulled over again to let another car pass.

"Nearly there," he said, accelerating away and pointing to the signpost saying "Fionnphort", the ferry terminal for Iona.

Shortly afterwards, they parked the car and strolled down the hill to the terminal.

"Damn," said Charles, as he saw the ferry pulling away from the quay. He checked the timetable outside the ticket office. "It's going to be very tight with the next ferry. Last visitors are let into the abbey at five. We've only got an hour or so to get there and check it out."

"We at least give it a try," said Mary, firmly. She touched her bag. "The Serpent Meteorite wants us to go today."

"What?" said Ben.

"You'll get used to it," replied Dan. "Mary and the Serpent Meteorite are running the show now."

"Can't you feel it? There's definitely something special in the air," said Charles, as the ferry edged into the dock after the ten-minute journey.

"Can we please get a move on," said Ben, as they disembarked.

They walked as fast as possible from the terminal, past the ruins of a medieval convent and on to the abbey. Arriving at the ticket office, they had five minutes to buy tickets.

"We close at five-thirty. You've only got half an hour," said the lady at the service desk.

"That'll do," said Mary, firmly.

In the abbey church, they easily found the pillow stone in its metal cage. Rather unimpressive, it was oval-shaped, barely a foot in length, and had a crude stylised cross carved into it. A large chunk of the stone had obviously been broken off.

"Well," said Ben. "What's so special about it?"

At that point, a guide approached them. "Very sorry, but we're closing now," she said, pointing towards the exit door, before going on to talk to a young couple who were admiring the font.

"Hang on!" said Mary, suddenly. She swung her bag off her back. "It's the Serpent Meteorite! It's coming alive!"

"What do you mean, *alive*?" asked Ben, apprehensively.

"It wants us to stay, for crying out loud. Something's happening."

It was Charles who took action. He noticed the guide was momentarily out of sight. "Here," he said, pointing to a door without a sign written on it. He turned the door handle and opened the door. "It's only cleaning stuff," he whispered. "Quick! In here!"

"You've got to be joking," said Ben, incredulously.

Mary immediately went into the cupboard, moved a couple of brooms and edged a bucket over to one side. "Hurry up," she said. "There's room."

Dan looked at Ben and held out his arm. "After you," he said.

Charles pulled the door shut and in the blackness they heard footsteps slowly fading away. There was a dull *thud* as a door closed, then silence.

40

It was pitch black in the cupboard, very dusty, and almost immediately Dan felt a sneeze building up. He put his hand to his mouth and started to shake, trying to stop it. When he received a firm dig in the ribs from Mary, he spluttered, but didn't sneeze.

Ben remained dead silent and Mary sensed he was out of his mind with frustration.

For his part, Charles felt around until he touched a wall, leant against it and closed his eyes. He felt Mary's hand brush against his, only for it to be quickly pulled away.

It was barely five minutes, but to Dan it seemed like an eternity. He held his wrist up to his face, hoping to see the time on his watch, but couldn't even see his own hand. Shuffling his feet impatiently and turning around, he managed to hit the bucket. They all heard it teeter, and Charles put his hand to his face, saying, "Oh, no," under his breath.

Dan reached down, feeling around to steady the bucket, but only succeeded in knocking over a broom. The bucket toppled over with a *clank*.

"Right, that's it," said Charles; he fumbled for the door handle and edged the door open. He peered through the gap and, not seeing anybody, opened the door wide and stepped out.

The abbey was deserted, but Charles couldn't help still speaking in a whisper. "I don't know what you have in mind, Mary, but we ought to be quick. There could be cleaners in here soon."

Mary stepped out, clutching the Serpent Meteorite in her bag. "Something's definitely happening with it," she said. "I always knew it was alive somehow, but in the hotel in Oban, it sent me a message – like a subliminal message. I couldn't get it out of my head – it was urging, directing me to come here to the abbey. That's why I insisted on coming here. Maybe it's St Columba's Pillow that's behind it. It felt as if the Serpent Meteorite had somehow been communicating with the pillow stone, which wanted us to come here."

"Well, here we are," said Ben, looking around worried. "What now?" The effigies of the 8th Duke of Argyll and his wife, lying on top of a tomb in marble splendour, caught his eye. He half expected them to turn around, wondering who could dare to disturb their peace.

Mary didn't say a word, but took the Serpent Meteorite out of the bag.

Shaking his head in disbelief, Ben followed Charles and Dan behind Mary, as she strode to the pillow stone, holding the Serpent Meteorite in front of herself.

Reaching the pillow stone, she carefully placed the Serpent Meteorite beside the metal cage, stepped back and closed her eyes, seeming to be meditating.

It was actually Ben who noticed it first. "Something is definitely happening," he said, shocked. "Look at the cut surface – it's changing colour." As if an unknown force were energising it, the crystals in the Serpent Meteorite were starting to shimmer and sparkle.

Ben reached out and held his hand over the cut surface. In the shadow created by his hand, the phenomenon became more obvious. "See, something's affecting the crystals – some of the crystals are glowing green. That could be the olivine crystals."

"And look at the pillow stone," said Dan, incredulously. "It's not just me, is it? That's starting to glow as well."

Mary stood there, her eyes still closed. Her head fell downwards and she stumbled, mumbling something at the same time.

Charles jumped forwards and placed his arms around her waist to steady her. She kept on mouthing words, but they made no sense.

Ben went up to the cage with Dan and peered at the pillow stone. "I can't believe it," Ben whispered. "Look, it's glowing more strongly."

Conscious that he had his arms around Mary, Charles gently released her.

She stood still, her head hanging downwards and her lips moving as she spoke quietly. The words were still impossible to decipher.

"I think it's some kind of spell she's saying," whispered Charles.

Suddenly, as if a switch had been thrown, both stones lit up together.

Mary seemed to receive a jolt of some unknown energy. She shuddered, raised her head, opened her eyes and stared, unblinking, at the pillow stone.

Now both stones were glowing brightly, the Serpent Meteorite emitting an eerie greenish light while the pillow stone shone like an electric light bulb.

Charles almost fell backwards as Mary abruptly lifted her hands high in front of herself, her fingers spread, like a priestess of some ancient religion. Now her voice echoed around the church as she started chanting in an unrecognisable language.

The men moved away from her, wondering how to react. The pillow stone was now so bright that it was almost impossible to look at it directly. Mesmerised, Charles and Dan kept looking as long as they were able, then turned away, half-blinded.

Only Ben kept on staring at it. Shielding his eyes with his fingers, he peered between them to see that a ball of light had silently formed and was hovering above the pillow stone.

Then, as if it had a life of its own, the light rose and grew in size to float there, giving the impression that it was inspecting them all.

Mary raised her arms higher as if in encouragement and the light grew in size to cast deep shadows behind everything immediately around it. Keeping her hands high in the air, she stared transfixed, as it floated higher, growing brighter and brighter, until it shone like a miniature sun. Now Mary closed her eyes and appeared to enter into a deep trance.

The light was so dazzling that Ben completely covered his eyes, fearful that the brilliant light would damage them.

It was only when Dan and Charles noticed the shadows had become less dense that they dared to turn around.

Charles nudged Ben. "It's fading now," he said.

Ben took his hands away from his eyes and watched as Mary slowly lowered her arms.

The sphere hung there in the same place but became smaller and dimmer, until it finally disappeared. Looking down at the Serpent Meteorite, he saw that the crystals had stopped glowing and that the exposed cut surface had returned to its normal appearance.

It was Charles who noticed Mary was shaking and, as her knees started to buckle, he rushed forwards to grab her. It seemed as if all the energy had been drained out of her and Charles now had difficulty in holding her upright.

"Get something for her to sit on," he called out to Dan, who immediately rushed away, grabbed a chair and swung it around behind her. Charles gently lowered Mary into it, took her right hand and rubbed it gently. Dan and Ben stood behind him, half-concerned, half-confused.

"What happened, Mary?" said Charles, quietly. "It seemed as if you were having another vision."

She opened her eyes, shook her head and looked up at him. "It was more than that, Charles," she said, quietly. "I don't know exactly what happened, but I do know the Serpent Meteorite was communicating somehow with St Columba's Pillow. They must have been communicating with each other before. Same old story – the Serpent

Meteorite seemed to know that it had to come here to the abbey and has been using us to get itself here."

"It did enter my mind that perhaps you were seeing what St Columba thought was an angel," said Charles.

"No, no," said Mary. "I didn't know what was going on at first. I thought it was like an angel, myself. But it was greeting the Serpent Meteorite as if they were old friends – I could actually understand what they were saying. Then it dawned on me what it really was…"

Charles didn't say anything and Dan and Ben edged closer.

"It was St Columba. That light was St Columba. It was the spirit of St Columba."

The men looked dumbfounded, unable to believe what she had just said.

"Don't you see?" said Mary. "That isn't any old grave marker in that cage. It really is St Columba's pillow stone. It must have been set up beside his grave when he was buried. His spirit, his soul, is in it."

Dan briefly caught Ben's eye and they looked at each other in total bewilderment.

"So it must be true," said Charles, eventually. "The cross was carved into the pillow stone later in a style to disguise what it really is. It must have been carved when Columba's bones were disinterred and put in the reliquary. That's why the pillow stone is treated with such reverence here. That's why it's not with all the other grave markers in the abbey museum."

Dan didn't respond, but went up to the pillow stone in its cage. Inert and cold-looking, it was now like any other stone.

Ben walked over, picked up the Serpent Meteorite and gave it to Mary.

She held it tightly. "St Columba himself must have been in contact with the Stone of Destiny at some time, because something else happened."

The others stared at her, wondering what on earth she was going to say next.

"It showed me where the Stone of Destiny is," Mary whispered. "The Serpent Meteorite asked the pillow stone to give me a vision of where the Stone of Destiny is."

"So, what did it show you?" asked Charles.

"Different images came into my mind – one after another. The first was a group of upright stones on the horizon, silhouetted against the sky."

"And?" said Dan.

"Then I was floating above them – lots of stones. They were arranged in the shape of a cross. The longest arm of the cross consisted of two lines of stones, forming something like an avenue between them. The other arms were much shorter single lines of stones. And in the middle, right at the centre of the cross, was a small stone circle with an enormous stone pillar in it, standing upright and shaped like the rudder of a ship."

"I know exactly where that is," said Charles.

Everybody looked at him.

"Callanish," he said. "Callanish on the Isle of Lewis. It's due north of here, and it's not that far. It's one of the most mysterious places in the British Isles. And it's actually documented that St Columba visited the Isle of Lewis…"

"I know what you're all thinking," said Dan. "You want

to go straight to the Isle of Lewis. But can we just get to grips with this first? For a start, we need to get out of this place."

"Hang on a minute," said Charles, and he walked to the main entrance. He tried to open the door. When he returned, the look on his face said it all. "Locked," he grunted. "But just a minute – I seem to remember there's an exit somewhere at the back."

He was right; the door was on the latch, but unlocked. He called to the others, held it open for them and quietly pulled it closed again. "Look – there's a gate over there into that field," he said. "We should be able to get to the coast and walk back to the hotel."

When they reached the gate, he stopped and looked back at the abbey. "Let's just wait a moment," he said.

They waited for a couple of minutes, looking for any human activity, but nobody appeared.

"I'm just wondering where Gráinne O'Connor is," said Charles.

41

"How on earth would we even start to explain this to other people?" said Dan. "They would think we were mad. I'm even beginning to question my own sanity. If I hadn't witnessed it myself…"

"I know it's unbelievable, but the experience in the abbey was very much for real," said Mary. She looked at Charles. "I'm just not sure how it's all going to end."

Charles didn't say anything, obviously deep in thought.

"To think we've actually been commandeered by a meteorite from Mars, which is somehow alive," she went on. "It's as if it wants to change the world and we've been chosen to instigate the change."

Ben had been sitting there, staring out of the window of the hotel at the blue waters of the Sound of Iona, his mind somewhere else. Now he suddenly sprang into life and swung around to face the others. "There is actually a scientific theory that's linked to what we've been witnessing," he pronounced. The others turned to him. "'The Stone Tape Theory'. The ability of stone to record and play back events. Admittedly, it is only a theory and it's been around for some time. But shall I explain?"

"Please," said Mary.

Dan looked unconvinced, but Charles turned to Ben with a look of hard concentration.

"Well, put simply, the theory supposes that crystalline rocks are able to capture past events and store them in the form of energy. Silicon dioxide, in its various forms such as quartz, would appear to be particularly favoured. Then, at a later time, people who are suitably sensitive can tap into this energy, so that the event can be played back. Perhaps it's only in their minds. But then, who knows? The Serpent and Antarctic Meteorites are, of course, crystalline rocks, and it seems both meteorites contain something extremely powerful. Somehow, whatever's in the Serpent Meteorite is manifesting itself to us – and Mary and Holly would appear to be especially sensitive."

"But how does it work?" asked Dan. "What do you suppose the mechanism is?"

"I assume you all know about crystal lattices?" said Ben.

"You'll have to keep it simple," replied Charles.

"Okay, you asked for it," said Ben. "Crystals have lattice structures consisting of an array of atoms shaped by electrical forces. The theory is that defects in the crystal lattices allow for reservoirs of energy where *memories* could be stored and potentially accessed later by the brains of sensitive people. For instance, the music you say you heard at Scone Palace – that could be an example. Perhaps sightings of ghosts, time travel, hearing things that nobody else does, are all part of the phenomenon. You could see the process as analogous to the recording process used to record and play back a television programme..."

"But surely what we saw in the abbey on Iona is in a different league?" said Charles. "Mary says what we saw was the actual spirit of St Columba. We all witnessed what happened there with the Serpent Meteorite and the pillow stone. Mary says they communicated with each other and that she could understand them."

"It could be the same principle, though," continued Ben. "As I said, it's only a theory and it could be shot down by any scientist worth his or her salt. We can't replicate what happened and there is no physical evidence of psychic forces or whatever in nature. But you're quite right, Charles – the point is that it happened. All of us witnessed it. The truth is, we don't really know what's going on, but it does seem that the Serpent Meteorite is somehow alive."

"Maybe it's not all that far-fetched," said Charles. "Take animism, for example. It's a belief still found around the world in so-called primitive societies. Animists believe that *everything* is alive, including stones. In fact, the belief that stones contain spirits is probably one of the world's oldest religions."

"I'm no philosopher," said Ben, "but I've been reading about the renewed interest in panpsychism – the idea that everything is conscious, right down to sub-atomic particles. That would fit in nicely with animism."

Dan shook his head. "I guess it's all rather outside my remit. But if we're talking about the ability of some people to have these strange experiences, what is it about red hair? Why you, Mary? Why Holly, Ben? Why are their experiences so extreme? The visions, for example?"

"I'm still wondering, myself," said Mary.

"Don't laugh," said Charles, "but it could all be tied up with the Atlantis myth."

"I'm beginning to think I could believe anything now," said Dan.

"Okay," said Charles. "Plato got it second-hand, of course, but the story is that Atlantis was destroyed by a cataclysmic event that certainly involved flooding. And of course a great flood is described in the Bible. And it's not only in the Bible – great floods crop up in mythologies, all around the world.

"For example, in Greek mythology, there's the story of Pyrrha of Thessaly. *Pyrrhus* means 'red' in Latin, and Horace and Ovid describe Pyrrha as a redhead. Anyway, the myth is that Pyrrha and her husband were the only survivors of a great deluge. Her husband was told by an oracle that they should both throw rocks over their shoulders. They do, and the rocks become human beings. In other words, the rocks were, or became, alive. It does sound very familiar, doesn't it?"

"Holly would have loved this," said Ben. "She's always going on about how special redheads are."

"She could be right," said Charles. "Since the earliest times redheads have been popping up all over the world in places where you wouldn't expect them. For instance, remains of redheads have been found in China. On the other side of the world, the aboriginals of the Canary Islands, the Guanches, are claimed to have had red hair. The Maoris say that when they arrived in New Zealand there was a redheaded tribe already there. Redheads are found as well in the Pacific Islands – look at the Easter

Island statues with their red stone topknots. They must have been brilliant sea voyagers.

"Could that be the result of a diaspora of people with red hair, after their civilisation was destroyed by a great flood? Atlantis, for example? Could it be that they were so advanced, so clever, that they rose to the top of just about every field of endeavour? Art, science, politics, monarchy... You name it, there's always a redhead around at the top."

"All good stuff, I'm sure," said Dan. "But no proof whatsoever."

"But it does fit in with my visions, doesn't it?" said Mary. "The vision where I was in the boat with what I believe was the Stone of Destiny – the same stone that was used in the coronation of Eremon. If that vision reflects reality, then I could be descended from the same Scota who gave her name to Scotland."

"I'm sorry, but it's all too much for me," Dan said. "And shouldn't we be talking about tomorrow? For instance, I'm still not sure what's so special about the Standing Stones of Callanish?"

"You'll see when we get there," said Charles. "The site's at the centre of a sacred landscape – it's very special. The Standing Stones of Callanish is the main monument you saw in your vision, Mary, and all the other monuments surrounding it – the stone circles, stone rows, standing stones – somehow relate to it in the landscape.

"And there is something else that is very relevant to our experiences. During the morning of every midsummer day, local folklore says something called *The Shining*

One walks the length of the stone avenue. Odd isn't it, considering what we've just witnessed?"

He yawned. "Listen, I've ranted on enough. If we're going to get to Callanish tomorrow, we need to make an early start. And I'm off to bed."

"We all have to be on the ball tomorrow," said Mary. "We may not be alone. I'm sure Gráinne O'Connor will be up to something."

In the car park at the ferry terminal just across the Sound of Iona, a woman in a red cagoule was walking along the lines of cars. Recognising the hire car, she stopped abruptly and smiled to herself. Reaching into a pocket, she found a red marker pen. After checking around to make sure she was alone, she carefully started to draw something on the front windscreen.

42

Mary again found that she couldn't sleep. She was now petrified of having another vision and was dreading whatever might lie ahead. Her mind instinctively flitted backwards, and this time settled on the normality of the life she had known back in Houston. She thought about the job she loved and how she used to look forward to each day.

Then reality kicked in again and she opened her eyes, only to see the unfamiliar, anonymous hotel room. She lay there, her mind racing, tossed and turned and finally gave up to lie on her back and analyse the frightening situation she was in.

Seeking solace, again she reached out in her mind to recollect memories of Bryan. This time she forced her mind back to the time when he was a cuddly baby, his shyness as he grew older, his moody period as a teenager, and then her delight when he went to college and blossomed. He was full of life and a sense of adventure; as a student he had always kept in regular contact, even if it sometimes involved phone calls in the early hours of the morning. It was the thought of his smiling, affectionate face that finally relaxed her and she drifted off into a dreamless sleep.

She woke to the sound of birdsong. Her awareness of nature and herself as part of it encouraged her to steel herself to be positive in facing the difficulties ahead. She reached out and touched the Serpent Meteorite. If it had shown strange powers before, at that moment it seemed inert, completely switched off.

Still needing mental support, she couldn't help thinking about Dan and Charles. Dan, who seemed so strong, she knew was vulnerable underneath the brash persona he presented to the world. Charles was the opposite. She felt his strength in his determination to support her in the totally weird and petrifying situation she was in, despite real danger to himself. But, also, she felt that he needed her, and she was somehow reassured by the thought.

Glancing at the clock on the bedside table, now showing five-thirty, she forced herself to focus on the day ahead, and she climbed out of bed.

The others were already waiting for her in the hotel lobby. Too early for breakfast, they collected the prepared packed lunches they had ordered and quietly left the hotel to walk to the terminal for the first ferry of the day. Early in the morning, the crystal-clear air, the tranquil blue sea and the welcoming sunshine seemed at odds with an apprehension about the uncertainties that lay ahead. They spoke little.

On the ferry, they stood together, their eyes drawn to Iona Abbey, subconsciously drawing strength and spiritual comfort from everything it represented.

"Calm before the storm," said Charles, quietly.

A few minutes later, the ferry docked and they climbed up the hill away from the terminal to the car park.

It was Dan who saw it first, inscribed in red on the windscreen of their car. "Is that what I think it is?" he said.

"It's a pentagram," replied Ben. "A symbol used in witchcraft."

"I knew it," said Mary. "I knew O'Connor would be around somewhere."

"We press on," said Charles, wiping the symbol away with his handkerchief. He handed the car key to Ben, saying, "Would you like to drive?"

Ben nodded and opened the door for Mary.

To their relief, the drive across Mull and the ferry to Oban proved uneventful, but as they began the long haul north to Ullapool, the ferry terminal for the Isle of Lewis, there was an air of tension and the conversation was desultory.

Approaching the town of Fort William, the tension increased. They were all aware that this was the town closest to Ben Nevis, where Bryan had lost his life. Nobody spoke as they caught sight of the mountain in the distance, but Mary's face reflected a deep sadness.

Dan noticeably took an interest in Loch Ness. He was clearly thinking about the monster that allegedly dwelt there, and he stared intently at the calm, dark water as they drove the length of the loch. It was only when they reached the end that he spoke. "At least we haven't got to contend with the Loch Ness monster," he said.

Charles couldn't help laughing.

Again, the sea was calm for the ferry trip from Ullapool to Stornoway, the main town on the Isle of Lewis, and they were soon on their way to the Standing Stones of Callanish.

A few miles short of Callanish, just outside the village of Achmore, Charles asked Ben to pull over and park. "There's something I want to show you," he said. "It's only a short walk up the hill."

At first sight, Achmore Stone Circle was unimpressive, and Dan was clearly underwhelmed. The landscape was barren and the site itself sodden, with pools of brackish water sitting in a peat bog. A solitary radio mast further up the hill merely added to the sense of desolation.

There were only two stones still standing and they were both leaning over at a drunken angle. Other stone pillars lay scattered around the site, half-buried in the peat. It seemed that if the stones were in any way alive, as Ben had theorised, then they had yet to recover from some wild Neolithic party.

Three black-faced sheep approached a prone megalith and eyed them warily, giving the impression that they were guarding something they knew was special. Mary waved to them as if to acknowledge their presence as kindred spirits.

"Is this it?" said Dan.

"There is more than immediately meets the eye," said Charles.

At this point Dan stepped sideways and his foot disappeared up to the ankle with a *squelch*. He muttered an expletive under his breath. Mary looked at him disapprovingly, but Ben couldn't stop himself from smirking.

"Come over here," said Charles, who was standing on a dry patch. "There's something I want to show you."

As they all approached Charles, he pointed towards the distant south-west horizon. "See that range of hills…"

"Where exactly?" said Dan, stamping his foot on the ground in an attempt to shake the muck from his shoe.

Charles fumbled in a pocket, took out his notebook and rapidly drew an outline of the horizon. "There," he said, showing them the drawing and pointing again into the distance with his finger.

"So?" said Dan.

"That's what this whole landscape is about," said Charles. "What we're looking at is the Old Woman of the Moors and she's as old as the hills, literally. I prefer her other name, though – Sleeping Beauty." He showed them the drawing in his notebook again. "See, it's like a woman resting on her back. Look, here's the pillow she's resting her head on. And here's her head, her body and her knees. What we're seeing on the horizon is created by mountains, valleys, ridges – all coming together when seen from a distance."

"To be honest, it's not exactly impressive," said Dan.

"Oh, there's much, much more," said Charles. "Since time immemorial there has been the belief that the whole of this landscape is sacred, especially because of its close association with the movements of the sun and the moon. And this is not the only site. Around here the whole landscape is covered in Neolithic monuments. So far, some twenty are known, though who knows how many are buried in the peat waiting to be discovered.

"See here," he said indicating a swelling in the stomach region of the figure drawn in his notebook. "From this site, you see the Sleeping Beauty as being pregnant. You can see her from all the other sites as well, but at each place she presents a different aspect of herself."

He put his notebook back in his pocket and continued, "I just wanted to point out the importance of the sacred landscape. But wait until we see the Standing Stones of Callanish. They really are something else…"

He shivered as a sudden gust of wind whipped through the site, and he looked upwards to see a dark cloud inching its way over the sun. "Weather's changing," he said. "We ought to press on."

Charles slowed down as they approached the village of Callanish, and Mary excitedly pointed out a line of stones standing silhouetted on a ridge. "That's it! That's exactly what I saw in my vision at the abbey."

Like giant soldiers resting, before continuing their march to a destination they would never reach, they stood there, starkly outlined against a menacing sky.

The Callanish visitor centre beckoned with its café and offers of food and drink, but Charles wanted to go straight to the stones themselves.

"This is going with us," said Mary, clasping the Serpent Meteorite.

They stopped before they reached the stones. It was difficult to discern the pattern of the Celtic cross, and beneath the gathering storm clouds the stones themselves looked jumbled, forlorn and rather sad.

Dan seemed decidedly unenthusiastic. "It's a long way to come for this."

It was at this point that the milky globe of the sun started to creep out from behind a cloud.

"Now you're going to see what it's all about," said Charles.

As if in response, the clouds parted and the sun burst forth into a small patch of blue sky. Now the stones seemed to come alive. Instead of solid, grey, heavy rocks, they looked ethereal and light as feathers. Hewn from Lewisian gneiss, the oldest kind of rock in Britain, each stone seemed to have its own personality, with veins of crystalline quartz and hornblende sparkling in the sunlight.

"Come with me," said Charles, and he led the way to the avenue. "All the sites around here constituted a vast lunar observatory, and this is the most important. We're so far north, the moon doesn't climb very high in the sky. So, from each site, it's possible to see the moon moving across the sky in close association with the Sleeping Beauty. But here, at the main site, the phenomenon is very special. Look at the horizon," he instructed. "Can you see her? The Sleeping Beauty?"

Mary and Ben immediately said, "Yes."

"Dan?" asked Charles.

Dan nodded.

Charles started tracing his finger along the horizon. "You can see that the Sleeping Beauty is exactly framed by the outliers of the stone circle. And that's significant, because every nineteen years or so, there's a lunar standstill. That's when the moon sets at its most extreme position in the landscape. It's special here, because as the moon sets, it dances along the Sleeping Beauty, appearing and disappearing, as if it's playing hide and seek."

He pointed to a dip in the horizon. "That's Glen Langadale. It's where the moon makes a last dramatic appearance before it finally disappears below the horizon. Can you imagine? It would have meant so much to Neolithic man that the whole place must have been an important centre for pilgrimage."

Far from being impressed, Dan was distracted. He was staring up at the sky. "I don't like the look of that," he said.

A huge black cloud had appeared and was edging its way over the sun. Within seconds, the wind gusted down the avenue, the sun disappeared and the stones reverted to grey, heavy inert blocks.

"Time to go to the visitor centre, perhaps?" suggested Charles.

He didn't receive a reply. In the distance, a flash of lightning shot down from the sky, and shortly after, there was an ear-splitting clap of thunder.

Reaching the entrance to the visitor centre, Charles stood back to let Mary and Ben enter before him. He turned back to the stones. "Where's Dan?" he said.

Neither Mary nor Ben had the chance to reply as Charles rushed away.

Dan was standing, rigid, in the stone circle and staring unblinking towards where another bolt of lightning struck the same place.

Charles put his arm around Dan's shoulder, just as a roll of thunder passed over them. He felt Dan shudder. "Mary told me about what happened in Afghanistan," he said. "But this is Scotland and you're with friends – friends who need you, Dan."

Charles took his arm away. "Mary and Ben will be wondering what's happened to you." He took a few steps towards the visitor centre and waited for him.

Dan slowly turned to face Charles and visibly relaxed. Taking one last look towards where the lightning was striking, he started walking towards Charles.

43

To the north-west of the Standing Stones of Callanish, on the coast of the Isle of Lewis, lies Dalmore Bay. A place that would have normally attracted the more adventurous tourist, it was now deserted after the few visitors who had been on the beach had noticed the gathering storm clouds and rapidly departed. Mary would have instantly recognised the beach as where she had landed in her vision and where Holly was trapped in a cave.

The northern end of the beach was protected by rugged cliffs and a jumble of rocks. It was here that Gráinne O'Connor brushed back her windblown hair, felt the meteorite in the pocket of her cagoule and clambered through the rocks until she came to a large boulder at the base of the cliffs. Now she crouched down in front of the boulder and put her back against it. Flexing her legs, she heaved hard. The boulder didn't budge at the first attempt, but with a second push, it rolled to one side and the entrance to the cave was revealed. She crawled inside on her hands and knees.

The cave opened up immediately, so that she was able

to stand upright. She reached up to a ledge, grabbed the torch she had previously left there and switched it on. Confidently, she walked through the cave until, deep inside, she came to the rock face and kicked the wedging stone from under the blocking boulder. With one heave, she dislodged the boulder.

The first thing Holly Fraser saw was the flickering light of the torch. She was seated, her back against the wall of the cavern, surrounded by several empty bottles of water and a neat pile of sandwich wrappers.

She shrank back in terror against the wall as the light approached and she discerned a solitary figure behind it. "What's going on? Where am I?" she stammered.

"Doesn't matter," O'Connor replied, coldly. "There's no time to waste – something's about to happen here."

She shone the torch towards the huge black meteorite on the ledge. It stood there, inert and giving away no clues as to what might happen next.

O'Connor took Holly by the elbow and pulled her upright.

"Where are you taking me?" Holly said, shaking.

"Not far. Somewhere where you'll be okay." O'Connor shone the torch at Holly's baby bump. "We need to keep you safe."

As she crawled out of the entrance to the cave and staggered to her feet, Holly blinked in the sunlight.

O'Connor appeared after Holly, put her hand in the small of her back and firmly pushed her towards the beach and the path to the car park.

Holly swung around to face her. "Don't push me!" she

spluttered. "What's all this about? Where are we going? You've clearly got the wrong person…"

O'Connor responded by pushing Holly again, so that she staggered forwards. "There's a holiday cottage near here," she said. "It's unoccupied at the moment and I broke the lock. You can hole up there – you'll be safe enough. But I can tell you right now that nobody will know where you are and there's no one around here to help you."

O'Connor looked up at the scudding black clouds and in the distance saw a flash of lightning. Shortly afterwards, a roll of thunder bounced off the cliffs.

Stopping, she looked back to the cave entrance. She could barely make it out, but it was definitely there. A faint wisp of mist was emerging from the cave.

Set back from Dalmore Bay in splendid isolation, the holiday cottage was the perfect place for the holidaymaker who wanted to get back to nature. For Holly, it was like escaping from one nightmare into another. When they arrived at the cottage, the door handle was hanging loose.

Holly was distraught. "Look! I just want to go home," she pleaded. "Don't you understand? People will be going crazy trying to find me…"

O'Connor flared. "Just stay in the house. Don't even think about trying to leave."

"But why are you doing this to me? Why was I kidnapped? I don't understand – you don't even know me. All I was doing was taking my dog for a walk. And why did you dump me in that foul cave in the dark? Please, please, let me go! You know I'm pregnant!"

"We need you," said O'Connor, bluntly. "Leave this place and you're dead."

"But when are you going to let me go back home?" cried Holly in desperation.

"I can't tell you," said O'Connor. "There's food, milk and water in the fridge. Just don't try to escape." With that, she left without looking back.

Holly went to the front door and watched the yellow car speed away. Desperately searching around for possible help, she realised that the house was totally isolated. Then she couldn't help it, and the tears coursed down her cheeks.

44

Mary jumped as a loud clap of thunder shook the cups of coffee and plates on their table. "This can't be a normal storm, surely," she said.

The only other customers in the café, a young couple in hiking gear, looked over and grimaced.

The waiter, a middle-aged man, came over and placed a large slice of walnut cake in front of Dan. "Enjoy," he said, in a strong Scottish accent.

"But I didn't order this," said Dan.

"No, your friends did," replied the waiter.

"Is this weather usual for the time of year?" asked Charles.

"It's not that rare in this part of the world," the waiter said. "It will probably pass soon."

Mary got up and walked to the window. There were two flashes of lightning in quick succession. "It's odd, but the lightning seems to be hitting exactly the same place," she said.

This time there were two cracks of thunder that were powerful enough to rattle the glass.

Mary shrank back and went to return to the others.

She had nearly reached their table when she stopped dead in her tracks, staring at the Serpent Meteorite, which was sitting in its bag in the middle of the table. She didn't say anything, but apprehensively took it out of the bag. Sitting down, she held it cupped between her knees like a crystal ball. She checked the young couple weren't watching, but they were busy studying a map. "Look," she whispered, "I think it's coming alive again."

Though the phenomenon was weak, the crystals were definitely starting to glisten.

"What's happening?" asked Charles.

Mary's brow furrowed as she studied it. "I don't know what's happening," she said, eventually. "But something's going on. Something is bringing it to life, but I don't know what."

When Dan looked apprehensive, Mary seemed to read his mind. "No, Dan, don't worry – I'm not having another vision. But I feel it's definitely trying to tell me something."

In response there was another flash of lightning.

Ben was sitting there, staring at his wristwatch. This time the thunder rumbled on and on. As it faded away, he looked up. "A smidge over ten seconds," he said. "If my calculation's correct, that makes it just over two miles away where the lightning is hitting."

"But which direction is it in?" asked Dan. "If we knew that, we could check on the map to see where it's striking."

"Hang on," said Charles, easing himself up. "I'll be back in a minute."

He practically ran to the stones and lined himself up behind the main stone in the middle of the circle. Fetching out his notebook and pen, he did a quick drawing and waited until there was another flash of lightning. Then he drew a line in the notebook and waited for the next lightning strike. It happened in less than a minute and in precisely the same place. He walked quickly back to the café, smiling smugly to himself.

The others studied him quizzically as he returned.

"The lightning is striking practically due north from here," he announced. "Just slightly west of due north."

"How did you work that out?" said Dan.

Charles looked pleased with himself. "Okay. I just happen to know that the main stone in the circle is orientated exactly north–south. Does anybody have the map?"

"It's in the car," said Dan.

Charles groaned and turned to go outside once more.

The waiter stopped wiping down the counter and started walking over to them again.

Mary quickly slipped the Serpent Meteorite into her pocket.

"You should have asked me," the waiter said. "Airigh na Beinne Bige."

"Come again?" said Dan.

"Airigh na Beinne Bige," the waiter repeated. "That's the name in Gaelic. Otherwise known as Callanish Site XI. It's a single standing stone just up the road, near Breasclete village. Some archaeologists have done a lot of work there with their equipment – real technical stuff. And guess what? They found evidence of other stones hidden under the peat that would have made a stone circle. Mind you, the villagers could have told them that – the locals had been pinching the stones for years to build their houses. They shouldn't have done it, though. They do say there's something magical about that place. One house where they used a stone was supposed to be haunted. The owner emigrated in the end." He eyed each of them in turn. "But the archaeologists found evidence of something else…"

They all stared at him, waiting.

"Well, the bedrock underneath the stone circle showed clear evidence of magnetic disturbances. The archaeologists say they were caused by repeated lightning strikes. And that must have happened before the peat was laid down, meaning it happened over four thousand years ago. That place was obviously very special to the ancients."

The café lit up with another flash of lightning. "You see? Definitely the same place," said the waiter, and he walked back to the counter.

Mary touched the Serpent Meteorite in her pocket. They all saw her hand twitch. "It just pulsed," she said quietly, trying not to draw attention. "I felt a tingle. It must be telling us to go there. I know it."

Dan looked at Ben and raised his eyebrows, as if to say, *here we go again.*

As he walked to the exit with the others, Dan suddenly stopped, turned and rushed back to the table to take a large bite of his walnut cake. "Coming," he said, waving goodbye to the waiter.

"Weird, isn't it?" the waiter called out to Dan as he disappeared. "Good luck."

45

It was immediately obvious that they had come to the right place. As they parked the car by the roadside and got out, the lightning flashed down, followed instantly by a crash of thunder that rocked the car. Any hint of blue sky, let alone the sun, had disappeared. Dark, angry clouds were now racing over the sky, the wind was gusting furiously and spots of rain were hammering into their faces.

Ben looked up at the heavens. "Are you sure we're doing the right thing?" he said.

Mary steadied herself as the wind buffeted her and then she started to climb up the slope ahead of the others. "Yes," she called back. "Do you really think this is natural? Something very strange is going on." She felt the Serpent Meteorite in her pocket. "I know this is what we're meant to do."

As if in response, another flash of lightning hit down immediately ahead of her. The thunder was so loud that she clapped her hands over her ears. Making sure that the others were following her, she pointed ahead and forced herself on upwards.

Charles halted to get his breath back. The sky was

now completely dark and a strong gust of wind made him stumble.

Ben grabbed his arm. "Let me help," he said.

"Don't worry – I'll make it," Charles said; he took a deep breath and continued.

When they saw it, they all stopped together and stared in awe. About five feet tall and leaning over at an angle, the stone stood alone, as strike after strike of lightning struck it, like a boxer defiantly taking blow after blow from vicious punches.

They approached it cautiously, praying that the lightning would only hit the stone.

"That's enough," said Dan. "No closer. It's too dangerous."

Even as he spoke, the wind dropped dramatically and the clouds seemed to freeze in the sky. A deep silence fell around them.

"I don't like this at all," said Ben, looking around. "It really isn't right." Everything was still. The lightning had stopped and the wind had suddenly dropped; it was as if all nature were waiting for something to happen.

"What's that smell?" Dan said. He automatically lifted his foot and inspected the sole of his boot.

Ben saw it first: a faint wisp of mist creeping up the hill towards them.

"I think we've seen this before," said Charles, under his breath. He instinctively moved closer to the stone, as if it could offer protection.

Like a tide coming in, the mist was remorselessly creeping up the slope towards them. In the distance, they could see a swirling sea of mist becoming ever thicker and starting to block out the landscape.

"I think I know what's going to happen next," said Charles.

Just as it had happened before at the Serpent Mound, tendrils of mist now started to curve and encircle them in a flanking movement. The smell of putrid, rotting flesh grew stronger. Together, they all edged towards the stone and stood with their backs towards it.

"That smell – I can't stand it," said Mary. She put her hand against her face and coughed.

It was as if the mist decided to pounce. A wave of mist formed and rolled forwards, then rose in height and curled over them.

Mary, being the shortest, was engulfed first. She reached out, touched Charles's arm and fumbled around to find his hand.

Charles squeezed her hand hard and put his arm around her, just as he himself was swamped.

Ben stood there defiantly, like a soldier facing an enemy charge, until the mist rose above his head.

Dan fought to the last. He stood on tiptoe and then jumped up and down to gasp clean air. "Dammit," he spluttered, as he finally succumbed.

"What's that in the mist?" Ben shouted.

"I can't see anything," replied Dan. "I wish I could."

"Over there." Ben pointed. "Like two red lights. They just came and went..." He didn't say anything else as once more they flashed into view. They were stationary at first, two red lights close together.

"They're like eyes," said Charles.

Even as they watched, the eyes moved up and down in unison, slowly growing larger. Now they stopped and moved sideways to circle around them, as if assessing their strength, their resolve and the best point of attack.

Charles moved in front of Mary, but she still couldn't resist peering round him to stare at the eyes.

For just a moment, the mist thinned and the outline of what appeared to be a huge black dog came into view, only to immediately disappear.

"Did you see what I believe I just saw?" said Dan.

"I think I know now what frightened Warren to death," replied Charles.

Ben seemed calm, almost philosophical. "There's a legend of a Black Dog associated with the Rollrights," was all he said.

In response, the eyes came closer, the outline of the dog became clearer and the stench stronger. They all knew the dog was approaching them, stalking them.

Charles felt Mary stiffen as the dog opened its mouth, bared its yellow teeth and snarled.

Hearing a faint click, Ben spun around and saw the red light of the eyes reflected in the blade of a pocket knife that Dan was holding. As he pointed it towards the dog and moved it slowly from side to side, the eyes followed it, as if the dog were being hypnotised.

Charles took advantage of the distraction and carefully edged Mary around to the other side of the stone, so that it was between them and the dog.

When Dan stopped moving the knife, the dog stopped, its eyes fixed on the reflection of its own eyes.

Dan turned to Ben. "Here we go," he whispered. "Get ready."

They watched as the dog crouched. Then it snarled viciously and leapt towards them.

Dan dropped the pocket knife, shoved Ben to one side and leapt aside himself so that the dog smashed into the stone. Immediately, as if planned, a bolt of lightning flashed down and hit the stone, hurling everybody away from it and onto the soft peat.

Dan picked himself up, went over to Ben and hauled him upright.

Ben stood there dazed.

"Are you all right?" asked Dan.

Ben nodded and turned to check on Mary and Charles. They had already clambered to their feet and were standing there, looking totally bewildered.

"Was that real?" said Ben.

Dan walked around the stone in the mist. There was no sign of the dog.

"Well, if it was real, it's not here now," said Dan. "That dreadful stench has gone too, thank God. But the mist is as thick as ever."

Mary wasn't listening. She was studying the stone. "Look – it's coming alive," she whispered.

Even as they watched it, the rock crystals in the stone were glistening in the mist.

"It must have been all that lightning," said Ben. "It's energised the crystals somehow."

It was as if a match had been struck. The stone glowed a faint blue at first, before an unearthly blue flame suddenly appeared and played ethereally from the top.

46

When the flame flared, they all leapt back from the stone. Then, to their amazement, as if it were taking on a life of its own, the flame detached itself and hovered above the stone. For a while it flickered different shades of blue, before growing brighter. The flickering stopped as it assumed the shape of a sphere, to float there in the mist, turning slowly and pulsing like a beating heart. Now a beautiful sky blue, it resembled some miniature stellar life form.

Charles still held on to Mary, but he could sense that she was completely mesmerised.

"It's the stone – it's feeding it with energy," whispered Ben, as the sphere rapidly grew in size and brightness to cast a blue light around it.

When the light started to penetrate the mist, the mist seemed to react. Initially, it swirled around the ball of light, but each time the sphere pulsed, the mist fell back so that it was possible to catch a glimpse of the surrounding landscape.

It was as if the mist had decided to fight. The temperature dropped dramatically and crystals of ice appeared in the air. Out of nowhere, frost formed on the peat and they all felt it becoming frozen solid beneath them.

Mary started shivering uncontrollably and Charles hugged her.

Dan wrapped his arms around himself. "If I know this bloody mist, it's still got a few more tricks to play."

He was caught off balance by the response of the sphere. Suddenly, it turned red and started emitting a steady warmth. It almost seemed to be saying, *Come closer*, and they instinctively moved in towards it.

Ben shook his head. "There has to be a scientific explanation for this. If the stone is really feeding it with energy, then where's the energy in the stone coming from?"

The mist reacted as if it had decided to exert its own power. Slowly, it started to swirl around the stone.

"What are you playing at now, you bastard?" said Dan.

The mist responded by moving faster.

"It's angry," said Mary, as it turned more and more rapidly.

Charles tightened his grip on her as the mist began to buffet them.

"Lie down!" yelled Ben. "Get down on the ground!"

Charles practically pushed Mary flat on to the peat.

"Dig in with your feet and fingers," shouted Ben.

Now the mist unleashed itself, developing into a full-scale whirlwind.

Charles put his arm over Mary's back, only to feel his arm being lifted upwards. He forced it down again and held it there. Turning his head, he noticed the sphere was still sedately turning and pulsing, as if at the calm centre of a tornado.

The mist stopped swirling as quickly as it had started and thickened again. Now an eerie silence settled.

Warily, they eased themselves up.

Like a ball of fire, the sphere was still turning slowly and silently. Warm, friendly and protective, it seemed to be waiting for the next move from its opponent.

Dan raised his arms high in the air. "Bring it on, you bloody loser," he yelled into the mist.

It was only a murmur at first, coming from the direction of the road. Indecipherable, it resembled a couple whispering together in some unknown language. A moment later the same murmuring seemed to come from the opposite direction.

Dan spun around, but could see nothing through the mist.

Now different voices joined in from other directions, but louder, creating the sensation that they were closing in on them.

A loud *screech* came out of nowhere. Ben jumped, only to spin around as something moaned, long and low, from the opposite direction.

It was at this point that the voices started yelling, unseen but insistent, and coming from all around them.

The sphere stopped turning, giving the impression that it was analysing the situation.

When the voices came nearer, the sphere seemed to brace itself and draw more energy from the stone. Again, it started to slowly turn.

"Are you thinking what I'm thinking?" said Dan.

"To me, they sound like souls of the dead," answered Mary.

In response, the mist immediately behind Dan congealed and formed a disembodied hand.

"Dan!" cried Ben. "Behind you!"

Dan whipped around and swiped at the hand, but his own hand went right through it.

Instantly, the voices faded to a whisper and stopped. The mist hung there motionless and the red ball revolved steadily.

It was the stone itself that made the next move. A line of blue flame, like a strike of lightning in reverse, shot up from the stone into the sphere.

The sphere burst into life and went from red to orange. The line of flame surged again into the glowing ball, so that it turned bright yellow and finally glowed with the fiercest white heat. Rising higher into the mist, it sat there, pouring out a blinding light.

In what seemed a final act of defiance, the mist swirled around the stone, before beginning to thin. Just faintly, they were now able to glimpse sunlight reflected from lochs in the distance.

"Look up there!" cried Dan.

High in the sky, the sun had appeared. It was dim, but it was there, fighting its way through the haze.

Emboldened, as if it were now confident of victory, the shaft of flame poured upwards from the stone to feed the sphere.

With a final dazzling flash, the flame seared into the

sphere and, like a nuclear explosion, the sphere exploded into a blinding light. Simultaneously, the sun burst through the clouds into a patch of blue sky. The remnants of the mist trailed away and sunlight poured down on to the landscape.

It took a full minute before their eyes could adjust and focus. There was no sign of the sphere; the ball of light had disappeared and the sun shone high above in a cloudless sky. The stone was standing there, now looking like any other unexceptional pillar of rock, as if nothing had happened.

From the direction of the sea, a lone seagull appeared and wheeled above them. It cried out, giving the impression that nature had given it permission to lead a celebration of a return to normality.

Ben approached the stone and held his hand close over the top. Not feeling anything unusual, he touched the stone lightly, ready to pull his hand away. "Completely dead," he said. "Something fired it up, though, didn't it? It was drawing on some intense source of energy. It's gone, though. Whatever activated the stone has completely disappeared. And I don't think lightning by itself could have caused what we just witnessed."

"Am I alone in suspecting what it was?" said Mary.

47

"Haven't we seen that bird before?" said Dan, pointing at the sky. A large black bird had appeared and was circling directly above them.

Mary looked towards where Dan was pointing. She didn't say anything, but watched it closely.

"Looks like a crow," said Ben.

"No, it's not a crow, it's a raven," said Charles. "We saw one at the Hill of Dunsinane, Ben. I wonder..." he continued, half to himself. He watched it as it drifted lower and in tighter circles.

Mary didn't say anything but glared at it and seemed to be steeling herself against its presence.

As if in response to Mary, the bird broke away, swooped down the hill and disappeared out of sight.

"Who's that?" asked Ben. He was watching somebody walking up the hill towards them.

He received an answer he wasn't expecting. "Leave this to me," said Mary, before anybody else could speak.

"Are you sure?" said Charles.

"*I said leave it to me.* This is personal." She patted the Serpent Meteorite in her pocket and started to walk purposefully down the slope towards the figure.

Gráinne O'Connor was dressed exactly as before, in her red cagoule and blue jeans. One of the pockets of her cagoule was noticeably bulging.

About fifty yards from the standing stone, Mary MacDougall and Gráinne O'Connor confronted each other.

Mary could hardly stop herself from shaking with anger. "Where is Holly Fraser?" she demanded.

O'Connor looked her straight in the eyes. "She's all right."

Ben looked down the hill at the pair, confused. He turned to Dan. "Is that who I think it is? The woman you told me about?"

"Yes," replied Dan.

"Then she'll know where Holly is," he shouted, and made to run down the hill.

Dan grabbed him by the shoulder. "Let Mary deal with this!"

"But I have to find Holly!" yelled Ben, trying to shake him off. He bristled as he watched Mary talking to O'Connor. His face contorted with rage, and after struggling free from Dan, he darted down the hill.

O'Connor spun around to see Ben pounding down towards them, before coolly turning back to face Mary. "If you want to see Fraser back again alive, tell him to back off."

As Ben stumbled to a halt in front of them, Mary stepped in front of O'Connor, stopping him with her arm. "Don't!" she commanded. "Let me deal with this."

It was O'Connor who spoke next. "Your girlfriend is

safe and well," she said, calmly. "But if you dare touch me, you won't see her again."

She turned back to Mary. "You come with me!" Then, expressionless, she turned to Ben. "You can follow us if you want," she said, and started to walk back down the hill.

Ben stood there glowering as he watched O'Connor.

Mary turned to him. "We have no choice, Ben," she said, squeezed his hand, and followed O'Connor.

He closed his eyes, took a deep breath, beckoned to Dan and Charles to join him and headed downhill in the direction of their car.

48

Mary climbed into the yellow car and glared at O'Connor. "What have you done with her? If anything happens to her…"

"I told you she's all right," O'Connor said, starting the engine.

"Then where is she?" Mary demanded. "She's pregnant, for God's sake. She's at great risk – she could lose her babies. Don't tell me she's still in that cave?"

O'Connor slipped the car into reverse and started to turn it round in the road, noting the men climbing into their car. "How do you know about the cave?" she asked.

Mary didn't say anything.

"So you've been having visions as well," said O'Connor. "The cave is at Dalmore Bay – about five miles from here. But she's not there any longer."

"Where is she, then?"

"She's in a holiday cottage near Dalmore Bay. It was empty and I took her there for her own safety."

"You mean you wanted to use her as a hostage," Mary spat out.

"True," said O'Connor, checking that the other car was behind her and starting to drive towards Breasclete village. "But nothing was ever going to happen to her. The Stone of Doom and the Stone of Destiny both needed her to be kept safe."

Mary looked confused. "Stone of Doom?"

"The meteorite in the cave. I assumed you knew all about that."

As they came to Breasclete village, she turned right on to the road north to Dalmore Bay.

"It's all about twins, isn't it?" continued O'Connor. "The Stone of Doom and the Stone of Destiny – twins." She patted her pocket. "Like your meteorite and my meteorite – twins. And all of them from the same place on Mars." She turned to Mary. "Holly Fraser is expecting twins – and twins are special to the Stone of Doom and the Stone of Destiny. Or at least they were…"

"What do you mean 'were'?"

"The stones have gone, haven't they? The Stone of Doom knew you were about to find the Stone of Destiny, so it provoked a battle. Except it lost. It disappeared. It completely dissolved away into that mist – all gone now. You won't find it in the cave."

"How do you know?"

O'Connor patted her pocket. "My meteorite – the one that was found in the Antarctic. It told me. It no longer has any contact with the Stone of Doom."

Mary felt the Serpent Meteorite in her pocket and closed her eyes while she concentrated.

O'Connor glanced at her. "Your meteorite – the one found at the Serpent Mound. It's not in contact with the Stone of Destiny, is it?"

Mary looked shaken. "No," she said. "The Stone of Destiny – it was under the standing stone, wasn't it? How did you know it was there?"

"The same as you, I expect. I saw the lightning. That was just the start of the battle. But when I saw the ball of light burst into sunlight, I knew the Stone of Destiny had won. It cost it its life, though. It made the ultimate sacrifice."

Mary didn't speak for a while. "How did we all get drawn into this?" she said, eventually. "Why did all this happen? What's it all about? Why me? Why you?"

"You don't know?" said O'Connor.

"Should I?" said Mary.

"Where does your mother's family come from?"

"Ireland, originally. The west coast of Ireland. My mother always avoided talking about it for some reason. She never said exactly where."

"It was the Dingle Peninsula in County Kerry," said O'Connor.

Mary looked startled. "How do you know that?"

O'Connor tapped the Antarctic Meteorite in her pocket. "I said I've been having visions as well."

"I still don't get it," said Mary.

"You probably don't know, but it's to do with my great-great-grandmother and your great-grandmother – you're a generation older than me, remember. They were twins, almost identical in appearance. Both of them even had the same green eyes we've inherited. There was one difference between them, however. Quite a big one, actually. Your great-grandmother had red hair. But my great-great-grandmother had black hair. In character, though, the twins were very different. My great-great-grandmother was a witch. Your great-grandmother was very religious and hated her. They fought like cats and dogs – it was visceral.

"Witchcraft has been passed down to me through the generations – it's in my blood. When your family left for the States, mine stayed and battled it out through the famine. There was no love lost."

Mary didn't know what to say.

"We've both been used," continued O'Connor. "The real Stone of Destiny was buried under the standing stone back there. Its twin, the Stone of Doom, was in the cave at Dalmore Bay. They've been fighting for dominance since time immemorial. They slightly overdid it this time, though."

"But why here? Why Callanish? Why were they hidden here?"

"This is a sacred landscape dedicated to the moon and sun. Always has been. That's why they were drawn here, I suppose. What better place for good and so-called bad to battle it out?"

"How long had the Stone of Doom been at Dalmore Bay? Where did it come from?"

"Nobody knows. The Stone of Doom is the foundation of our sect – *The Order of the Black Dog*. It's *our* sacred stone. Each generation of the sect has been initiated into its existence and its whereabouts through the High Priestesses. I'm the latest."

"What about the dog – the black dog? Was it real? It has gone, hasn't it?"

"Are you asking whether it was a thought-form generated by the Stone of Doom? To terrify people and maintain control? I don't know. But it always seemed very real to me. I couldn't stand the smell."

"I still don't understand," said Mary. "Why a black dog?"

"The Black Dog is something deep in the human psyche. The fear of the rabid dog, the wolf, the jackal – the wild aspect of the dog before it became domesticated. Perhaps it's something lodged in our primaeval mind that's never gone away. It crops up everywhere in mythology, like Black Shuck, Barghest, Hairy Jack, Shug Monkey, Bogey Beast… There are countless examples here and around the world. And there's one thing they have in common – they are always associated with death. That's why the Stone of Doom and my meteorite manifested it. Your friend in the States should have left your meteorite where he found it. He got himself involved in something he didn't understand and he paid the price."

Mary didn't say anything for a while.

"So how did the Stone of Destiny end up under the standing stone up there?" she asked eventually.

"By force of its will, I suppose. Ultimately, the real Stone of Destiny needed to be near its twin. It manipulated people to get itself under the standing stone, because it knew that the standing stone was in a sacred place near to the cave at Dalmore Bay. It could have been one of any number of people who took it there – Fergus, son of Erc; St Columba; a MacDougall owner of Dunstaffnage Castle; Abbot Henry of Scone; or the monks… Maybe even an owner of Dunsinane House. Who knows? One thing's for certain, though – the Stone of Destiny in Edinburgh is definitely a fake."

"Do you really think I don't know that?"

O'Connor checked the rear-view mirror to make sure Ben's car was still behind them. "Perhaps that's why we were destined to meet each other. We were drawn together somehow because of our ancestor twins. We balance each other."

"So what now?" said Mary.

"It goes on, doesn't it?" She touched the Antarctic Meteorite in her pocket and pointed to the Serpent Meteorite in Mary's jacket.

As they approached Dalmore Bay, O'Connor slowed down, switched on her warning lights, pulled over and stopped. "This is where I leave you," she said, and pointed ahead. "Take the first right. Holly Fraser is in the cottage down the road about a mile on the left. You can't miss it – it's the only building for miles. Now, get out of the car."

Ben drew up behind O'Connor. "Where is she?" he shouted, jumping out of the car. But he didn't get the chance to say more.

O'Connor strode up to him. "This is where your girlfriend is. I've told Mary exactly where to find her. Take care of her – she's very important to us all." She turned away from Ben before he had a chance to respond, and faced Charles. "Look after Mary, Charles. She's going to need your support."

Finally, she turned to Dan, her green eyes glinting. "If

you ever feel the urge to indulge in the dark arts, Dan, you know where to find me."

"Dark arts?" replied Dan. "What makes you think I'm cut out for the dark arts?"

"I mean a Guinness or two, of course. What did you think I meant? Bye for now," she said cheerfully, and before anyone could react, she walked back to her car. Ignoring everybody, she calmly turned the car round and drove away back down south.

49

Ben skidded the car into the driveway of the holiday home in Dalmore, leapt out of it, ran to the front door and burst into the house. Dan, Mary and Charles followed him.

Holly was lying on the sofa. Her eyes were closed and she was visibly shaking. At the sight of Ben, she broke down completely.

He rushed over to her and hugged her. "We're here. You'll be all right now," he whispered. The others immediately left them alone and disappeared into the kitchen.

After a while, Charles came back. "We've just checked the fridge," he said. "There's food – bread, butter, cheese – milk, coffee, tea… Would you like some tea, Holly?"

She smiled wanly and nodded.

Charles very gently asked her for the details of what had happened, while Ben sat with his arm around her.

Still in shock, Holly hesitatingly related how she had been kidnapped at the Rollright Stones, how her phone had been snatched away and how she had been driven in a locked van to Cornwall. There, at night, she had been dragged onto a fishing boat, which eventually landed the following night at Dalmore Bay. Gráinne O'Connor had been there, waiting for her.

Holly now needed to be cajoled into talking about her terrifying imprisonment in the cave with the Stone of Doom. The memory of her nightmare in Long Compton had kept flooding back and she had been terrified that she would share the same fate as the red-haired girl. Worst of all, she had no idea why she had been kidnapped nor why she had been taken there.

"You were being kept as a hostage, Holly," explained Mary. "O'Connor wanted the Serpent Meteorite in exchange for you. She knew it could lead her to the Stone of Destiny…"

Holly now looked completely confused. "I don't know what you're talking about." She turned to Ben. "Can you tell me what this is all about?"

Ben took in a breath. "There's a lot been going on here in Scotland…"

Holly suddenly glared at him. "That's a bloody understatement, if ever I heard one…" Tears welled up in her eyes. "Why didn't you keep me out of it? You don't know what the hell I've been through. I'm pregnant with twins – just in case you've forgotten!"

"Can you leave us alone for a while, please?" Ben said to the others. "There's a lot I'm going to have to explain…"

"We'll go and make the tea," said Charles.

Fifteen minutes later, when Mary peeked around the door to check, Ben was sitting with his arm around Holly. Neither was speaking and she was nestling into him.

Mary quietly entered the room with a tray of tea and food, which she placed on a table. "Shall I pour the tea?" she said.

Ben nodded...

50

Charles unobtrusively glanced at Holly, who was sitting with Ben's arm around her, sipping tea. She caught his eye and smiled at him.

Charles sat down in a chair beside them. "We should still check the cave," he said, quietly. "We need to make sure the so-called Stone of Doom really has gone. You said, Holly, that O'Connor left the cave entrance open. Could you explain where this cave is? Don't worry, we can leave you and Ben here. Dan, Mary and I will go and have a look."

When Charles, Mary and Dan reached the car park, the sun was already starting to sink in the sky and they were relieved to see that the car park was deserted.

"Holly said it was in the rocks over there," said Charles, pointing and leading the way. They found the cave, exactly as Holly had described, with the blocking boulder rolled to one side.

Dan sniffed the air. "Can you smell it?" he said. "There's still a whiff of the mist. It must be the right place." He stepped back. "After you," he said to Charles.

Mary shook her head at Dan, while Charles knelt down and crawled into the cave. "I've found the torch," he called back. "Right where Holly said it would be."

Mary immediately went down on her knees and crawled in after him.

Dan took a last look at the empty beach and the sun hanging over the horizon of the calm sea, then followed Mary.

Stunned by the fact that somehow the place had remained the secret of an ancient witchcraft cult for many thousands of years, they moved, cautiously, deeper into the cave, until they came to the rock face. They froze when they saw the rolled-back boulder and the entrance to the inner cavern.

Charles looked back at the others, then knelt down and shone the torch into the cavern. "This is definitely the place," he said, and immediately crawled through the entrance.

Dan took a deep breath and went through after him, followed by Mary.

It was when the torchlight fell on the water bottles and sandwich wrappers that they realised the full horror of Holly's experience.

Charles shone the torch around the cavern, until the light fell on the rock ledge. "That must have been where the meteorite was," he said.

"No sign of it now," replied Mary. "At least O'Connor was right about that. Let's get out of here. This place reeks of evil – I need fresh air."

They emerged as the sun had sunk about halfway

beneath the horizon, glowing bright red and the focal point of a clear sky.

"Dan, help me push this back," said Charles, touching the boulder. "I don't think we want this place to become a tourist attraction." He and Dan rolled the boulder back until it fell back into place, a perfect fit.

Charles stood back. "Never to be opened again, I hope."

Dan grunted in agreement.

Intensely relieved to be outside again, Mary didn't say anything. Instead, she walked slowly down to the shoreline. Standing there, she breathed in the fresh air and gazed far out to sea.

Charles and Dan walked down after her, standing next to her, not speaking. It was as if they were seeking a return to some sort of normality after all the other-worldly events.

Together, they watched the sky as it reddened and the sun dipped lower and lower. They remained silent while they stared at it, conscious of its raw beauty.

Suddenly, something caught them by surprise. At the exact moment that the sun finally disappeared, for just a split second a bright green light flashed out towards them.

"Hey! Did you see that?" said Charles.

"It must have been some kind of optical effect," said Dan. He turned and started to walk back up the beach. "Ben and Holly will want to be getting away from that house," he called out.

Charles turned to Mary. "Shall we go, Mary?"

She didn't budge.

"Mary? Come on! Ben and Holly will be wondering where we are."

Mary was still staring straight ahead to the spot where the sun had set.

"Mary?" repeated Charles, looking worried.

She slowly turned to him. "Something just happened, Charles. It happened with that green flash. It was as if for a split second a door opened in my mind. I think the sun just spoke to me…"

He looked stunned. "What do you mean, the sun…?"

"The sun, Charles. Just for a moment I had the feeling my mind was in direct communication with the sun itself."

51

"'Bed and breakfast' in Stornoway this time," said Charles cheerfully, as Mary, Ben and Holly squeezed into the back of the car parked outside the holiday cottage. "I've tipped them off that we'll be arriving late. Too late for a meal, I'm afraid, but I've brought all the food out of the fridge here."

"I just need a beer," said Dan, as he settled in the front passenger seat alongside Charles.

Nobody was inclined to talk; they were still too stunned. Even as they drove through Callanish, there was no hint of the tumultuous event that had occurred there. Now there was an air of deep peace in a landscape that was at ease with itself.

They were welcomed by the landlord of the guesthouse with the words, "Have you heard? There's been the most terrible storm and an incredible sea mist at Callanish. They say it smelled awful. Probably rotten seaweed that got stirred up by it all."

"Yes, we got caught up in it," said Charles. "It was quite dramatic."

Mary touched Charles on the hand. "Charles, I'm sorry, but I'm completely exhausted. It's all been too much for me. I think I'll go straight to bed." She turned round as she made to go up the stairs to her room. "Please don't say anything to the others about what happened to me on the beach. I can't face talking about it yet."

Charles nodded. "I quite understand."

In any case, Ben and Holly excused themselves and Dan was last seen questioning the landlord about where he could get a drink.

In her room, Mary lay back on the bed and stared at the ceiling. This time she didn't put the Serpent Meteorite next to her head. She sensed she didn't need to; it had fulfilled its task.

Outside the guesthouse she could hear the sounds of traffic and the occasional voice as people passed by. She listened for a while, then closed her eyes.

Without really trying, she found she could shut down the immediate sensations of the world. She wondered whether her profound experience induced by the green flash at Dalmore Bay had been an extreme reaction. Perhaps it was associated with a sense of relief that, at last, she had been released from the hold of something totally strange, almost incomprehensible, and outside her control. She prayed that her life could now return to a state that approached normality.

It didn't happen. For just a moment, her mind was lit up by a flash of white light and she sensed that something in the far recesses of her mind was reaching out, trying to break through into her consciousness.

Then the sensation faded. She couldn't help thinking again about her recent experience at Dalmore Bay. Maybe the feeling of communication and oneness with the consciousness of the sun had always existed in her mind, latent but out of reach. Maybe it was an ancient form of consciousness in humanity that had been superseded by the evolutionary process. Or maybe it was something completely new, planted there somehow by the Stone of Destiny and activated by the green flash from the sun.

At this point, all she wanted to do was to rest, to calm her mind and adjust to the new situation. All these recent happenings had been too overwhelming, too frightening.

It was as if whatever had instigated the flash of white light in her mind had decided that she wasn't quite ready for yet more new experiences. Instead, other powerful images from the day flooded through her brain: the sun lighting up the Standing Stones of Callanish, the storm, the lightning, the mist, and the sphere of light that finally defeated the mist. It was difficult now for her to believe that these things had actually happened, yet she knew that not only had she witnessed them herself, but others had witnessed them as well.

The thought of Gráinne O'Connor making her bold appearance burst into her consciousness and a wave of intense anger flooded through her. Yet after a few minutes, even that subsided. Yes, O'Connor was a nasty piece of work, but she couldn't escape the fact that O'Connor was family, even if distantly related.

Now she could see that she and O'Connor were like the twins they were descended from. She began to understand as well that the battle between them would go on. The Stone of Destiny and the Stone of Doom might have disappeared, and yet they lived on through the Serpent Meteorite and the Antarctic Meteorite. Like the twins that they were, sometimes one meteorite would be on top, sometimes the other, but ultimately in their love–hate relationship, they balanced each other, as did O'Connor and herself. She only hoped the meteorites could now find other ways of conducting their affairs and leave her and O'Connor out of it. She had had enough.

Reassured by the thought that, just possibly, she could return to her old self, she unconsciously relaxed and freed her mind. The memory of the turbulent events of the day began to fade, but after a few peaceful moments, the image of the dawn breaking over a tranquil sea floated into her consciousness. She instantly realised that, in her mind, she was standing yet again on the golden sand of the beach at Dalmore Bay.

Slowly, the sky became suffused with pink and then yellow. It was at this point that she became aware, for a second time, that the being of the sun was about to break through into her mind.

When it happened, it didn't surprise her. Just as the sun rose over the horizon, once again there was a sharp green flash. This time, though, like a spiritual balm, sunlight poured into her mind to bathe her in a warm glow. Slowly, the sunlight grew stronger but, unlike before, she did not blink or resist it. Now she accepted that her experience at Dalmore Bay had not been an aberration and that something permanent had happened: her mind, her very consciousness, was once again at one with its progenitor, the mind of the sun, and was at peace with it.

She could feel that, at this stage, the sun was somehow

holding back its full power, concerned not to overwhelm her, not to drive her into a kind of madness. Instead, it was exerting a more calming effect and she basked in the sense of its essential goodness, feeling its concern for its offspring: life on Earth.

It was as if the sun were wishing to give her a glimpse of her future. Somehow, she felt her very being was engulfed, deep inside the body of the sun itself.

As with her own brain, infinitely sophisticated electrochemical forces were at play, yet she was well aware that those in the sun were incalculably more powerful. What she did not realise was that she was being primed for something so profound that, for her, there would be no going back.

In her mind, she sensed the barely discernible murmuring of myriad voices, coming and going, like the gentle sound of leaves rustling in a light summer breeze. Slowly, as if in anticipation of some cosmic event, the voices became animated with mounting excitement. Mary knew, even if she couldn't understand what they were saying or what was happening, that the sounds were emanating from individual entities in some way communicating with each other. Suddenly, it all stopped and there was a profound, deep silence.

It was so faint at first that she could barely perceive it: like the voice of some celestial choirboy, there was a sound so beautiful that as it grew louder and richer, her heart leapt. Other voices now joined it one by one, and then, as if floodgates had been opened, she was filled with the sublime music of a heavenly choir. She listened, entranced, until she was overwhelmed and found herself singing with the choir.

The heavenly music didn't stop suddenly; it faded away gradually, leaving her with the sense of an infinite space that was somehow alive.

It was now that the full magnitude of what she had witnessed dawned on her. She realised that she was being gently introduced not only to the very being of the sun, but also to its place in the universe. For a single divine moment, she had been at one with the stars themselves.

52

Mary was in a state of complete mental disarray when she went down for breakfast the next morning. She knew she had undergone a profoundly cosmic experience outside her control and it had overwhelmed her. Afterwards, she had fallen into a deep sleep. Waking, she had still felt stunned, trying to come to terms with what had happened to her.

Going downstairs, she was comforted to find the other four already sitting there, engaged in earnest conversation. They stopped talking the instant they saw her and Charles immediately pulled out the empty chair beside him. "Here, sit here, Mary."

"So what exactly happened to you at Dalmore Bay, Mary?" said Dan. "I know by now when you've had another 'experience.'"

Charles looked at her, expectantly.

Mary couldn't stop talking. It all poured out: how she had seen the green flash and how, for just a second, her mind had seemed to expand to communicate with the sun, so that she began to feel at one with it. Then, once she was in bed, how the experience had returned, but more profoundly than before. Fearing they might think she had gone completely mad, she held back about telling how she had witnessed the heavenly choir. She looked at each of them, bewildered.

"It's not a new idea," said Ben.

"What's not a new idea?" said Dan, still looking incredulous. "I haven't got to grips with the concept that stones can be alive, let alone this."

"I'm talking about the idea that the sun is conscious. Okay, so what's happened to Mary is awesome. But we've been prepared for it, haven't we? What's been happening to us, and especially Mary, hasn't been exactly normal. From what I can make out, it's as if the sun has been involved in everything we've been through, culminating in Mary's experience last night.

"Look at it this way. The sun is full of electric currents, just like the animal brain. And all life on Earth has evolved because of the sun. Consciousness is part of that evolution, so why shouldn't our own consciousness have come from the sun? The ancients knew it, didn't they? They recognised the power of the sun and worshipped it. Perhaps we've been taking the sun for granted for too long."

"Then why didn't it happen to me?" said Holly. "I've got red hair and I've had some pretty weird experiences, too…"

"It was the green flash. It all happened after I saw the green flash," said Mary. "It was as if the sun had somehow decided I was ready and was using the green flash to trigger the change in my level of consciousness. Maybe it's the sun's way of communicating something special or unusual."

"But what is this green flash?" asked Dan. "What's so special about a green flash?"

"Actually, it's a well-documented phenomenon associated with the sun," said Ben. "It normally happens with certain weather conditions and it can occur at sunrise as well as sunset. Pilots sometimes see it—"

He was cut off by Charles. "There's a book by Jules Verne called *The Green Ray* – surely you must have read it? All the action takes place in Scotland and, in the story, if you see the green ray when the sun sets, the true intentions of your heart and of others will be revealed. It's quite romantic, really…" He avoided looking at Mary.

Mary looked as if she were going to burst into tears. "I wish you would all stop talking about it as if something almost normal has happened. It's not normal at all, and I'm feeling petrified. I don't know if I've got the courage to deal with it all. If I'm supposed to be some sort of 'chosen one', I don't know if I can cope with it."

They all sat there in stunned silence.

It was Charles who spoke first. "You're not alone, Mary. We are all here – and we've been on the journey with you. We're all in it together."

"But what do I do now?" said Mary. "Do I have to set myself up as some sort of guru who's seen the light? Do I start giving talks about what happened to us? And, anyway, who would ever believe any of it?"

"I suggest we let nature take its course," said Charles. "We should all just get on with our lives. Perhaps, if the sun ordains it, other people with the genes for red hair will come to see a green flash. I suspect you may not be the only one, Mary. Possibly, the sun has some plan for humanity – maybe for all life on Earth."

"It's still very difficult for me," she said.

"Once you have had a bit of time to get used to it, it will start feeling a little less strange to you," said Charles. "Your mind could get used to what's happening to it. Perhaps, one day, you will want to tell the world about all this. Of course, we can't pretend it hasn't happened, but in the meantime it is probably a good idea to try to return to some sort of normality."

There was a long silence, finally broken by Holly. "If we're talking about some sort of normality, if you don't mind, I would just like to get back home," she said, touching her baby bump.

Ben nodded. "Yes, we should get back. If anybody needs a lift, we'll be getting flights from Edinburgh tomorrow."

"Count me in," said Dan. "I suppose there'll be flights to Dublin from Edinburgh, won't there?"

"Why Dublin?" asked Mary, looking suspicious.

"They do draught Guinness there. It's so much better than bottles."

Mary put her hand to her forehead, closed her eyes and slowly shook her head.

"Maybe just a couple of days in Ireland," said Dan. "Then back to Houston, I suppose. Just think of all those meteorites waiting to be categorised."

"What about you, Mary?" said Charles. "This might be a good time of year to look around Oxford. I could show you my old college – I might even be able to swing a meal at the High Table…"

Mary pondered. "Why not," she said.

53

St Michael Cemetery, Boston

"What's that raven doing here?" said Mary, her face hardening.

Charles took one look at the bird sitting on the tombstone in a secluded part of the cemetery. "That's not a raven – it's a crow," he said. "You should be able to recognise an American crow, Mary."

With a loud *caw*, the bird flew clumsily upwards and settled in a tree, from where it looked down on them.

Charles and Mary walked up to the plot in front of Warren's tombstone and stood there in silence. There were still a few faded bunches of flowers on the soil, together with several cards and notes, now indecipherable.

"His family have just had the tombstone erected," Charles said. "But they haven't yet arranged the plot. Perhaps they'll just grass it over."

He read the inscription carved into the granite, detailing Warren's full name, qualifications and dates.

Looking around, he took in the trees, the landscaping and finally stared at the crow. It seemed to take the hint and swooped away, but other birds were singing and a butterfly was fluttering from flower to flower.

Charles squeezed Mary's hand. "I think he's at peace here," he said.

Mary touched the tombstone and whispered something that Charles couldn't hear. Tears started to well up in her eyes.

She was about to take her hand away from the tombstone when she froze and turned bright red.

As Charles looked at her quizzically, she burst out laughing.

"Hello, Warren," she said.

Charles tried to look surprised. "Is he there, in the tombstone?" he asked.

"Yes, he really is," Mary replied.

"What did he say?"

Mary laughed again. "Oh, I couldn't possibly tell you that."

"The old rogue," said Charles. "He obviously hasn't changed a bit." He reached into his pocket as his phone buzzed; he checked the number.

"Ben," he said, putting it to his ear. His face broke into a broad smile and he gave a thumbs-up sign to Mary. "When did it happen?"

He listened again.

"How are they doing?"

He nodded, smiling, to Mary.

"What? How about that? Thanks for letting me know. Yes, you must have a lot of people to tell."

He put the phone back into his pocket, looking slightly puzzled. "Twin boys and everybody's fine."

"Are they identical?" asked Mary.

"Yes. Well, almost. Identical, except that one's got red hair and the other's got black hair. Perhaps it's not so surprising, given their parents. He said they both smiled at him together – great big beaming smiles."

Mary didn't react at first. "That's odd," she then said. "Newborns don't smile…"

APPENDIX

Letter in The Times, 1 January, 1819

MACBETH'S CASTLE.-- (CURIOUS DISCOVERY.)
-- A letter from Dunsinane, in Scotland, states as
follows:-- "On the 19th November, as the servants
belonging to the West Mains of Dunsinane-house, were
employed in carrying away stones from the excavation
made among the ruins that point out the site of Macbeth's
Castle here, part of the ground they stood on suddenly
gave way, and sank down about six feet, discovering a
regularly built vault, about six feet long and four wide.
None of the men being injured, curiosity induced them
to clear out the subterranean recess, when they discovered
among the ruins a large stone, weighing about 500L which
is pronounced to be of the meteoric or semi-metallic kind.
This stone must have lain here during the long series of
ages since Macbeth's reign. Besides it were also found two
round tablets, of a composition resembling bronze. On
one of these two lines are engraved, which a gentleman has

thus deciphered –– 'The sconce (or shadow) of kingdom come, until sylphs in air carry me again to Bethel.' These plates exhibit the figures of targets for the arms. From time immemorial it has been believed among us here, that unseen hands brought Jacob's pillow from Bethel, and dropped it on the site where the Palace of Scoon now stands. A strong belief is also entertained by many in this part of the country, that it was only a representation of this Jacob's pillow that Edward sent to Westminster, the sacred stone not having been found by him. The curious here, aware of such traditions, and who have viewed these venerable remains of antiquity, agree that Macbeth may, or rather must, have deposited the stone in question at the bottom of his Castle, on the hill of Dunsinane (from the trouble of the times), where it has been found by the workmen. This curious stone has been shipped for London for the inspection of the scientific amateur, in order to discover its real quality."

ACKNOWLEDGMENTS

This book would not have been written without the help of many people, but there are those to whom I am particularly indebted.

At the outset, I especially want to thank my wife, Maggie Burr, ex-Fleet Street journalist, who has been unstinting in her support through constant editing and as sounding board.

Two people stand out in terms of making invaluable contributions to the plot, namely Alan Bowers and Pamela Giese.

Alan made my hair stand on end and provided major inspiration with his description of a bizarre event he witnessed in the early hours at that most mysterious of places, the Rollright Stones, near Oxford.

Pamela generously shared her intimate knowledge of the Great Serpent Mound in Ohio, without which the scenes set there would have been incomplete.

Special thanks to Celia Harper, musician and composer, who explained musical concepts, supported on one memorable occasion by her skilful demonstration of overtone singing.

Frank Breslin not only read through a draft, making corrections and invaluable observations, but managed to make the whole process a lot of fun.

My sister, Jo Bull, read the book as it was being written and never faltered in her encouragement.

Finally, I must thank Berni Stevens, herself an author, who must be one of the best cover designers around.